Susan Alison lives in Bristol, UK, and writes and paints full-time. She paints dogs, especially Border Collies. Every now and then she paints something that is not a dog just to show she's not completely under the paw. Mainly she's under the paw... Short stories of hers (*not* usually about dogs) have been published in women's magazines worldwide.

She has a dog blog (with the occasional non-dog painting) at www.MontyandRosie.blogspot.com

Also by Susan Alison and available soon...

Out from under the Polar Bear
(first scene at the back of this book)

Author's website: www.SusanAlison.com

See the author's blog at
www.MontyandRosie.blogspot.com
for book excerpts, news, paintings
and contact details.

This book can be bought from the publisher at:

http://stores.lulu.com/SusanAlisonArt

Susan ALISON

WHITE LIES
and
CUSTARD CREAMS

Author's website: www.SusanAlison.com

and dog blog: www.MontyandRosie.blogspot.com

ACKNOWLEDGEMENTS

My special thanks go to Jill Mansell for reading my book all the way through, for using her time on my behalf and for the wonderful quote that resulted.

Remarkably, considering the time I spend in front of my computer, I have some real life friends – and family - and thanks go to them for their encouragement – you know who you are!

Thanks also to collective cyber support received from the Internet Writers Workshop, who read the first couple of chapters, and from Friends and Writers who cheered me on when the going got tough. They also voted for my slipper-wearing-dog painting 'Because it's Bedtime' – and helped it win! What more could I ask?

And thanks to my dogs, whose presence has made my life that much more full of love, laughter and, er, fragrance…

Cover art by Susan Alison

For Helen Alison, my mother
With love.

Chapter One

As soon as he said, "Hello, Liz," she knew Hugh was in trouble.

She still had that heart-shaking little jumpy feeling when she saw him. He really was quite a hunk in a big, solid, charcoal-grey-suit kind of way. But Liz's heart wasn't jumping about now. In fact, it had taken a lie-down in her stomach, its head covered with a pillow.

Stalling for time she pulled her front door wide open to allow her ex to come in. Determined to keep to their usual standard of greeting, she grinned at him, poked him sharply in the chest and yanked his tie crooked, nearly throttling him in the process. "Helloo there, you scruffy thing you. To what do I owe this unexpected, but delightful pleasure?" She leant forward and gave him a quick hug and a peck on his immaculately shaved cheek. He didn't exactly recoil, but nor did he grab her bodily and give her his usual, I'm-lost-without-you hug.

Ever since they'd split up, Hugh had wanted them to get back together, but although Liz loved him, there was no way she could live with him.

It was great the way he always appeared when needed, though, and just now she really needed his advice on various lodger-related incidents. And here he was on her doorstop, as if by magic. What a good ex!

He usually greeted her with something like "Well, hello there, my little short-necked swan," or "Hiya, my little drop of summer," or something equally as nauseating – anything but plain old, 'Hello, Liz'. Maybe it was because he couldn't honestly use the 'little' word any more and he was too kind to say, "my large but luscious dumpling" or "my blooming flower, how nice to see more of you", although she didn't think she'd put on *that* much weight. But that could be it. How thoughtful he was. How kind.

Except that he then shouted at Moocher to get down, whereupon that poor, affectionate pooch slunk off under the table all hurt and rejected. He brutally savaged his rubber rat to show he didn't really care.

"That was a bit mean, wasn't it?" Liz said.

"Not at all," he said, beating in exaggerated fashion at his trousers. "I'm sick of being covered in dog hair when I come here."

He had a point about the dog hair, of course, but he'd never seemed to mind before. Liz decided not to argue. There must be something very seriously up for him to behave like this. She leant under the table and reassured Moocher that everyone else in the world still loved him, and then she set about making coffee.

"Milk?" she queried, pouring it in before he replied.

"No. I take it black these days," he said, which was a bit of a bummer because she'd just

2

used the last of the coffee. She'd give him herbal tea and hope he didn't notice.

"What's going on, then?" Liz asked as she sat down opposite him, noticing he'd taken his jacket off as though this was still his home. Mysteriously, the thought warmed her, but the heat could have been down to the fact that he looked so good in a white shirt.

"I'm learning to stand up for myself around here, that's all," he said.

The top of Liz's head immediately got hot. "And what the hell's *that* supposed to mean?" She stared at him disbelievingly and wondered if it really *was* him. They were on the verge of a silly row – their problems had always stemmed from Liz being too scatty and independent for Hugh, and Hugh being too possessive and tidy for Liz, but they'd never had silly rows. Only worthwhile ones. Liz felt quite ill. "Forget it," she said and realised he'd spoken at the same time. "Pardon?"

"I said, 'it was a stupid thing for me to say'. I'm sorry." He looked as appalled as Liz felt. That made her feel a bit better, especially when he bent down and made a fuss of Moocher. Moocher forgave him instantly. He was like that. Couldn't hold a grudge for any time at all, that dog.

Liz started to say, "I'm glad you came over..." just as he started to say, "Liz, I wanted to tell you about..."

"Oh, we've done it again," she said. "Tell you what, you go first." Liz felt unaccountably jittery.

"No," he said. "You go first."

Liz grinned, conscious that her smile wobbled. "Okay then..." and as she was about to launch into the whole sorry tale about the lodger who'd just absconded with three months' rent, her collection of vintage Bonzo Dog postcards and all of one of the other lodgers' knickers, the doorbell shrilled out. Left to herself she would have ignored it, but Hugh couldn't stand it when she did that, so, sighing mightily, she dragged herself out to the front door. Opening it she found two weeping little girls and a fraught looking woman, presumably their mother, clutching one of those baskets you put your small pet in.

"Sorry to disturb you," the woman said. "But we're visiting Mrs Noakes..."

"Oh, yes. I know Mrs Noakes. She lives at the bottom of our back garden, doesn't she? Well, I don't mean like a leprechaun or something. She has her own back garden – and her own home, come to that..." Liz was conscious of waffling on like a complete idiot and realised with a shock that she felt nervous – not of the trio facing her, but of Hugh. How very peculiar, but there was something about him today that had put her on edge. Something very definitely Not Right.

She tried again. "It's just that her back garden backs onto our back garden... And that's why it seems like she lives at the bottom of our back garden..."

The three of them stood there like one, their mouths open to the same fish-like degree as her wittering finally petered out.

All this time her voice had been rising, as it tended to when she got in a state. So it was all Hugh's fault that now the whole of Bristol knew Mrs Noakes was a leprechaun.

Liz waited for them to say something, but the mother seemed at a loss, maybe even a trifle alarmed. The girls, whose sobbing had reached the hiccupy stage, hid behind her, no doubt trailing snot down the back of her skirt.

"So, maybe she *is indeed* a leprechaun after all," Liz said, to prod them into something resembling life again.

"Uh," the woman started, squaring her shoulders and lifting her chin. "Mrs Noakes is a trifle incapacitated at the moment because she's recently had a knee replacement so we came round to get her tortoise."

"Her tortoise?"

"Yes, her tortoise is quite a handful. Always getting out when he sees the opportunity. She turns her back for a moment and he's off. She thought he might be in your garden."

"We have a solid brick wall between our gardens."

"Oh, he can climb walls."

"This is a speedy, wall-climbing tortoise." Liz hadn't heard of one of those before. "Well, then, no doubt he's made previous forays into my garden. So speedily I've never noticed. In which case he'll make his own way home again won't he? The way he's always done it before." She didn't make it sound sarcastic or anything but even so Hugh was there, doing his, now-Liz-behave-thing. He had appeared and laid a hand on her arm in a compelling manner, which did nothing to help her already-shredded nerves.

"Let them come through and get the tortoise, Liz."

"Why don't I just find it and put it over the wall for you," Liz said. A perfectly good suggestion, she'd have thought. She really didn't want her tête-à-tête with Hugh ruined so completely.

5

They all looked at her as though she'd said, 'Why don't I just find it and put it in the oven to roast on high with a few sweet potatoes?' Which she hadn't. And she wouldn't. Of course. (But it wasn't a bad idea.) She gave up, stood back, and three complete strangers and a wicker pet basket stampeded – slowly, as it turned out – through her house, taking far too much interest in everything around them on their way. In fact Liz ended up standing on their heels, trying to get them to hurry through and out the back. If they had to go, why didn't they get on with it?

Moocher thought it was hilarious, especially when the little girls, whose names, at a guess, just had to be Pink and Fluffy, screamed thrillingly. He was only saying hello to them, but they backed away from him as though afraid of catching something, shrieking, "Dirty. Dirteee. Mummy. Mummeee…"

Liz heard her say, "It's all right, Darlings, just hide behind Mummy." And then Liz had this brilliant idea that the back door should stick shut, so she barged ahead and grabbed the door handle. "Damn," she said. "Why can't I get this back door open when I need to? This poxie door, it always sticks when I need to get outside in a hurry." She banged it a few times and kicked it a few times and made quite a racket thinking if they couldn't get the door open they'd have to go and she could get back to Hugh. Liz was increasingly certain he had something awful to tell her, like he'd contracted leprosy or was moving to the outer, lesser-spotted islands-of-the-damned, never to be seen again or that he was foreclosing on the half of the house he still owned and wanted his money right now and she'd have to sell up to give it to him or…

Of course, Hugh came up behind her, turned the key and the door swung freely open. Liz might have felt a fool, but was far more anxious about what was going on behind that handsome but too serious face of his.

He gave her his look that meant she'd be hearing about this later. No wonder they weren't married any more.

Luckily they were interrupted by Pink and Fluffy's wailings. Their mother stared up an apple tree, cooing, "Tinkerbell, Tinkerbell…"

Tinkerbell the Tortoise?

Up an apple tree?

Pink and Fluffy were in fits of despair because Moocher, realising he was unwelcome, had decided to play by himself. He'd picked up the remains of an old rawhide shopping bag and thrashed it about his head, whipping it from side to side, spraying Pink and Fluffy with the mud, leaves and general winter garden detritus that had collected in it since he'd last paid it attention.

Liz had a wild desire to laugh and as her face, totally out of control, started to fold up at the edges, Hugh clenched his hand on her arm hard enough for her to know that if she wanted to make thirty-three she'd better force her face to behave. It was a battle, but finally she must have looked at least pained, rather than hysterical. That was mainly because she had hold of the inside of her cheeks with her teeth. It was the only way.

Hugh spent some time with his handkerchief returning Pink and Fluffy to a state they considered reasonable. Moocher would have been happy to do the same, but for some reason these people preferred a strange man's spit to a friendly dog's lick. Life was very odd.

Liz found herself staring down at the back of his neck – at the bit where his hair just refused to go where he combed it and it sort-of squiggled down one side. She might even have had her hand out to run her finger over that dear little bit, before she realised what she was doing. Good grief! She snatched her hand away and stuffed it in her back pocket. Her jeans were a bit tight just now – all those custard creams – so her hand wasn't going to get out of that pocket in a hurry.

As she watched him, she wondered about Hugh and children. He'd have made a good Dad. He'd have been perfect. Pity really, about them, but too late now. There was still time for both of them to find other, more suitable mates, though.

Mind you, if any child of hers was likely to turn out like Pink and Fluffy, she'd stick with Border Collies. Liz determined to keep her mind on the business in hand and looked for Tortoise-Woman – there she was, just sidling down from the patio that ran between Liz's house and her neighbour, Lydia's – having a damn thorough look in her breakfast room window whilst she did so. Liz supposed it was possible Lydia had invited the devil-tortoise in for a cup of tea.

In fact, it was obvious that Mummee was rootling around the garden very thoroughly indeed. She checked up the other side of the house, looking in any windows available whilst she was at it, and into Liz's other neighbour, Git-Next Door's place. He wouldn't like that, but any opportunity to annoy him further than just by Liz's very existence, was welcome, so she wasn't about to stop the woman.

Liz shook herself. She was being too critical. The woman must be anxious about Mrs Noakes's tortoise.

Finally, she tracked Tinkerbell down. He, or maybe it was a she, must have been cowering behind the compost bin because Tortoise-woman emerged from there, a triumphant smile on her face, holding aloft this poor ol' tortoise, his bid for freedom foiled, and locked him in the pet basket. They all trooped back inside. She checked over her girls, tweaked this ribbon here, that bit of lace there, before setting off, a chastened Tinkerbell once more back in possession.

In an attempt to avoid any awkward questions about her recent past behaviour with the door, Liz raced into her story about the absconding lodger, but didn't get very far before Hugh gave a sorrowful shake of his head. "How do you do it, Liz?"

"Do what?"

"Get into these situations."

"I don't. They just happen, that's all. It's nothing to do with me. Anyway, that's not the point. I was hoping for some advice."

"You're just going to have to not get into these situations, Liz. What if I weren't around to help you out all the time?"

"What?" There was that strange, unpleasantly dislikeable tone again. "I don't want you to help me out, thank you very much! I just wanted your opinion." Liz stared at him, appalled. When did he get this stuffy? How had it happened? He wasn't like this last time she saw him. Something must have happened to him. "Uh, Hugh, sweetie. Have you been in any road traffic accidents recently? Fallen down the stairs? Hit your head somehow? Been possessed?"

"Don't be silly, Liz," he said in a real I-want-my-face-slapped tone.

Stoically, she kept her hands to herself.

He regarded her expression, which probably wasn't her friendliest. "Now, Liz…"

"Don't 'Now, Liz…' me," she said. "Why are you being so poncey? Why is it everyone thinks you're the person to turn to when they're in trouble, if that's the best you can come up with?"

He sighed, shook his head slightly and looked at her as though she were the source of all the trouble in the world. Why *did* people do that? As though she could help it.

The doorbell chose that moment to shrill out again and he suddenly glanced at his watch and stood up, grabbing his jacket as he did so. "I'm sorry, but I must go. I had no idea I'd been here this long."

And he went haring down the hall as if he had to get away from her now, right this minute, or his head would explode.

Just as well, really, as Liz had completely forgotten the potential lodger coming to view the room so recently vacated by Melvin, the Bonzo Dog postcard pincher. She was puzzled, though. She'd never seen Hugh so ill at ease, something so obviously on his mind. Well, whatever it was, it'd have to stay there for a while longer - if there was any room for it to perch in there now he'd become so narrow-minded.

Chapter Two

Even though Hugh got himself out of Liz's house as fast as he decently could, he still noticed that the young girl on the doorstep looked more like the sort of lodger Liz *should* take in, rather than the motley types she usually ended up with. But he kept his mouth firmly shut. It wasn't his business, and she would tell him that quickly enough if he gave his opinion, and so would Charity.

Charity...

"Damn. Damn. Damn." If only he wasn't such a coward. He'd gone round to Liz's with the express purpose of telling her about Charity and in the event he'd been unable. How he wished he could work out why. It didn't make any sense to him, but then, he was no good with the whole woman and relationship thing. Successful at business, quite a hit socially, and at merely dating, but serious relationships and he was adrift. Perhaps he should take an evening class.

He was wrenched from his musings by Lydia-next-door. "Hugh! Oh, how lovely to see you! Were you about to call in? Of course you were. Dear boy, do come in with me. I'll put the kettle on."

Hugh opened his mouth to put her off. Firmly. He hadn't come here to see Lydia. He didn't have time to see her now. He *had* to get back to Charity who waited to hear the outcome of his visit to Liz. "That would be very pleasant, Lydia," he said. "I can't think of anything I'd rather do than have a cup of tea with you."

Her beaming smile rewarded him while he berated himself for his weakness. It was pathetic. He was ruled by women who confused him. Still, Lydia always had brandy snaps, so there was some consolation to be had. He followed her up the path.

Seated in Lydia's breakfast room while she moved around her hand-crafted oak kitchen, Hugh sank lower into glooming about his inability to deal with women who mattered. Even his mother knew he couldn't refuse her anything although it might make life very difficult for him. The difference with his mother was that, knowing this, she wouldn't ask him for anything that made life difficult for him. That was because she truly loved him. Apparently no one else did, not really. Viciously he ripped off a hangnail and it pulled right down the side of his nail and along the bottom and now would be sore as hell for days, and then it'd probably get infected and then his finger would swell up and then his hand and arm and then everything would fall off. "Bastard thing," he hissed under his breath, trying to bite if off before it went further and made even more of a mess. He'd always had neatly manicured hands until recently. He was a disgrace. Hastily he put his hand in his pocket as Lydia approached with a laden tray. Of course, he should have carried it for her. He was forgetting his manners, now, as well.

Lydia put out a couple of Chinese rice pattern cups and saucers and lifted the matching teapot, pouring from it at the same time as milk from a little jug.

"I'm assuming you take your tea the same way you always have, Hugh," she said.

He stared at the cup of fragrant brew and his mouth almost watered, but guilt kept him from answering immediately and Lydia caught it. 'Oh, you don't! Never mind. I'll get a fresh cup.' And she was off with the full one and back with a clean one before Hugh was able to object. She started again and poured him a milk-free cup of tea.

"On a health kick, Hugh?" Lydia enquired, seating herself with her own cup of tea so white she must only have shown it the teapot. She ladled in three sugars, stirred briskly and laid the spoon gently on the saucer. She picked up a gold-rimmed plate covered in rose buds and stacked with brandy snaps. "See, I always keep your favourites in case you drop by." She held it out to him and, miserably, he shook his head. Somehow if he had one Charity would know. She just would.

"Good heavens, Hugh. It's not as if you need to lose weight."

"They'll clog my arteries," he mumbled without looking at her. He knew she'd have a disbelieving look on her face and he didn't want to see it.

Quiet shrouded the room. Hugh could hear birds outside, the tick of a clock further into the house, wind chimes in the garden. He tried very hard to drink his tea without making a noise that would reverberate around the place like water going down a plughole.

"Hugh, my friend. Have you met another woman?"

He brought his head up so sharply his whole body jerked and tea slopped into the saucer.

He gazed mutely at Lydia. He didn't want to tell her when he hadn't told Liz. It wouldn't be right.

"You haven't told Liz, yet, have you?" she asked gently.

How could she read his mind? Charity could do it, too.

"Don't worry," Lydia added when Hugh didn't reply. "I won't tell her if you don't want me to."

"No, thanks Lydia. I want to tell her myself. That's why I called round today but someone came to the door before I could tell her."

In the face of Lydia's slightly amused expression he relented. "You're right. I chickened out of telling her. I don't know why. How did you know anyway?"

Why she should look at him so pityingly he had no idea. She merely said, "I think you should relax a bit, have a nice cup of tea with milk in it, and a few brandy snaps. No one will know and you'll feel better for it. Tell me about your woman."

"Fiancée," he corrected. "She's my fiancée. But I'm not quite sure how it happened." The familiar feeling of puzzlement swept over him. Glancing at Lydia he added hastily, "I do love her though." Gratefully he accepted the fresh tea and crunched happily into a brandy snap.

"Well, it was time to move on, Hugh," Lydia said gently. "You and Liz have been apart for a few years now."

"Two and a fifth," he said absently. Two years, seventy three days, to be exact. Not that he was counting of course. He just had a thing about numbers, that was all. "Life is much more peaceful. And my new fiancé is much easier to deal with and completely different to Liz. And look how I failed with Liz – I mean, a more serene relationship is better all round, don't you think?"

"More serene? Do you mean less passionate? Or less exciting?"

"No, I mean less rows and aggro and discomfort."

"Is it love?"

"How can one tell? I thought it was love with Liz, but look how that turned out. Maybe what I have now is the way it should be. Quiet contentment."

"With no brandy snaps in your life."

He flushed.

"I'm sorry, Hugh. I wish you all the best. I truly do."

"I tried to suffocate Liz, tried to stifle her and she rebelled. Now I'm with someone with all the opposite personality traits – *and* she's tidy - I should be more successful." A wave of sadness threatened to overcome him, but he knew he'd been bad for Liz and he also knew it was time to move on. Talking of which…

"I must go now, Lydia. Thanks for the tea – and the brandy snaps."

"Anytime, Hugh. You know you're always welcome."

"And if you could keep my news to yourself I'd appreciate it."

"You can rely on me."

Hugh pecked her on the cheek and hurried off to Charity's. On the way he stopped at a newsagent to get some mints in case she could smell brandy snaps on his breath.

Chapter Three

"Is yours the kind of house where one cleans the bath before one gets in it or after one gets out of it, Mrs Houston?"

Julie Carrington-Smythe watched Liz carefully from across the bedroom she'd come to see. She was absolutely serious.

So Liz lied.

"We *always* clean the bath when we get out of it." Trying for a crisp, no-nonsense tone, Liz knew it wasn't exactly true. Simon hardly ever cleaned it. He forgot on a regular basis. But it wasn't worth mentioning the odd foible of her longest-lasting lodger. In Liz's experience, people Julie's age (twentyish) barely registered the existence of people Liz's age (thirtyish) and were totally incapable of seeing people Simon's age (fiftyish) at all. Nah, it wasn't worth mentioning.

Especially as there was the most enormous gas bill to pay and Liz wanted Julie Carrington-Smythe to help her pay it now she'd lost the knicker-nicker's rent.

"Oh, and do call me Liz," she said. "All my lodgers call me Liz."

Julie gave her a cold glance and stalked from the room. Liz followed her across the landing into the bathroom where she glowered at the bath so fiercely Liz was surprised its enamel didn't cringe. So she looked at it too.

A faint but inescapable ring around the bath announced Liz a liar and told her that Simon had chosen today, of all days, to bathe in the morning.

Liz tried for a smile, but it faltered and died in the glare of Julie's accusing, I-just-knew-it gaze. So she burst into waffle instead. "We *are* reasonably civilised here you know. We have various other house rules including stuff like no incoming phone calls after ten, for example. It's not fair for everyone to be woken up…"

"I have my mobile and will only use that."

"Right. Okay. And what you do in your own room is your own affair, as long as you do it reasonably quietly… And you have to like dogs, and you must clear up after yourself in the communal rooms and do your bit to keep them clean and tidy and empty the bin every now and then. For some reason no one ever empties the bin. We all wait for everyone else to do it. What else? I know. This is a non-smoking house, as you know. Oh, and you should help keep the garden tidy…"

She said, "I don't like dogs."

Oh. So much for that, then. Liz immediately led the way from the bathroom and started down the stairs. There were many points on which she'd bend, but not this one. Mooch the Pooch was too important for her to allow anyone in the house who might do him harm. Just not liking him was enough for that – he was a very sensitive dog.

But Julie stopped Liz with her next words. "Unless it's a collie type, largely black and mainly comatose."

"Oh! It is." Liz turned to look at her. She could feel her face stretching around a big grin. "What a marvellous coincidence!"

Liz refused to consider what an outright, unbelievable coincidence it was, because maybe the gas wouldn't be cut off after all if she refused to consider what an outright, unbelievable coincidence it was…

"You still want the room?"

"Yes," she said.

Phew! "When do you want to move in?"

"Now?"

"Oh! Um, yep, fine," Liz said, striving to keep a straight face and not show surprise at Julie's urgency. "There's just one other thing. For various reasons, anyone living in this house has to be able to get in and out, with or without their keys."

"What do you mean? Break in?" Julie raised a finely shaped eyebrow in a way that had Liz itching to smack her. She was obviously feeling quite violent today. Hugh had definitely put her on edge.

By this time they were back downstairs in the breakfast room. "Look," Liz said. "I'll show you how easy it is to get out and back in again." She walked through the kitchen to the back door, and crouching down, she dived out of the dog-flap in one fluid movement. The flap did its usual 'clatter-thunk' before resting back in place. With practiced ease she regained her feet and walked along the side of the house to the breakfast room window. Liz looked at Julie through the grubby glass and, raising her voice she said, "And now I'll come back in again."

Which she did.

Julie simply stood there, only now both her eyebrows had reached her hairline in such a smackable way that Liz had to put her hands in my pockets to prevent them getting out of control.

"I didn't know you could get dog-flaps," she said. "Let alone ones that size."

"Yes, handy isn't it."

"And now you want me to prove that I can get in and out of it, too?"

"Yep, that's right."

"Well, that won't be a problem." She started towards the back door and stopped. "Hold on a moment. What's to stop anybody getting in off the street?"

"Good point." Liz was about to launch into an explanation when the familiar 'clatter-thunk' announced Simon's arrival home. Her first and oldest lodger had obviously forgotten his keys. Again. She turned back to wish him a good morning, but didn't wait for a reply. There was no use expecting speech from Simon before noon.

"I thought you said this was a non-smoking house!" Julie peered past Liz, her face screwed up as though she'd stood in something unpleasant.

Liz looked at Simon, and sure enough, his pocket was smouldering. "Simon. Simon! Your pocket!"

He jumped as though he'd been poked with a sharp celestial stick, and danced around, slapping frantically at his body.

Sighing, Liz turned back to Julie and said, "He doesn't smoke in the house – parts of his body might, but he doesn't. If he wants a smoke he has to go outside. I'll introduce you properly later in the day, if you don't mind. We want to get on with this before it rains."

Julie seemed bemused, but she would soon realise that getting in the house without a key was a much more pleasant little adventure if it wasn't sleeting or blowing a gale. Actually, if the weather was nice, you could pretend you were an explorer on an expedition to new and exciting lands, even if it was only into a couple of back gardens.

"The reason that not just anyone can get in from the street is that you have to go through the house next door," Liz said. "I'll take you in now and introduce you to Lonely Lydia. She's a Poor Thing and always pleased to see people, so don't feel you're disturbing her. In fact, you could view the getting-in-the-house-with-no-key exercise as part of what we put back into the community. Anyway, she'll let you out of her back door. Just nip over her wall, drop into my garden, pop through the dog-flap and then you'll be a fully qualified lodger of number nine Malvern Road. Simple."

"Right," she said.

"Um, Liz, wait a minute, Liz," Simon said. (And it wasn't even noon yet.) "I don't think you can ask her to do the key-less test...."

"Everyone has to do it, Simon. No exceptions."

"But, Liz...."

"Don't worry about me, Simon.... Do you mind me calling you Simon?" Julie watched Simon as though truly concerned about his answer.

He didn't look at her. "Um, no. That is, no, not at all," he mumbled.

"Well, Simon," she said, switching on a high-voltage smile. "It's sweet of you to worry, but there's no need. I'm quite athletic."

Simon's head went down and he seemed to study, with deep concentration, the texture of the grain in the floorboards. A dark maroon wave washed up the back of his neck. Liz, too, was silenced by the unexpected charm on display. It hadn't been turned on for her benefit, but then, Liz was female. She was also old enough to be Julie's mother, probably. Well, no, not *that* old. Big sister, perhaps. Well, a few years older anyway.

"I must confess that it seems a little odd, but if it's all part of the initiation ritual here, then I'm game. We can't have our landlady worrying about us getting burnt to a crisp inside, or frozen stiff outside, just because we've mislaid our keys, now can we?" She laughed merrily.

"I'm not *that* worried," Liz muttered, apparently unheard, but pleased that she had in fact insisted on this part of the initial interview for potential lodgers. She could just imagine what the newly poncified saint Hugh would have to say about it if a lodger of hers did actually get burnt to a crisp. Oh, yes, he'd be there, leaning back on his heels, staring above her head, going, "Now, Liz..." Ooh. She could just hear him in her mind. Ooh!

Simon distracted her from her growing fury by digging his toe into the floor and twisting his body from side to side, mumbling, "Umsmoke. Neesmoke..."

"Right," Liz said, throwing off all thought of poncey ex-husbands and their bigoted views. "Simon needs a cigarette. Let's get to it."

She led the way. Throwing open her front door, she was struck afresh by the loveliness of the day, which was cold but bright, just beginning to think of spring. And, perhaps, rain. But suddenly it was as if optimism was breathable and they couldn't help but fill up on it. That's what comes of *not* thinking of one's ex, obviously.

They hurried down the path, only to be stopped by Simon's shout of glee as he passed their recycling box. Recovering from his temporary, Julie-induced paralysis, he pounced on a couple of battered old shoes. Funnily enough, Liz had seen them earlier when she was putting out the wheelie bin and she'd thought at the time how strange it was that he'd thrown out two different shoes. He must have just realised his mistake. She checked his feet and, sure enough, he had odd shoes on.

"Hang on," he muttered and disappeared back into the house with the salvaged shoes. He reappeared, a smug look on his face, and the same odd shoes on his feet. Liz knew Simon well and didn't want to risk a comment which would get her bogged down in his particular brand of logic. She turned away.

Julie was still watching Simon without looking where she walked and fell over another recycling box. This one lurked at the end of Liz's wall. It was piled high with wine bottles that, no doubt, covered a couple of chunkier spirit bottles underneath.

It was Lydia's, of course. She always 'accidentally' pushed her box over to their side because she didn't want the neighbours to know she drank so much, whereas it was only to be expected of a house full of unwashed lodgers. They didn't bear her any ill will for this. She was a Poor Thing.

Simon gallantly helped Julie to her feet, but she shrugged his hand from her arm and beat non-existent dirt from her clothes with exaggerated movements. Then she peered into the box and sniffed audibly, casting a contemptuous look Liz's way. Liz knew she'd been consigned to the 'drunken, sluttish landlady' compartment in Julie's brain. Probably the same compartment existed these days in Hugh's brain.

Damnit! Why did she keep thinking of him? He always ruined things, he did. Anyway, she didn't care what he thought. And she wasn't going to think about what he thought. Oh, no!

It put her right off explaining to Julie that the bottles weren't theirs. She, and Hugh, would think what they wanted, whatever she said. People usually did. Especially if their minds had somehow shrunk to the size of a shrivelled mushroom, like Hugh's must have.

They proceeded on to Lydia's, who, as usual, welcomed them with open arms. The trick was to kiss the air on both sides of her face without actually touching her cheek with your own. Otherwise you came away with a landslide of powder down your face, dribbling onto your shoulder like frenzied dandruff. Lydia was well turned-out all the time, even first thing in the morning, immaculately dressed, coiffed, accessorised and made up. Liz was always tempted to suggest she use less make-up, but as she used none what did she know?

Today, Lydia wore a navy-blue skirt suit with a cream silk blouse. The style was a couple of decades behind the times, but she looked very elegant. Although Liz thought the really thick tights she wore spoilt the effect a bit but maybe she had varicose veins or regretted tattoos from her youth. Liz stifled a snort, trying to imagine what sort of tattoos Lydia might have around her ankles.

Fluffy kittens with bows round their necks, or little puppies chasing butterflies. She wasn't the skull and crossbones or set of fangs type.

Anyway, they came through Lydia's greeting unscathed except for Julie who ended up with powder drifts on both her cheeks, but at least they matched.

"How lovely to have a new face next door," Lydia said. "You make sure you come in just whenever you want to, dear. Don't feel you have to wait until you forget your key."

"I won't forget my key," Julie said. Ungraciously, Liz thought, but Lydia didn't seem to notice.

Lydia's hospitality was obviously going to make up for Liz's lack of it. She retrieved many and various packets of biscuits from her cupboard and set them out on pretty plates - a different one for each different type of biscuit and a running commentary for them all.

"We'll have the custard creams on this little frilly one. Got this one from Clapham market many years ago when I had a boyfriend there…"

"The lemon puffs will do nicely on this little one – go with the primroses, don't they? Just right for today…"

She put the ginger creams next to Simon, on a paper plate. Her crockery had already suffered because of his clumsiness and he was very fond of ginger creams. She learnt quickly, did Lydia. Liz had often wondered if the special attention she paid him was only about protecting her china. They must have been about the same age… Not that Simon had noticed. Liz fancied he'd run in the opposite direction, screaming, if he thought Lydia, or anyone, had designs on him.

And then it started…

"Now then, Julie. Where did you say your parents lived? How do you keep yourself, dear? Are there any young men you particularly favour? I can't see any rings on your finger, dear."

Poor Lonely Lydia seemed to live her life through theirs. It was enough to make sure everyone remembered their key.

Eventually they made it out into the garden. Lydia led the way through her newly sprouting bulbs, shoved aside a promising clump of some grassy thing and showed them her wall. It wasn't a high wall. If it was, Lydia wouldn't be able to see straight into their breakfast room. She wouldn't be in a position to telephone and let them know when the fridge door wasn't shut properly. Even so, Julie looked taken aback. Perhaps it was the state of the wall. It was pretty soggy, looked slimy and probably infested with dead woodlice and maybe a slug or two.

Liz took a moment to appreciate Julie's rather nice jacket - suede and leather, the kind that had broad shoulders but tapered down under her bum. Well, that was in for a rough ride if she kept it on. Lydia, Simon and Liz stood there expectantly.

Julie looked at the wall. She looked at them. "Go away!" she said. "I'm not doing this for your entertainment. I'm doing this so I can have the room."

Pity, that. Especially if she fell foul of any devil-tortoises on her way over. Liz would have liked to clap eyes on Tinkerbell the tearaway tortoise in action.

"Okay," Liz said. "You just climb over the wall and limbo in through the dog-flap like I showed you. By the way, I take it you have got the deposit and a month's rent to give me up front?"

Julie turned and snapped, "Yes, I have."

Oh, very crabby. "Good! I'll see you next door, then."

Liz had to chivvy Lydia and Simon inside and then drag them away from Lydia's breakfast room window. She left Simon to more coffee and biscuits. It saved him shopping and cooking meals. Pity she couldn't stay, but she wanted to get back to welcome Julie properly into her new home. Also, Liz didn't want Julie wandering about in her house until she was a fully paid up member of it.

When Liz got back outside, though, she found a man waiting on her doorstep.

"How can I help?" she asked. She was aiming at polite, but coldly distant.

"I've come about the room," he said.

Liz was fitting her key into the lock and spoke over her shoulder to him: "Oh, I wasn't expecting anybody else today..."

He put his arms right around her, effortlessly picked her up and walked them both over Liz's own threshold. He put her down in the hall. He was tall, large and unsmiling. She was short, reasonably slim and gobsmacked.

Chapter Four

To give herself some time she made a production of straightening her clothes and brushing off imaginary specks of dust and not so imaginary biscuit crumbs.

For the first time in her brief-but-interesting history of having lodgers she really wished some of them were home.

She wouldn't even have minded if there just happened to be a shrivelled-mushroom-for-a-brain bigot handy. Even if he couldn't help himself and came out with that, "Now, Liz..." thing.

He wasn't handy, though. Might have known he wouldn't be any use when she *really* needed him. Too busy being narrow-minded somewhere else, probably.

Finally she looked at this chap with what she hoped was an icy and un-intimidated glare. "That was a bit enthusiastic, wasn't it? What's your game?"

He wasn't at all put out. "I don't have all day and I've been waiting around already," he said. "You quite clearly said to be here at ten-thirty."

"No, I didn't. I've already said I wasn't expecting anyone else today. There isn't a room for you to have, I'm afraid. They've all gone." Liz stared hard at him. She could feel the top of her head getting hot. She wasn't at all keen on his

27

high-handed attitude, although another, alien part of her, was sizing him up. Hmm, rather nice, and he'd certainly made her heart wake up and take notice, the way it was thundering round in her chest. That could have been fear, or it could have been animal lust. Fear had the edge, though.

"It can't have gone so soon," he said. "I'm here on time. It was only this morning we arranged this." His voice had hardened.

Liz backed away from him a bit, in a casual, very, very relaxed kind of way.

He was obviously totally bonkers.

"I haven't spoken to anyone on the phone this morning," she said. "And I'm sorry, but I don't have a room spare either."

He was looking all round him and Liz wished someone would come into the house, but it was unlikely that her wish would be answered at this time in the morning. Everyone would be at work, just getting into their stride. Moocher would recently have got up, stretching himself and yawning, tail waving slowly from side to side, but she willed him to have a lie-in. It'd be awful for him to come to her protection and get hurt.

Hugh, damnitalltohell, was who she really needed. He was at least as tall as this chap, and just as wide and solid-looking, and he could do intimidating with the best of them.

She thought she might be able to sidle around the madman, open the door and somehow push him out of the house, but he suddenly shot off down the hall. Liz could see him peering around the breakfast room. He then disappeared into the kitchen.

She made off after him. "Hey - what do you think you're doing?" Stupid question - he was obviously looking for something. "Who are you anyway?" That was better.

By this time, they were both in the kitchen and squaring up to each other, if you can call it that when one of the protagonists was about a foot shorter than the other.

Liz's heart really was making a hell of a fuss about all this, thundering away as it was, and she didn't think it was because he was a bit of a hunk. Although he was. Anyway, she wished it would shut up and let her think.

The madman's nose began to quiver and wrinkle. Liz became aware that there was a silent war going on between the members of the household as to who should empty the bin *this* time. But then, why should she worry about what a madman thought?

"So - who the hell are you?" she managed through gritted teeth. She was trying not to draw too deep a breath in case the fumes from the overflowing bin got in and rotted her lungs. She didn't usually spend much time in the kitchen, and this was one good reason.

"My name is Tony Armitage. I have an appointment to see the owner of this house, a Liz Houston, at ten-thirty. I intend seeing this Liz Houston and I intend seeing this house. I need a room. This house is in the right area. I have the deposit and one month, two month's rent if need be, to give in advance. Where is Liz Houston?"

She said, "I am Liz Houston and I definitely did not make an appointment with any Tony Armitage person!"

He drew back from her all of a sudden, almost recoiling. What a relief! He was tall enough that she'd been developing a nasty crick in her neck looking up at him.

He appeared so dismayed Liz nearly felt sorry for him. "Come through into the breakfast room and let's sort this out." She was glad to leave the decomposing veg smell behind and took the opportunity to gulp in some fresh breakfast-room air.

They sat down at the table and she pulled her diary towards her. There was no appointment at ten-thirty. Could she have arranged this appointment and then forgotten it and failed to put it in her diary too? She didn't think so. But there was no denying his certainty. Although he could have been lying.

But he must have thought *she* was because he gave her a strange look and demanded, "Are you really Liz Houston?"

"Of course I am. I've just said so."

"I expected someone a lot older."

Oh! What a nice man! He could move in any time he wanted if he kept that up.

"If you think flattery is going to get you the room you can think again." Liz wasn't afraid of him anymore. Not now he was sitting down. Not now he seemed like such a nice man.

"It's not flattery. I really was expecting someone in their fifties, not their twenties."

He was getting better all the time. He was still looking around though, sizing everything up. Maybe he was a burglar with a different approach. Hugh's voice flashed through her brain: "Now, Liz…" Yeah. He probably *was* a burglar.

Liz took the offensive based on the notion that flattery is very nice, but you can't trust the flatterer. "I don't have a room. And don't start all

30

that rigmarole again. Whoever you spoke to this morning, it wasn't me. I'm sorry, but you must be in the wrong place." Hugh would be proud of her. Suddenly Liz kicked herself in the ankle. Why the hell did she keep thinking of Hugh? She didn't care if he'd be proud of her or not!

Dragging her attention back to Tony Armitage, she wondered how he knew her name, and why he was really here?

"Can you make room? Have you a lodger who's leaving? Could I pay one to go?"

Besotted though she might be about her house she would not describe it as luxurious, or the facilities it offered as particularly desirable.

"Why are you so desperate to be here?" Liz demanded.

He wasn't forthcoming. They stared at each other, deadlocked. Now Liz could inspect him openly she could see that he was indeed a pretty fine specimen of a man. He couldn't be a burglar and look like that. Liz knew all that stuff about not telling a book by its cover, but really, this chap looked too hero-ish to be interested in silver spoons and second-hand tellies. Cashmere was his camouflage, not stripy jumpers and swag bags.

Not that Liz was interested. Oh, no, not her. She was not interested in men and relationships and all that stuff anymore. She just managed to keep her snort of derision to herself. So that made another good reason to get rid of him.

Strange that there'd been two weird people in the same morning wanting to get lodgings in her house, not to mention someone searching her garden too thoroughly for a speed-crazy tortoise. Anyone would think there was a conspiracy

31

between them... Julie! Ohmigod! Where on earth had *she* got to?

She looked wildly around the breakfast room as though Julie might suddenly materialize on the mantelpiece. She had disappeared somewhere between Lydia's back garden and hers. She'd lost a potential lodger.

Aargh. Liz could hear it echoing all around her skull: "Now, Liz..."

She jumped up and rushed down the hall. No, Julie wasn't in the downstairs bedroom that used to be a lounge. Liz dashed into the front room that was now the communal sitting room. She wasn't in there. Where could she be? Liz spun around to find her view reduced to an expanse of crisp white shirt split down the middle by a tie that looked very old-school. Criminy - he could move quickly and quietly. Spooky.

"Don't do that," Liz snapped. "Don't creep up on me like that!"

He looked crestfallen. "I thought you'd decided to give me the tour after all."

"Oh! Well, not exactly." Liz could hardly offer the information that she'd lost her newest lodger.

"Never mind, you can show me which room was on offer, even if it's taken. I could probably persuade whoever's taken it to let me have it."

"I find your certainty rather off-putting, Mr Armitage. Not only that, but it's me who decides whether you live in this house - not you - not anyone else. Me."

But her mind was on Julie Carrington-Smythe's disappearing act.

Perhaps she'd given up the whole idea of limboing in through the dog-flap. Maybe she'd gone back into Lydia's for more coffee, cake and sympathy. That was probably it. So she wasn't in league with this chap and Liz would have a room free for him. She wasn't sure that was a terrifically good idea, but it would give him what he wanted and get him off her back. Also, the gas bill was rather large and he did say he could pay two months rent up front. Why do people say that stuff about money being the root of all evil when it's patently obvious that it's the *lack* of money that's the trouble?

So Liz pushed past him and headed back the way they'd come. She opened the door out of the kitchen. And there the vanished lodger was.

Half in and half out of the dog-flap.

Stuck.

Chapter Five

She must have been there all that time. Liz looked through the upper, glass part of the back door and saw Simon and Lydia over their side oohing and aahing and being totally useless. Lydia also had a mobile phone cradled between her chin and shoulder. Liz hoped she wasn't calling out any fire and rescue teams to liberate Julie. She could just imagine that being plastered all over the local paper. *Now, Liz...*

She looked back at the heap on the floor. "Why on earth didn't you shout?"

Julie slowly raised her head, gave her a venomous look and flopped it back down again.

Fancy getting stuck in the dog-flap. Liz hadn't thought Julie was *that* chunky, for Pete's sake, but that explained Simon's objections to the exercise. Even so, being chunky doesn't stop people from forgetting their keys.

How irritating it all was.

Liz sighed.

Then she jumped about a metre in the air as a voice bellowed in her ear, "What the hell's going on? What have you done to this poor girl? Don't just stand there – we've got to get her off this floor before she gets hypothermia."

"Hang on a minute," Liz said. "Hang on! Blimey – what makes you so sure it's anything to do with me? I can't help it if she chooses to get stuck in my dog-flap. Why the bloody hell didn't she yell about it?"

She glared at the heap on the floor. "Not only that, but if you hadn't kept all your clothes on, Julie, it would have been a doddle."

Julie stirred, gave her a nasty look and came back with: "You didn't tell me that part of the deal was to crawl through here naked."

"Oh, very witty. Talk about exaggerating! If you'd taken off that huge jacket of yours and thrown it through first you'd have come through that dog-flap without touching the sides. Anyway, *why* didn't you scream for help when you got stuck?"

"What - to be ripped to pieces by that ravening animal of yours?" Julie was obviously recovering.

"Don't be silly. I don't know this man."

"Your dog," she snapped. "I'm talking about your dog."

"You don't know my dog."

Tony joined in. "You've got a dog?"

The world was going mad around her unsuspecting head. "Well of course I have. Why would I have a dog-flap if I didn't have a dog?"

He looked grave as though he was seriously considering the question. "I don't know, perhaps to indulge a strange habit of getting people stuck in it."

"It's not a habit. It's never happened before and wouldn't have happened now if she'd taken that enormous coat off. And I still fail to see why the hell she didn't yell out."

But she could see Julie was going to get sulky rather than answer her questions. Pity, she'd seemed like a good sport for a while. Liz watched with interest as Tony inspected the frame of the dog-flap.

The whole situation raised rather worrying concerns. It had never occurred to her before that there might be potential lodgers who were just too big to go through the dog-flap. Liz couldn't discriminate to that extent could she? She couldn't say to people, "No, sorry, but you're too big to go through my dog-flap. Therefore you can't have a room." Although it might make perfect sense to her, she could see that to some it might not. She could even be had up by the equal opportunities people, maybe, for discriminating on the grounds of size. She could be accused of sizism. Life gets complicated sometimes.

Some instinct made her look up. Lydia was transfixed by the tableau and was making unmistakable hand signals. She wanted to know who the hunk was. Liz shrugged exaggeratedly which seemed to make Lydia even more excited. Simon in the meantime had obviously taken the opportunity to have a few smokes and was in the process of rolling the lit end out between his thumb and forefinger in that absent-minded way he had. And, yes, into his pocket it went. When he started to dance around on the spot clutching his leg, Liz found herself glad that she was in here and he was over there. The smell of burning leg hairs is not nice.

After wallowing in another deep sigh, she returned her attention to the present and realised that Tony Armitage had taken it upon himself to remove the entire dog-flap from the door, frame and all, with Julie still stuck in it. Julie stood there, in her kitchen, wearing the dog-flap as if it was some sort of fashion accessory. Why she should be able to extricate herself more easily from a loose dog-flap than from one anchored firmly in the back door was beyond Liz. But by this time she was too tired of the day to object. She put the kettle on instead. Let them get on with it.

No one was taking any notice of her so she scoffed the rest of Sandra's chocolate biscuits. Hers was the only tin that rattled when Liz shook it. Liz hated it when the lodgers pinched off each other, but there were only four biscuits anyway and Liz would replace them. Her need was greater than Sandra's at that moment.

Now Tony was removing Julie's clothing. She just stood there, a life-size doll with a sea of discarded clothes around her feet like wrinkled waves. Tony continued taking her clothes off, pulling a sweater gently out from between her and the dog-flap frame, to reveal another sweater beneath.

The door bell rang out. Liz was glad to have a good excuse to leave them to it.

Except, it turned out to be Hugh. Trust him to turn up too late to rescue her from a madman who had bodily carried her over her own threshold - but not too late to witness the spectacle in her kitchen. Neither of them spoke. He simply followed her into the house. But he took one look at the tableau in the kitchen and turned on his heel to leave, still silent.

She trotted after him. "Hugh. Hang on. What's up? What did you call round for?"

He stopped halfway down the garden path and looked at her as if totally exasperated by something. "I'm on my way to see a client and had quarter of an hour spare, so I thought I'd drop in to see you. I still want us to have a chat. But I can see you're far too busy at the moment. God knows what you're up to now. But I no longer want to know. What you get up to is your business."

For years Liz had wanted him to believe that, and behave as though her business was truly hers, but she didn't want him discontinuing all interest in it in quite this contemptuous manner. What *was* going on with him that his attitude towards her had changed so radically? Liz couldn't fathom it, but was determined not to let it rile her. At that moment, though, she knew if she tried to sling together a whole sentence she'd probably start shouting. He was bugging the hell out of her with his newly stuffy ways. So she merely opened her mouth to squeeze out a squeaked, "Okay. See you then,", gave a brief wave and marched back into the house. It was impossible to slam her front door because it didn't fit properly. It was very annoying.

She stomped back down to the kitchen just as Moocher turned up looking displeased. His lie-in must have been badly disturbed by all the hoohah. Liz tried to stroke the wrinkles out of his forehead. "Ooh, lookie, lookie. Here's the ravening creature," Liz announced.

Tony stopped what he was doing, and Julie and he both glanced around at the ravening creature, briefly, before hurriedly looking away.

Of course, Moocher had chosen that historic moment to perform his morning toilette, thoroughly and noisily. Criminy. Liz went for another biscuit, but in the stress of it all she'd finished them. She wet her finger and tried to get the crumbs out of the bottom of the tin.

The clatter as the dog-flap hit the floor jerked her attention out of the biscuit tin. The pile of discarded clothes was enormous. This explained why Julie'd had no luggage with her - it was all on her back. It must be easier to carry it that way. Tony continued to peel yet more layers of clothing off her.

Liz thought it was time she stepped in. "Leave her be. She might want some of those clothes left on."

"They're soaking wet, Mrs Houston. She's in a state of shock. Look at her. We must get them off her and get her into something warm." He certainly seemed keen to get them off her, and if they were wet, Liz supposed the basic idea was right. More clothes slapped onto the floor.

"How did you get so wet, Julie? It's not raining."

"I fell in the pond."

"How did you manage to do that? The pond's nowhere near the back door!"

Liz wondered if Julie felt too stupid to admit being scared into the pond by a rampaging devil-tortoise.

"I was just looking around."

"You can't have been looking that thoroughly, then."

"I was, but your pond is so overgrown I thought it was a cabbage patch or something."

"It's a pond for wildlife isn't it? You can't expect to see water if it's for wildlife can you? Oh, that reminds me - lodgers have to contribute some effort to the upkeep of the garden, too."

"Well that shouldn't be difficult if you want it to remain at its present standard," Tony said.

"It won't be a problem of *yours*, don't forget," Liz said, feeling the need to remind him that he wasn't going to be a lodger of hers anytime soon.

She could see that Julie was shuddering with cold, so she went upstairs, started a bath running, found a towel and dressing gown, and trudged back down the stairs. As she passed through the breakfast room, she glanced out of the window and saw Lydia opposite, sitting in her own breakfast room in regal splendour, a cup of tea in one hand, a biscuit in the other, watching the drama in Liz's house unfold. Simon leant against her back door, smoking. He had a sizeable hole in his trouser leg.

What did startle her was that Hugh was there, too. He must have left her house and gone straight next door. He stood just behind Lydia's shoulder as though at attention, and his face could have belonged to one of those avenging angels that come down to moralise at you, finger wagging. He looked at her as though they were complete strangers. Actually, Liz thought they were at that moment. She had certainly never met her ex in his current, bigoted guise. She wondered what on earth he was doing in Lydia's, but she turned away in what she hoped was a 'stuff-you' gesture.

Moocher was leaping in and out of the hole in her back door as if to say that swinging the flap had been too much effort all along. Tough! It would have to go back in. The temperature of the house had dropped considerably and God knew what was happening to the next gas bill right at that moment.

She was amazed to see that Julie now looked about half the age she'd thought her. She was positively stick-like, very young and very cold. Liz thought Tony had gone far enough and took charge. "Come on, let's get you in the bath and then bed perhaps."

"Can I have the room then?" she asked, her voice wobbling as it came out between quivering jaws.

Liz sighed again. "Yes. Come on. You have passed the test, after a fashion. I don't believe you'll get stuck again. You don't have to walk around clad in your entire wardrobe any more." Liz turned to Tony, "And I want that dog-flap back in the door forthwith!" She was fresh out of social niceties by then.

Liz took Julie upstairs, made sure she had everything she needed and left her in the bathroom. She would put herself to bed when she got out of the bath. Liz wondered if she'd clean it.

She could hear hammering from downstairs. Where had Tony got a hammer from? Perhaps he came prepared. She went on up to her attic and stood in the doorway, looking longingly into the room. The attic was the very hub of her business empire. In the attic Liz could be alone and undisturbed by all the irritating influences of everyday life. However, this was not the time, so she left it again, shutting the door firmly behind her.

Coming back down the stairs she heard the familiar screech of the front door as it dragged across the flagstones. Must be Sandra at this time of day. She worked early shifts and came home for lunch when civilised people were having elevenses.

"Hellooo…"

She always yelled when she came in the house.

Why?

Liz completed her descent to the hall. "Hello," she said in what she hoped was a repressive tone of voice. Sandra was one of these unbearably bouncy people, even first thing in the morning. Especially first thing in the morning. Awful.

"Oh, Liz. I meant to tell you. I'm moving out today," Sandra said, watching her carefully with her slightly protruding eyes. Liz hadn't really taken note of them before. Nor had she noticed before what a very sly face Sandra had. "Today," she repeated. "I'm moving out. You can keep the deposit."

Liz was startled. Sandra had no intention of moving out last time they'd spoken. That had been the previous night. As for offering to forego her deposit, that didn't fit with her grasping nature at all.

"You're moving out? Today? And I can keep the deposit?" Liz just wanted to be sure she'd heard aright.

Sandra was already galloping up the stairs. "Yup," she yelled over her shoulder. "By the way, there's a woman outside looking for a tortoise." Liz heard her door open and shut and then heard her singing. Singing! Out of tune. Thank God she was going. It meant Liz didn't have to buy a replacement pack of chocolate biscuits. Viciously she wished there'd been more biscuits in Sandra's tin and then Liz could have eaten them all. That would have served her right.

She didn't want to think about the drop in income straightaway.

By that time tortoise-woman, thankfully minus Pink and Fluffy, had appeared at the door, swinging her pet basket as though it was an admission ticket to Liz's house and garden. She merely lifted an eyebrow. Liz merely nodded and tortoise-woman cantered off down the hall.

Then Liz realised how she'd been set up. She wondered if the clunks and clicks were audible as her brain finally made the connections. She sprinted up the stairs after Sandra. She could move pretty fast when she wanted to, even if her brain lagged behind by a few weeks. She had barely begun to beat on Sandra's door before she threw it open. "It was *you*, wasn't it? *You* rang this man, this Tony Armitage, pretending you were me. You told him to come round here at ten thirty, told him there was a room. How much did he pay you for your collusion? And why did you do it? And how did you know to ring him?"

Sandra was busy piling heaps of clothes into black rubbish bags, but she looked up and said, "I didn't do anything of the sort."

Liz had never before noticed how crab-like her mouth was.

Sandra started to fill another bag, hurling into it many-coloured boots, pastel-shaded shoes and extravagantly-strapped sandals. "Someone I know who knows him knew he wanted a place in Bristol in a hurry - he seemed particular about being in this area - he asked her if there were any rooms going here and I said there might be for a price. And he paid it. I said I would arrange with you for an appointment. I had meant to tell you of course."

"Of course."

Taking in lodgers can be a disillusioning experience.

Liz studied this ex-lodger's activity with sneaking admiration. She'd never seen anyone pack up their life in such a short space of time. Sandra had lived there for about a year and, just like that, she was ready to move on.

"How much did he pay you?" Liz was genuinely curious because for Sandra to voluntarily forfeit her deposit and take off at a moment's notice, it must have been an absolute fortune.

"Mind your own business," Sandra said, outrage colouring her voice.

"Have you still got it all?"

"What's it to you?" she demanded, but she stopped, momentarily, the process of stuffing a shelf full of hideous rag dolls of different nationalities into another black bag. She looked at Liz speculatively as if wondering if she might be on to another deal.

"I'm only asking because when I tell him he can't have your room he'll probably want it back. He strikes me as someone who won't want to have parted with that kind of money for nothing."

"He won't want it back because you'll let him have the room," Sandra declared, as though she could read Liz's mind with utter certainty. "I saw the gas bill come through yesterday."

Perhaps she *could* read her mind with utter certainty.

Liz didn't ask Sandra where she was going. Sandra didn't offer a forwarding address.

Going back up to the attic Liz looked in. Yes, her little world was still there. Waiting for her. She shut the door with her on the outside of it and went to confront the future, pulling a fiercely gruesome face at Sandra's bedroom door as she passed it.

Liz wished she'd remembered to tell her that when she'd been on the phone to Tony Armitage, he'd thought she was in her fifties. That would have been a crushing blow to such a vain twentyish person. It still gave Liz a pleasant glow to think of it. Maybe things were looking up.

Tony had finished fitting the dog-flap back into its hole in the door and was sitting at the breakfast room table with two mugs of coffee in front of him, presumably for him and for Liz. She wondered if he came prepared with coffee in his pocket, too, and walked straight past him to minutely inspect the dog-flap. As if she knew what to look for by way of carpentering jobs. She pushed it out and watched it swing back in with its usual 'clatter-thunk'. He'd done a tidy job as far as she could see. Liz glanced out of the window, but Lydia and Simon must have retired into her front room, no doubt to recover from all the excitement. Hugh was still there, though, and stared at her as though his look alone was enough to make her see sense about whatever it was she was supposed to have done *now*. Liz gritted her teeth, gave a little fluttery wave, and endeavoured to produce a light-hearted grin. Neither his stance, nor his expression, changed one iota. Sod him, then.

She truly wished she could put up a fence between the two houses so that her affairs weren't quite so open to Lydia's view on an everyday basis, and Hugh's just now. But Poor Lydia would have felt shut out. Liz sighed and sat down opposite Tony. The sunlight streaming in through the window showed her he was older than she'd first thought.

"I decided to make us some coffee," he said. "I'll replace it."

Spoken like a potential lodger with all the right attitudes.

"Thanks," she said.

"That's a helluva dog-flap you've got there," he said. He had a nice, clean and even smile.

"Moocher's a helluva dog." Liz's answering smile felt a touch strained and self-conscious and was mainly for Hugh's benefit.

"You're not bothered about anyone else coming in through it?"

"Nah. What would you think if you saw a dog-flap that size?"

"I'd think that one helluva dog lived in that house."

"Quite so." Her smile, this time, came more easily.

"Julie still in the bath?"

"She's in bed now."

"Why do you think she was wearing all her clothes?"

"Oh, I dunno. Easier to carry? She was in disguise? She was cold? Thanks for helping with her, by the way, and with the dog-flap. You were right about the need to get her warm again."

"You know there's a man watching us from next door, don't you?"

"Yeah. Just ignore him."

"I will. Oh, by the way, a strange woman with a pet basket came marching in here, stopped, looked across to your neighbour's, muttered something, rushed out into the garden, ran around it, rushed back in, muttered something else and ran out of the house."

"Oh, that was Tortoise-woman. Don't worry about it."

"Is it a daily occurrence - a tortoise-woman rushes around your property and rushes out again?"

"No. Well, it didn't use to be. Don't worry about it. I can't imagine she'll be round *again*."

"I won't worry. Did you know she's in next door now, standing next to the man we're ignoring?"

Liz couldn't help herself. She immediately looked up. Hopeless. She got so mad when she said to other people, "Don't look now, but..." and what did they do? Yeah. They looked. And here she was behaving in the same undisciplined way. And Tony was right. Tortoise-woman was next door talking to Hugh. What on earth was going on? As Liz watched, Tortoise-woman made her way through Lydia's kitchen and out of her back door. She must have decided devil-tortoise was raping and pillaging in next door's garden when she couldn't find him in Liz's.

Tony and Liz fiddled with the handles of their mugs, took miniscule sips of coffee, crossed their legs and uncrossed them again. Liz wondered if Tony was worried about varicose veins too.

Suddenly he asked: "Do I get the room?"

"Why do you want it so much?"

"I need somewhere to stay in Bristol."

"Yeah, but there's lots of places. Why are you so anxious to be here, in this house? You must have paid Sandra a fortune to get her to leave."

"You'll need someone else now that Sandra's leaving."

"Why do you want to be in this house so much?"

"It must cost a lot of money to keep an old house like this one going."

"Mr Armitage! Please answer my question. Otherwise how can you expect me to give you the room? You're making yourself more and more suspect by avoiding the issue."

He straightened up and looked directly at her. "I want to be in this particular area. Are there any other houses with empty rooms in Malvern Road?"

"Not that I'm aware of."

"Well there you are. It has to be in this house then. But I can assure you that, if there *was* a room in the house next door for example, I would take it. Does that reassure you that it's nothing to do with you personally?"

"Yes." Liz couldn't say anything else. His reasons were his concern and anyway she didn't usually ask such questions of her lodgers. There were things she wouldn't like people to ask her. And he appeared to be well able to pay the rent...

"Do I get the room then?"

"Yes. You've gone to a lot of effort, not to mention expense, to get it."

He beamed, positively beamed and Liz felt warmed.

She would have to watch that.

She seemed to have come out of it quite well - two new lodgers and Sandra's deposit. The gas bill, huge though it was, could be paid, no problem. Tony was very good-looking and seemed like a useful chap, if a tad used to getting his own way. Julie, as it turned out, was a mere babe. Liz could cope with her. Two months rent up front. Yes, all in all, it had worked out okay.

"However," she said, endeavouring to get back to business. "There are certain house rules to which you must adhere..."

"I gather that the dog-flap business is about if a lodger forgets their key - I have no intention of doing the dog-flap trial, I'm afraid."

There was that unmistakeable high-handedness again. Pity. Liz shrugged, but before she could say something silly like: "Well, you can't stay here then," he said, "I hate to draw your attention to it, but do you think my shoulders would get through?"

She gazed at the parts of his anatomy in question and realised, sinkingly, that he was right. Not only that, but although his shoulders wouldn't get through, his hips certainly would. Perfect. However, she had her resolutions to think of and one of them was to not think of such things.

"If you put one shoulder in first and sort of twisted your way in, I expect..."

"No." He did something nice with his eyebrows. A sort of a twitchy, appealing thing. "How about if I get some more keys made up and give one to your neighbour?" He flicked his eyes sideways to indicate Lydia who now stood next to Hugh in her window staring their way.

"No!"

There went the eyebrows again. Liz must ignore them in future.

"No?"

"No. She's very sweet and a Poor Thing because she's so lonely, but she's a damn nuisance. She has no life of her own and lives what little she does have through us. She's always around, always calling, always peering through this window from her window."

"Why don't you put up a fence?"

"Because it would be too much of a slap in the face." She knew she'd just contradicted herself, but really, there were some things you just couldn't do. "It would be like slamming a door on her foot. Anyway - the key - I can't have her having one - God knows if she would, but I can just imagine her prancing in here any time she felt lonely which is about once every quarter of an hour. It would be a nightmare." Her shudder was real.

"All right then, can I give one to the neighbour on the other side?"

"Git-Next-Door? Certainly not! What a creep that man is! What a pain. He'd use it to come in here and poison Moocher."

Tony looked interested for a second. "Git-Next-Door? No, I don't want to know." He lowered his eyes and absently pulled a long black dog hair from his sleeve. The Moocher Effect had rolled into action. "What about if I kept a key in my car? Or just hid it somewhere anonymous?"

Liz couldn't think of any better suggestions. "Oh, all right. You can keep a key somewhere else. But you're not allowed to tell anyone that I've let you off the trial or I'll never regain my authority and house rules are house rules."

"So - you're definitely letting me have the room?"

She nodded without looking at him again. She needed to build up some defences against Tony Armitage's charms, that was for sure.

Moocher had no such reservation and ambled over to lay his head on Tony's lap in order, no doubt, to share around some more hairs. Tony idly pulled Moocher's ears - a sure sign of a dog-man. He was okay. Moocher had given his seal of approval. In fact, as Liz watched, his approval became rather too enthusiastic and she jumped up to drag him off and make him sit at her feet in obedient-dog fashion. She refused to be embarrassed. He was a full-blooded dog after all, although, it had to be said, that was only because he'd chosen to enter and brighten her life when he was too old to be safely done.

"And Mr Houston?"

Considering Liz'd just been thinking about neutering the dog, this query took her by surprise. It would probably have taken Hugh by surprise, too. "Pardon?"

"Mr Houston? Doesn't he have to okay the lodgers?"

"No," Liz snapped, not prepared to actually tell this man Mr Houston had nothing to do with her lodgers whatsoever. Except, of course, that if Mr Houston was still there no lodgers would be required, but it was her fault for chucking him out. She started to sink into her usual swamp of self-pity when thinking of the break up of her marriage when she realised that Tony must only have asked to see if there was a Mr Houston at all, and also, Sandra would probably have told him there wasn't.

Slightly flustered as she wasn't sure of his motives, or even whether she was interested, especially as she'd sworn off all that stuff, Liz launched into landlady mode. "Anyway, there *are* other rules, you know," she said to try and regain some authority over the proceedings.

"Yes, Sandra's told me them - no phone calls after ten, clean bath after get out not before get in..."

Sometimes she knew when she was beaten. "Right, well, I can get back to work then..."

It was a relief, too, to get away from Hugh's regard. From the corner of her eye she could see he still stood there, next door, like a great black looming mountain, waiting to fall on her with so much disapproval she'd suffocate under it. Tortoise-woman was nowhere to be seen.

Hugh watched Liz leave the room and was surprised to see the man who'd been ignoring him until now turn directly his way and smile. What did that mean? Alarmed, but naturally polite, Hugh gritted his teeth and managed an answering grimace. Did he think Hugh was someone else? Why would he be smiling at him? Hugh turned away from the window even more worried about Liz than before. What on earth was he going to do about her? She had this knack of getting in trouble, just falling from one perilous situation to the next. How could he keep an eye on her when he wasn't supposed to be seeing her anymore? He knew it was a bit lame of him merely to acquiesce to Charity's wishes in this, but at the same time he knew it was best to steer clear of Liz. Although he did love Charity, there was something about Liz that got him hot and bothered. And hot and bothered in an unsettling way he no longer wanted to feel.

Charity had known as soon as she'd seen him that he'd not told Liz about them and she'd made it clear, in her quiet way, that he needed to apprise Liz of the situation forthwith. Well, he'd failed again. He'd turned up at Liz's but somehow the sight of some man, who was now smiling at him, stripping some girl in the kitchen was not conducive to telling his ex-wife about his future wife. He was chicken. He knew it.

Of course, now that Simon and Lydia had filled him on the new lodger getting stuck in the dog-flap, it all made perfect sense. Except no one knew who the man was. Hugh had premonitions about him. He was bound to be trouble.

And as for the strange woman he'd seen before, minus children this time, but faithful pet basket in hand – what was that about? They'd exchanged a few words about uncontrollable tortoises and she'd gone but he was convinced that if Liz wasn't part of the picture neither would there be a mad Tortoise-woman.

"Hugh, do stop worrying about her. She is a full grown woman now and must fend for herself."

He flinched as Lydia came through to refresh the teapot.

"Yes, but she doesn't, does she? She's always getting in trouble."

"Nothing she can't handle."

"How can I not be around to help, though?" He felt powerless. Lydia put down the teapot.

"Hugh, I gather you're not supposed to see Liz anymore. That's your business. Why don't I just report in to you every now and then so you can feel reassured that she's fine?"

He felt immense relief at such a simple solution and could only stare at Lydia gratefully.

"Of course, Liz will feel that it's spying if she found out, but she won't find out." Lydia happily opened another packet of biscuits as Hugh's relief dissolved like butter on a hot plate. His scalp tingled. What if Liz found out?

Lydia glanced at him and laughed. She smacked him playfully on the arm. "She won't find out! Why on earth should she find out? I'm not going to tell her. Go on, go about your new start and stop worrying about Liz. I'll let you know if she really needs you, so you needn't worry about it."

Motionless, Hugh stared across at Liz's house and mentally said goodbye. Unexpectedly choked up he took his leave of Lydia and went to start his new life with no more loose ends from his old to trip him up.

Chapter Six

Liz stared for a long time at her computer monitor, but the spreadsheet glowing upon it failed to grip her attention. She tried so hard to cultivate a 'live and let live' philosophy, but this didn't switch off her curiosity. So, why did Tony want so much to live in this area? Why did he behave as though he could undress a strange young girl in someone else's kitchen and get away with it? Perhaps he was a doctor? Why would a doctor come to view a room with a hammer in his pocket?

What was Hugh doing in next door, staring into Liz's breakfast room?

Was it a coincidence that both times Hugh had turned up so had a wild-eyed woman looking for a vicious tortoise?

There were too many questions. The spreadsheet was easier.

Several hours later she was roused from futile efforts to make sense of her client's accounts by the most incredible smell of wholesome home cooking. It smelt like frying onions and spices and country kitchens. It filled the attic with an out of this world fragrance and set her mouth watering.

Moocher jumped off his bean-bag and padded around the room twitching his nose and pulling in deep noisy breaths of pure pleasure. But he wasn't getting any and neither was Liz. She didn't believe in all this let's-be-chummy-and-hang-out-and-have-all-our-meals-together stuff in a house like this - who does the shopping, the cooking, the washing up? Who pays, and for what? And then it means having to stop and eat when required, rather than on the go. It's pure disruption for someone trying to work at home.

However, it was Moocher's supper time so they trailed down the stairs to find a jolly party around the table. They were all there, Tony, Julie (looking much recovered), Simon and Melanie.

Melanie was the other lodger. She was very enthusiastic about everything – eating, talking, sport, good causes. And she was so honest her name could be in the dictionary instead of the word 'honest' and everyone would know what it meant.

So there they all were. Moocher and Liz were greeted with cries of: "Pull up a chair, there's a plate for you." How nice.

"No thanks," she said, heading resolutely into the kitchen. "I don't want to stop work. I'm only here to feed Moocher."

"No more Sandra, then?" That was Melanie.

"No," Simon muttered. "Thank heaven for that. No more pretending we're not embarrassed…"

Crumbs. Liz had completely forgotten she'd meant to add another item to her 'potential lodger' questionnaire, namely: Are you mad on sex and if you are, do you have somewhere else to go for it? Many were the times the other occupants of the house, their hands clamped over their ears, had hurried past Sandra's door doing a curious crab-like scuttle, trying to get away from what sounded like a porn movie set within.

It must be nice to be so uninhibited, though. Sandra seemed to have a different partner for each day of the week. They were just a blur leaving the house in the morning and seldom seen arriving at night. They just seemed to come and go, as it were, as regular as the days passing.

That'd be a relief anyway. Tempting though it was to ask Julie and Tony the question now, it didn't seem fair. Liz'd have to add it for the next lodger.

She took the lid off Moocher's pan of liver and cabbage and recoiled as the stench hit her. She often cooked his food because she thought it must be really boring getting the same old stuff out of a tin every day, not to mention all the E numbers and heaven knows what else they put in it. However, despite liver and cabbage being one of Moocher's favourite dishes, he was far more interested in what the others were having,

That was a shame because he couldn't have any. Liz ladled out his ration for the evening and put it in the usual place. He sat without her telling him. She always made him sit before he could have his food - like a silent grace. Actually, it was to show that at least for a couple of seconds, twice a day, she was indeed the one in control. He was kind enough to let her believe that. He sat obediently with his head turned about two hundred degrees, staring at the feast on the table. Liz wondered who'd cooked it. Probably Mr I've-got-a-hammer-in-my-pocket-and-am-prepared-for-any-occasion himself. Was there no end to that man's talents? She peered sideways and sneaked a look at the back of his neck. Hmm, it had a darling little cowlick of hair on it that didn't want to go the way the rest of his hair went. She shivered and tore her gaze away, uncomfortably reminded of Hugh in friendlier times. Moocher nudged her in the shin to keep her mind on the important things in life.

"Good dog, you can have it." These magic words weren't followed by the usual dash to get his snout in the bowl. She said it again, louder. He looked at her sadly and eventually staggered to his feet. He shuffled to his bowl, advancing on his supper as though she'd given him a dish of cold rat vomit.

She was staring at the droop of his tail, which usually waved gently like a heavy flag whilst he was eating his supper, when she distinctly heard the sound of breaking glass. Not a sort of tinkle-sound, but a sort of huge-big-pane-of-glass breaking sound. It was very close. Her first thought was that it was Lydia's breakfast room window, but looking over at it through her kitchen window she could see it was still in one piece. There wasn't another window closer unless it was one of Liz's. It wasn't the breakfast room. It must be the front room.

The front room! She raced down the hall. Barging into the front room she was brought up short by a hand grabbing her arm and pulling her abruptly backwards. Just as well because a missile came flying through the enormous hole already in the window and narrowly missed rearranging her features. It flew by her and disappeared into the lush, leafy depths of Abigail, the aspidistra.

It was Tony, of course, who had hold of her arm in such a manly I-will-protect-you way. She paused to take stock of a shooting feeling in her midriff of the warm and fuzzy type. But she didn't pause for long. Her house was under attack from some lunatic out in the road. Who the hell did they think they were? She noticed Simon dash past her towards Abigail. "Simon, hang on to Moocher," she shrieked. Liz plunged into the lobby and threw open the front door.

She sprinted down the path just in time to see the cloud of exhaust issuing from a car speeding down Malvern Road, obviously escaping from the scene of the crime. Too late to follow it, although there were a couple of men running down the road as though that was what they were trying to do. Maybe they'd get the registration number.

Feeling a nose push into her hand she instantly got mad. "Bloody hell, Simon, I asked you to hang on to Moocher. He might have been run over. You know perfectly well he's not allowed out the front!" She immediately felt ashamed. One shouldn't shout at the likes of Simon. They so rarely shout back. Moocher, also, has a mind of his own and it was her fault for opening the front door without shutting the lobby door. "Sorry," she mumbled. "Didn't mean to shout."

He appeared at her elbow, looking strained. Nevertheless, he was tolerant. "I know," he said. "You were caught up in the moment."

How annoying when people are so understanding. She wanted to shout at him again, but controlled herself.

Back in the front room Tony was already clearing up the glass. He was so efficient, that man. Her next gas bill must have been leaping skywards as any warm air the house might have contained was sucked out through the annihilated window. Who on earth would want to throw missiles through her window? What were they anyway?

They were bricks, or half bricks, or maybe the same brick broken in half. The two pieces had been placed tidily on the coffee table, each on its own coaster. Julie, hankie held to her mouth, and Melanie, face alight with lust, were standing around as though admiring Tony's efficiency, or perhaps it was his rear view. He did make a pleasant sight as he crawled around the floor checking for slivers of glass.

"Was there a message on those bricks?" Liz asked.

The room fell quiet at what she thought was a perfectly reasonable question. After all, messages and bricks traditionally went together. Like messages and bottles. And why throw two bricks if the first wasn't for gaining attention for the message carried by the second? Made perfect sense to her.

"No," Tony said, firmly. "Why should there be a message? It will just have been yobs who wanted you to have clean windows, probably."

"Oh, very funny," Liz said. He'd obviously checked out the state of her windows while he was waiting at the front door that morning.

Trouble was, he'd done it without the benefit of her illuminating theory. Liz's theory was that if the windows were so dirty you couldn't see through them then obviously the occupants of the house are not just lazy, but also broke. Therefore, burglars won't be at all interested, and, fingers crossed as she thought it, they were the only un-burgled house in all the time she'd lived in Malvern Road. Which, to be fair, was only a few years, but there was no way she was going to ruin her run of luck by washing the windows. No way.

Anyway, Liz wasn't amused and decided not to lower herself with explanations for her filthy windows. "It doesn't seem like yobs to me," she said. "Why two bricks? They're more likely to have been caught with two. Anyway, I'm calling the police or has anyone done so already?" She looked around in surprise at the sheepish expressions her lodgers suddenly exhibited. She looked at Tony for explanation. He'd only been there half a day and he was clearly the leader. A shade of uneasiness rippled through her.

"There's no need," he said. "I'll get it fixed."

"There's every need. The police should be called. This should be reported. I need a crime reference number to claim on the insurance. Apart from which, we shouldn't hide crime. It needs to be dealt with."

"I can assure you, they might put in a token appearance, but they won't be much interested and you can bet nothing will be done, least of all the yobs caught. That's the way it is. I'll deal with it. You don't even need to lose your no-claims bonus. If you call them, you'll have a late night and nothing to show for it."

Trouble was, Liz suspected he was right. But she didn't see why he was so anxious to settle the bill and deal with the hassle. And she didn't think she should let him, although it was very tempting to have someone else do the hassle bit. She thought of Hugh, the Hugh who had existed before Mr Stuffed Shirt took his place, and that was her undoing. He was so very good at sorting out hassle without even a frown marring his lovely face, or a crease his shirt. Whereas she knew only too well how easy it was to waste a whole day on the phone and get in a stinking bad temper and still not achieve what she wanted and she *did* have a deadline on her present work. She dithered and rather feebly allowed it to be taken out of her hands. It was all Hugh's fault. If she hadn't thought of him she wouldn't have allowed such weak thinking in herself.

"Let's call it settled then," Tony said, losing interest in her concerns and turning to Melanie. "Look, Julie's upset. Why don't you take her into the breakfast room and get on with your supper and the card game and I'll sort this out."

He chivvied them out of the front room. Simon had disappeared, probably outside for a smoke, and that seemed to be that.

Wondering why paralysis had gripped her usual determination to do everything herself, Liz grabbed a couple of apples and a chunk of cheese and went back to untangling her client's accounts. Moocher went with her. They got into the attic and Liz knelt down on the floor. Moocher took up his accustomed stance and she hugged him long and hard, her arms around his chunky shoulders, her face resting on the top of his head. He was such a huggable dog. And he was always there for her. The rest of her world seemed to be trembling around the edges, but she could always depend on Moocher.

But something bothered her about what had happened. She tried to ignore it for the time being but by the time she'd been hugging Moocher so long her knees had lost all feeling, she had developed an absolute certainty that there *had* been a message on one of those bricks. She had a very visual memory and she could see on the movie screen in her mind a rubber band on the floor in the front room below the sideboard that Abigail graced. She hadn't realised the significance of it at the time. So, who had the message? What did it say? Who was it for? Why did they keep it a secret?

Something was afoot and she really wanted to ignore it. All she ever wanted was to pay her bills and keep her house and get on with her new career, but these ambitions seemed to get further and further away from her.

Although it didn't seem right to ignore whatever was going on, she was tired. She was just going to go to bed and not think about anything until the morning. Especially, she wouldn't think about Hugh, whose ready presence, in his previous incarnation, in her mind seemed to take on more appeal the more the puzzles mounted.

The morning shone through her dormer window with an expectant, hard to ignore, gusto. Liz rolled over, and groaned. She hadn't slept much and felt pretty old.

Reluctance dragged at her, but she had to go downstairs. Apart from anything else, a slosh of grapefruit juice was urgently required to carve a channel through her morning-mouth and jolt her into some form of consciousness. Caffeine, too, would help to kick-start her thinking.

However, despite her lack of enthusiasm, the front room looked magnificent in the bright morning light. It was amazing the difference brilliantly clean windows made. Git-Next-Door would be pleased. He'd actually complained, once, about the state of her windows. Damn nerve.

Burglars would be pleased too. They wouldn't have to wade through the undergrowth of the front garden anymore to inspect the contents of her house. Everything was clearly spot-lit by the morning sun and could, no doubt, be seen from the other side of the road.

How Tony Armitage had managed to get all this sorted over-night was anyone's guess. Even now it was only seven in the morning.

The rubber band had disappeared from the floor. The bricks had gone too. This bothered her and brought all the unanswered questions rushing back to ruin her morning. She was so close to ringing Hugh it was frightening, so she visualised slapping herself a few times and imagined her head snapping from side to side with the force of her blows. That was better! She wouldn't want him thinking she needed him. Especially the new Hugh who wouldn't be able to resist the, "Now, Liz..." bit.

Reviewing the situation, Liz realized that, judging by the lack of response to her enquiries the previous night, information wouldn't be forthcoming. Simon always looked shifty, that was just his normal expression, but it didn't mean he was capable of anything more devious than copping a few sly smokes out the back of the garden shed. Even then, the unmistakable aroma of smouldering trouser pocket gave him away every time.

Melanie was incapable of anything underhand. She'd been Liz's lodger for over a year and was so straightforward that if she saw someone in the street drop a bit of paper she would return it to them and not understand why they weren't just as pleased whether it was a sweet wrapper or a fiver. If you wanted an opinion on your latest hair-style you didn't ask Melanie. Because she would tell you. No, impossible to imagine Melanie doing anything sinister.

Julie, on the other hand, was an unknown quantity. She was terribly upset which, surely, meant something other than just being a wimp. Tony Armitage, too, was not only unfamiliar territory, but he was just too efficient in sorting something that, on the face of it, didn't concern him.

Liz couldn't believe the bricks had anything to do with her. She led an entirely blameless, somewhat boring life. Or she used to.

She trailed out to the kitchen and put the kettle on. There was a note from Tony, 'All sorted. No worries.' Well, that was reassuring, except that it wasn't. She felt beleaguered somehow, uneasy, as though a storm was boiling up ready to burst out and scald all in its way.

The phone rang. "Damn and blast!" It was still only a little after seven, for crying out loud, and she realised what she hadn't done. She hadn't thrown herself on the floor so that she could crawl along under the level of the window to stop Lydia seeing her from her house. She did this every morning without fail. But she hadn't this morning. It just went to show how disrupted her little world had become.

Sure enough it was Lydia. "Just thought I'd ring, as I'd seen you and knew I wouldn't be disturbing you. But someone's left your fridge door open – I can see it quite clearly from here. Just thought you'd like to know."

"Thank you, Lydia. I'll shut it. Thank you. Must go - pressure of work, you know."

Jeez. Liz wished she had the guts to say to her, "For heaven's sake - get a life - preferably one of your own." But she didn't have the guts.

Someone had left the fridge door slightly ajar. Liz shut it firmly and turned to give the expected wave to a beaming Lydia who'd just done her first good deed of the day. This meant she could start her day in a good mood and Liz could start hers in anything but.

Then she realised that she needed her grapefruit juice wakener from the fridge so she opened the door and there, tidily, on a very pretty paper plate, covered in cling film, was a finger. A human finger.

Chapter Seven

Liz shut the fridge door with more force than perhaps was necessary and stood there, still gripping the handle, the blood thundering in her ears like a train going through a tunnel.

Some time later, she realised two things. One, she needed to breathe in soon; two, her fist had seized up around the door handle. She took in a huge noisy breath and the black spots disappeared from in front of her staring eyes. That was when she discovered that they needed to blink, which they did with some effort, happily lubricating her eyeballs. She then used her left hand to lever the fingers of her right from the handle of the fridge and stood there some more, vigorously flexing her hands, trying to restore some feeling to them.

Whoever had put a finger in her fridge had probably been whoever it was who'd left it just enough ajar to cause Lydia to ring her up at seven in the morning. Liz couldn't decide which was worse – a severed finger in her fridge or Lydia ringing her at such a Godforsaken hour. And Liz still didn't have her grapefruit juice. But then again, perhaps she didn't want it any more.

Her fridge was one of the sort that didn't shut on its own - it needed a no-nonsense push. So whoever put the finger in the fridge was obviously unfamiliar with it. That let Melanie and Simon off. Well, it let Melanie off. Simon quite often forgot to shut the fridge properly, but the worst thing he'd ever left in the fridge was some of that bait-stuff for fishing which was pretty revolting, but not in quite the same league as a severed human finger. Nah, it couldn't be him.

That left the new lodgers. If Liz waited, surely one of them would give themselves away. She sat down at the table.

Melanie came downstairs first, in a blindingly bright and embarrassingly short nightie. Liz leapt up and got the milk for her from the fridge. Or she thought she had. In fact she picked up a bottle of home-made ketchup and Melanie didn't fancy that in her tea so Liz had to try again. This time she looked at what she was doing and succeeded in getting the milk.

Melanie thanked her, but put the width of the table between them and proceeded to shoot strange glances at her. Anyone would think Liz never did anything for her lodgers. Melanie even went so far as to enquire, in a kindly tone, after her health.

"I'm fine, thanks," Liz answered. "You?"

"I'm fine."

"Good," Liz said. She was glad she was fine.

They ran out of conversation. She wasn't a morning person at the best of times and, this morning, Liz was only interested in her fridge.

She got the milk on her first attempt for Simon. Liz could do it with her eyes shut by then. He also gave her a strange, hunted, look. "Have I done something? Are you still angry with me for letting Moocher out into the road?"

"No, don't be daft!" Liz took another glance at him. He looked rough. He looked like he'd been up all night. "You all right, Simon?" He seemed more nervous than usual this morning, his head twisting around at any sound, his hands jittering in silent, jerky dance.

"Yes, yes, I'm fine. I'm just worried about what Stella's up to..."

"Stella?"

"Yes, you know, my ex."

"Of course I do. Sorry, Simon, my mind's on other things at the moment. You've heard from Stella?"

"Yes. Another message..."

And then Liz heard it. She heard the firm tread of manly footsteps descending the stairs. "Sorry, Simon. Later..." He sat down at the table.

Tony smiled at them as he passed. He went out into the kitchen and put the kettle on. Simon and Melanie looked at her expectantly. Liz smiled at them reassuringly. It must have come out more like a pinched grimace, because it prompted Simon to whisper, "Do you want me to get the milk for him?"

"No!" Liz yelled in a whisper. Yelling in a whisper makes your throat sore she discovered. Liz held Simon's arm down on the table. "No," she said in a more reasonable, less damaging whisper.

Liz decided he must still be upset about Stella because he shook her hand off and went out into the garden, probably for a smoke or five.

Tony came into the breakfast room with his coffee and sat down.

Liz looked at him hopefully. "You don't take milk?" She hadn't noticed yesterday. She must start being more observant now she knew she lived in a world riddled with crime.

"No."

Rats!

And then Liz heard more footsteps on the stairs. This time they were delicate, hesitant and timid. A monster arose within her and bared its teeth at her conscience. Liz could not let such a young, sweet and innocent girl see that finger. Could she? It might be her doing, that finger, mightn't it? Liz didn't know who, or what, she was dealing with here. She had to let her get on with it. Liz had set her trap and whoever fell in it was 'it'. Anyway, Julie had to boil the kettle and get the doings first which would give Liz a bit more time to fight this damned inconvenient voice in her head.

Julie didn't bother with the kettle. Oh, no - not a bit of it. She went straight to the fridge, pulled open the door, screamed so loudly it was impossible to believe it came from her tiny frame and keeled over backwards. She hadn't even given Liz a chance to stop her, even if she'd wanted to. Fancy her moving that fast! On her way down she narrowly missed bashing her head in on the table but, of course, Tony's timing was perfect. He caught her in his strong arms and crushed her to his hairy chest. No, no, not exactly. To be fair, it was more like he caught a falling sack of coal and cradled it in his arms because what else could he do with it? Yeah, it was more like that.

He sat down and settled Julie comfortably on his lap as though he was used to dealing with unconscious maidens and glared at Liz.

Why her?

"What the hell's going on?" he demanded.

"I wish I knew," Liz yelled, starting to her feet in frustration. It would seem she needed practice at this. She'd cocked up what she thought would be a straightforward and revealing incident. Instead of which, she knew no more now than when she first saw the finger. The only person to see it was Julie. She was out cold but not necessarily because she knew anything about it. It could have been simply because she didn't expect to see such a thing in the fridge. To be fair, there wasn't usually a finger in the fridge. In fact, Liz couldn't remember there ever having been one in there before.

Tony still watched her expectantly.

"There's a severed finger in the fridge. Is it yours?" Liz demanded of him thinking she'd take him by surprise. She registered a sharp, "Oh!" from Melanie, but Liz was more interested in Tony's reaction.

"I have all mine," he snapped.

"Is it your doing then?"

"Don't be ridiculous - why should I put a spare finger in the fridge? In case I forget one?"

"Very bloody funny. Not!"

"I'm not even sure I believe you," he said frowning at her as though Liz was in the habit of making up stories about fingers in the fridge just to amuse her lodgers first thing in the morning.

Liz didn't care whether he believed her or not. She was annoyed at the failure of her bit of detective work. Especially as she'd realised that if any of them had put it there then of course they wouldn't go to the fridge. Or would they?

Julie by now was recovering and removed herself from Tony's lap. She was sitting, unaided, on a chair at the table, emitting little squeaks

71

whenever her eyes crept fridge-wards. How very feminine. Liz noticed Tony still had a hand of his over a hand of hers. Hmm, was that the way the wind blew? Not that their love life was her business, of course, but it was a bit quick. Mind you, the way Melanie was hanging off his every word she seemed to think she was in with a chance so maybe he was still fair game.

Her mind was wandering. Liz snagged it and brought it sharply back to attention.

The telephone rang. Melanie answered it, spoke briefly and put it down. "Lydia says someone's left the fridge door open," she said and turned to give the obligatory wave through the window. She went through to the kitchen and Liz heard the tap run and the click of the kettle being switched on. Good idea.

She was at a loss. What to do next? What to do... She supposed the only thing was to call the police and they might be able to fingerprint it, or perhaps someone may have reported a missing finger.

Liz supposed one should call the police anyway if one finds a finger in one's fridge.

Okay, she'd call the police.

Chapter Eight

"What are you doing?" Tony demanded as Liz headed for the phone.

"Calling the police."

"No!" He jumped out of his chair and stood over her. He was so tall he blocked out the sun. "You don't want to do that. It's not a good idea..."

Her scalp heated up so quickly while she tried to make her tongue work, Liz was afraid it was going to blister off. Finally, she managed speech: "My God! Are you threatening me?"

"No, no! Of course not! I was just thinking that for someone to have done this must mean they're very close. Or, at least they must be keeping an eye on this place..."

Julie let out a heart-rending moan and looked over her shoulder, but he ignored her. He was concentrating on Liz. "And they know you didn't call the police last night, so they'll think..."

"Are you saying the two incidents are linked? What makes you think that? This is an entirely different thing to a broken window, for Pete's sake. What is it with you and the police anyway?" Her head was getting hotter by the second.

The phone rang. Liz snatched it up, convinced the police were into telepathy these days.

It was Lydia. "Your fridge door is still open, dear. Think of all that electricity going to waste and how bad it is for the things in your fridge..."

Liz gritted her teeth so hard she thought they'd splinter. "Thank you, Lydia," she said, her jaw aching from the effort of speaking fairly naturally. "I will shut it forthwith. Good bye."

She strode to the window, if a shortass like her could be said to stride, and waved. Lydia fluttered a lace handkerchief with one hand whilst the other girlishly covered her mouth, no doubt to stifle giggles.

"Yes. Ha. Ha," Liz said and Lydia suddenly disappeared from view. God knows what Liz'd looked like. A snarling shortass yeti probably.

"You can't go to the police," Tony said. His voice sounded much too satisfied for her liking. He continued in the same smug vein: "I thought I'd have a look for myself, but the *evidence*, if, indeed, it ever existed, has gone."

What was the man wittering on about? Liz went to the fridge, carefully walking around him, as though round a snake pit, and saw that he was right. The plate with its grisly burden had disappeared. Liz looked around the room, mystified. She *had* seen it. Julie had seen it – else why all the histrionics? Liz felt very unstable and even put her hand out to the wall to steady myself.

Tony continued, not bothering to disguise the amusement in his voice. "I could just see you trying to tell your local constabulary that you had a finger, you didn't know whose, in your fridge when you got up this morning. You had no idea where it came from or should I say, *who* it came from, and then suddenly it was gone. 'No, officer, no sign of forced entry.' I don't think even you could carry that one off, Liz."

No, Liz didn't think she could either. Nor could she think what she'd thought was fanciable about Tony. Well – actually – yes, she could – his back view in well tailored trousers. But the rest of him was turning out to be a severe disappointment.

Then Liz heard Melanie's enthusiastic voice floating out from the kitchen, "Oh, Moocher, you bad dog, what have you stolen now? Here give it to me - you'll choke on the cling film."

Liz's heart threw itself out of her chest and threatened to erupt from her mouth. She rushed out to the kitchen to see Moocher looking up at Melanie with one of his what-me-I'm-an-innocent-doggie looks on his furry face and a bit of cling film hanging from his front teeth, which Melanie plucked off as Liz watched.

Another very, very bad day had begun. How could five adults, in one room, have allowed a big black hairy dog to waltz in, help himself to a delicacy from the fridge and then retire to the kitchen to scoff the evidence without anyone seeing him at it?

Tony started to laugh, not delicately either. Uproariously was probably the word. Liz gave him her best you're-dead stare but it didn't stop him. He even had the nerve to say: "I'm sorry, but it *is* funny."

"It's not funny at all. I'm very picky about what he eats."

On reflection, maybe not the best thing Liz could have said. She hurried on: "Not only that, but you wouldn't think it funny if it was *your* finger, would you? Also, why are you so determined that I don't go to the police with anything that happens?" Liz stood there with her fists on her hips. This must be an automatic throw-back stance coming from her mother's side in situations of stress. Normally, she'd avoid such a fish-wife pose like she avoided men who dribbled.

"There's something very dodgy about you and I want to know what it is." Liz tapped her foot like people with their fists on their hips should be able to do. It's quite difficult to do it for any length of time with no practice. The muscles in your leg seize up. She stopped tapping her foot.

"I'm waiting." Her mother used to say that when Liz'd been particularly adventurous and she wanted an answer from her as to what she'd done. As if she didn't already know. What a horrible thought. Why was Liz thinking so much of her mother just now? It must be because Liz was in trouble and knew it. Same reason for thoughts of Hugh, no doubt. She removed her fists and sat down.

The phone rang. Liz leapt up, scooped it off its rest and yelled, "The fridge door is still open. I know the fridge door is still open. I like it open. Okay?"

The voice at the other end was not Lydia's. It belonged to one of her clients. "Personally," he said. "I shut my fridge door whenever I can. You never know what might get in it, or out of it, come to that. How often do you clean your fridge?"

Why do I get the demented people, Liz thought. Why can't I have the sort of clients who would simply say, "Oh, is this a bad time? Call me back when you're done." But, oh no, I get the smart alecks.

"I, er, I clean my fridge every month, thoroughly," Liz said firmly. Simon, who had just reappeared from the garden, stared at her, startled out of his customary coma. Liz made a face at him. "But as for your accounts..."

"No, seriously, do you find it best to use washing up liquid? My mother always told me that would taint the salad, so I use bicarb, you know. Of course you can't use anything scratchy, it would spoil the surfaces."

"Er, well, actually. I never clean my fridge. I was lying."

"Oh! Hahaha. Very funny."

"No, I'm serious. However, I might be tempted to clean it now because there's been a finger in it. A finger hacked off someone. Now then, your accounts are ready, but we do need to get together to discuss tax implications. When's a good time?"

"You are sooo funny. A finger. Hahaha. Seriously though, take my tip and use bicarb," he said. "Oh, hohoho, you keep finger food in your fridge - I get it. You nearly had me going there."

Liz wished he *was* going. "Tomorrow be all right, two-thirty?"

"Oh. Yup. Two-thirty. I'll see you then. Don't forget the bicarb."

"Thank you. I won't ever forget it again. Bye then." Liz replaced the phone and sighed. Unbelievable. This guy ran a construction company and he cleaned his fridge with bicarb. It would be in the forefront of her brain every time he made a pass at her now: Jeez, this hunky guy cleans his fridge with bicarb. His mum told him to. Liz turned around and fixed her oldest lodger with a piercing stare. "Simon, what do you clean the fridge with?"

"Bicarb of course." He almost saluted as he said it.

Everyone in the world except her knew that you should clean your fridge with bicarb.

"I think it's time for a clean, don't you?"

He leapt from his chair. "I'll do it. I'll do it," he said and rushed into the kitchen.

She turned to her newest lodger. "So, what have you got against the police, Tony?"

Liz was worried about telling the police there'd been a finger in her fridge. No sane person would believe her. And if they *did* believe her what would they do about it? They might decide to excavate Moocher's stomach to find the remains and Liz wasn't having that. She was an averagely law-abiding citizen but nobody was cutting up her dog in order to find the chewed up remains of a finger no one was claiming as their own.

She supposed they could wait until it went through his system, but would they? Perhaps she'd secretly bag up his poo over the next couple of days and keep it somewhere until this was all sorted out, in case it was any use. Question is, should finger-infested poo be kept in the fridge? Would it go off if it wasn't?

"They're after me," Tony said.

"What?"

"The police are after me for something which I'm trying to sort out at the moment. I didn't do it, but I have to prove I didn't do it and if they catch up with me I won't be able to prove it."

Liz had this strange and enchanted feeling that she was on the set of The Fugitive and Harrison Ford would come racing around the corner any moment, hotly pursued by Tommy Lee Jones and Liz would be whisked up in it all and come out the other end of a great pipe with a thousand metre drop into a paradise of richness and unparalleled splendour and she would live happily ever after with no lodgers, no bills and no bloody fridge at all.

Everyone looked at each other and then at her. The expression on their faces was clear to read. Liz had, in an instant, become the criminal of the piece. It would have helped if someone other than her had seen the damn finger! Julie had, but Liz knew without asking that she wasn't in a hurry to back her up.

She also knew that if Liz got the police in she would become Malvern Road's equivalent of a mad cow, and no lodgers would ever come here to pay her bills for her again. What had happened to her philosophy of live and let live? What had happened to that?

"Right. Right, then. Well..."

"Liz, you can't get the police in now. Tony has to get it sorted and then it'll be okay. After all, he got the window fixed and there's no finger to report or anything..."

This was a pretty impassioned speech from Melanie. Tony must make a mighty handsome casserole. There they all were, rooting for this man who had only entered the household yesterday. He probably bribed Moocher to pinch the finger, come to think of it.

"Thanks Melanie, for your support."

Liz was sure his voice didn't accidentally become a thrillingly husky bone-melting tone.

Melanie fidgeted and blushed slightly. Liz's bones melted slightly.

"Yeah, Liz. There's no need for the police, is there?" Even Simon was on his side. Liz would never shout "Pocket!" at him again. He could burn a hole right through his leg for all she cared.

"What about whoever the finger came off? What about them?" Liz asked, hardening her bones.

But no one answered. No one looked at her now. Simon, bless him, had gone a bright pink. No one believed her. Liz wasn't sure she believed herself anymore. She'd avoided looking at it after that one, brief, glimpse. She'd had a very bad night. She'd got up very early, perhaps too early. Could it have been a sheesh kebab on that plate? Had Moocher developed a taste for Asian cuisine?

"I've got work to do," she snapped, and stomped off before she collapsed in a gibbering heap. She wanted to repeatedly bang her head on the floor in the hope that the feeling of snow blizzards inside it would clear. She was still going to call the police, but needed some time to collect her thoughts. To do that she would have to get away from their accusing looks.

She headed for the attic. Moocher stayed downstairs, probably hoping for another snack. Actually, it was time for his walk and it was Sandra's turn today. He liked going out with her. She didn't tire easily. Must be all the exercise she got. Too bad he'd have to make do with Melanie instead.

Accounts were boring. Dead boring if the wrong person was doing them. And she was the wrong person. Liz only did accounts because she could, and because it was a way of earning money from home. She stared at yet another trial balance for quite a while before she realised she wasn't seeing it at all. She was actually running over in her mind the attitude Tony seemed to have towards Julie. It was a strangely familiar attitude he showed her and Liz wasn't really into coincidences. They'd arrived on the same day, both anxious for a room in her house. Julie hadn't objected to him virtually undressing her. Julie might have been in shock or was just incredibly wimpish and Tony didn't get as far as her bare flesh, but even so...

Liz wasn't happy with Tony's explanation of why no police either. What on earth could he have done that made the police think he'd done something else, but that he could prove he hadn't and they'd all live happily ever after? She'd have to rent that Harrison Ford video again and see if it gave her any clues.

Also, she had to admit, she was driving around with no insurance and no MOT last year for about three days without realising it. If someone had got the police in for something else and they'd asked her for her driving documents Liz would have been in trouble. Who, really, isn't a black pot sometimes? Or was it kettle?

She really needed Hugh. Her hand crept along her desk phone-wards as though it belonged to someone else. Liz watched it with a strange fascination as it moved quite independently of her brain. She certainly did not want to telephone her ex and ask him to come and sort things out. She would never show such weakness and anyway it would encourage him in thinking they might stand a chance together. And they didn't. So it wouldn't be fair. (Not to mention the, "Now, Liz..." thing).

Her hand had picked up the receiver before her other hand came to its senses and slapped the first one so hard it dropped the receiver back into the cradle. Comes to something when one's own hand was prepared to let you down and go behind your back. Maybe Liz should cut it off to stop it doing it again. And then put it in the fridge. Aargh.

It was no good. She wasn't getting very far in her deliberations. She wandered over to the dormer window and stood right in it peering down on Malvern Road. She loved this window. There was a little step up into it. It was like one small step up sends you giant-leaps into the sky and, once there, you could survey the rooftops, the little people in the street, the cats and the birds and other people's business to your heart's content. Sometimes it was like you were on a level with the hot-air balloons that came over, breathing heavily in that monstrous way they have. Sometimes you could wave to the little people in their suspended baskets and they'd wave back.

It didn't generally occur to people down in the street to stare upwards if they should be doing something they didn't want someone to see. They might look all around and over their shoulder, but they never seemed to look up. Oh, the power of it all! The things she'd seen!

For example, the chap with muscles across the road had some strange urge to pee in his front garden hedge. Liz had seen him doing it a few times. He would grin whilst doing it, waving to people and whistling. In general it made him very happy so there couldn't be anything wrong with it, although the hedge wouldn't agree. One day she'd check to see if there was a brown patch in that spot on his side.

The woman in the house on the other side of him took photos of him doing it sometimes, from the back. Why? Maybe Liz should take a photo of her taking a photo of him peeing in his hedge. But she couldn't think what for.

Anyway, there was the usual activity. In other words, there was no sign of brick carrying yobs, no one running down the street with carefully presented fingers. No, there were a couple of cats warning each other off, a keen gardener getting his patch ready for the planting of optimistic seedlings and, ooh, look, there was Git-Next-Door fiddling around with his gate. What was he doing? Liz leaned further forward until her nose squashed up against the glass and stared at him. Or rather, she stared at the top of his head.

There was something about Git-Next-Door that bothered her. More than usual. Liz stared until her eyes watered. She rubbed them and stared some more. And then it hit her. He was fumbling about with the catch on the gate and "fumbling" was the right word. He was having difficulty because there was a great beehive of bandage around his hand.

She didn't remember seeing him with a bandage on yesterday when she spotted him in his garden tweaking the odd blade of grass that had the nerve to grow out of line – in fact, it would have been impossible for him to get his very expensive, fawn-coloured leather gardening gloves on with a bandage like that on his hand. No, he did not have it yesterday. But this morning there definitely had been a finger in her fridge. Could that finger possibly have belonged, or, strictly speaking, still belong to Git-Next-Door? Liz felt positively light-headed with intuition. But did she need to know?

Not really, no. There was no longer a finger to know anything about. She would just make even more of a fool of herself.

But... What if it *was* his finger? What was she supposed to do, exactly? Attempt to return it? Duhhh... Before Liz could get too befuddled by sending her thoughts down that path, she saw something that put it right out of her mind. It was Hugh. She had never seen so much of him since they last lived together, a couple of years ago. Actually, she'd never seen so much of him when they *had* lived together than she had in the last day or so. And here he was again. So early again, too.

Her heart lifted, jumped a little, and then remembered he wasn't Hugh anymore. No, he was Mr Judgmental now. Drat. She'd have given anything to see the old Hugh. She even felt her throat start to swell up in remembrance of her old friend who was no more. Maybe that was why he'd come back so soon. Maybe it *was* the old Hugh come to apologise. Maybe Liz *could* unburden herself onto him of all the mysteries that had collected around her in the last twenty-four hours. Oh, how wonderful that would be!

But then, maybe he wasn't coming here. Liz watched him park and lock up and cross the road, surprised to see him not even check for traffic. In fact, he walked as though carrying a heavy load, feet loath to carry him, and fear caught her breath instead. There *had to be* something wrong with him. Maybe, this time, he would tell her what it was.

She raced as quietly as possible down the stairs and opened the door before he reached it, before he could ring the bell and bring others on the scene. She didn't want anyone else getting in on the act, and he'd be too polite to say so, even if he did want to confide something in her. Liz hurriedly dragged the door open, pecked him on the cheek, ignored his recoil and pulled him by the arm over the doorstep and into the front room, shutting the door firmly behind them. In fact, she locked it as well. She knew it was a communal room and therefore shouldn't be locked against other lodgers, but it was either that or take him up the attic and she felt that was too intimate and might make him feel they did stand a chance of getting back together when Liz knew they did not.

He remained silent for some time, walking around the room, fiddling with things. Liz waited.

Finally, he coughed. "Liz. I wanted to tell you why I came round yesterday."

"Oh, I thought you came round because you always do when we need you," Liz said, immediately forgiving him his previous pomposity.

"No, I came around to tell you I'm getting engaged to be married," he said.

As though it was a perfectly ordinary thing to be doing.

She felt her face flinch and her brain started to make strange, shrill noises that skidded around the inside of her skull.

Hugh wouldn't look at her. And Liz was glad. She had no idea what she must have looked like. She felt as though a rugby team had jumped on her stomach and stayed there. Doing some more jumping. Grinding their studded heels in.

"Hugh," Liz said. "That's wonderful news. I'm very happy for you. When's the wedding?" She was extremely proud of herself for getting this out, despite the Springboks' best efforts.

He still didn't look at her. "We haven't set a date as yet. I'll… I'll let you know when we do. In the meantime I probably won't be around so much. You know how it is."

"No, I don't know how it is. Why should you not be around so much?"

"Because I'll be spending a lot of time with Charity."

"Charity?"

"Yes," he said and finally he looked at her. Glared might be a better word. Daring her to say anything. As if she would. As if she could think of anything at all to say.

"Charity?"

"Yes. Charity."

Hysteria welled up and Liz knew she couldn't attempt much more by way of speech. Not without risking a wobbly voice and hot, leaking eyes.

"Right," she managed to creak out through a throat suddenly tight and pained. "I wish you well." She stood up and led the way to the door.

With him on the outside, curiously reluctant to go it seemed, and her in the house looking at him and Moocher pressed against the side of her leg as though he felt the unleashed, and unreasonable, hurt, Hugh held out his hand and Liz put her hand in it. They shook hands and he left.

That was the first, and probably would be last, time in their entire history that they'd ever shaken hands. They'd hugged and kissed and cried and shouted and hurled stuff. They'd never shaken hands. It must really be the end, then.

Chapter Nine

The whole concept of 'denial' crashed in upon Liz with all its advantages. She decided to try it out. If she didn't think about Hugh's impending nuptials then it couldn't affect her one way or the other. Okay then.

Staring out into the street, she realised she must had been standing on her own doorstep for quite a while before becoming aware of Tortoise-woman. Again. Unbelievable. And Hugh had just been there. It couldn't possibly be coincidence. Liz couldn't work it out, though, and gave the woman such a ferocious look she backed off, but not before Liz noticed a smug look on her ratty face. Liz shut the door, kicked it and stomped up to her attic.

She went back to the trial balance and gazed at it as if for inspiration. She wasn't thinking about anything. No, nothing. Nothing at all.

Then she remembered that she hadn't retrieved the black recycling bin after it'd been emptied. No one else would do it. The fact that she usually refused to do so on the basis that someone else should do it occasionally was neither here not there. It was urgent business to retrieve that bin now and if she just happened to run into Git-Next-Door as she did so, well then, that was Fate. In fact, she'd probably been given the gift of Git-

Next-Door's undoubtedly missing finger to keep her mind off other stuff.

She raced down the stairs, feeling the wind rush through her hair, and burst out of the front door. As luck would have it, Git-Next-Door was just about to shut his own door with him on the inside. Liz leapt lithely over the intervening, admittedly low, wall between his path and hers and yelled, "Git... Hello! Hello! I need to speak to you."

His door stopped moving. She'd caught his attention. She ran up his path and pushed her face into the narrow gap he'd left. "Good Morning, Mr Oliver, I must speak to you."

"Why should I speak to someone who calls me Git?"

Good question.

"I wouldn't blame you if you didn't," Liz said, on the basis that disarming candour might do the trick. Well, she'd seen it work for other people and it was time she tried the devious route too. "I just wanted to ask about your... how you are. That's all." Liz realised this must seem very odd to him. They'd been uneasy neighbours for a couple of years and never exchanged pleasantries. Unpleasantries, yes.

"Why should you be interested? You never have been before."

Quite so.

Liz struggled to make her face look politely concerned. "I'm making a new effort. After all, we *are* neighbours. It's silly for us to carry on the way we do."

The door opened a fraction more.

"You started it by bringing a load of unwashed students into an erstwhile nice street."

"I beg your pardon! None of them are students. My lodgers are all perfectly respectable people whatever they do." Well, that was open to question, but not to hers - or his.

"And you're always parking outside my house."

Liz strove for a peaceful tone of voice. "No one owns the street, Mr Oliver, and in a road like this one, you park where you can."

"But these houses are only a car width, give or take, and your house has several cars attached to it."

This was obviously a hit. And time was going on and Liz was getting nowhere. She would have to buckle. "You're right, Mr Oliver, so right. I'll tell my lodgers not to park in front of your house anymore. Okay?" Fat lot of use that would be, but there you go. She could imagine them rolling around the floor clutching their stomachs in a somewhat strained attempt at sarcastic mirth when she tried it.

Miraculously, the door opened fully and Liz was blinded by a broad grin. It only appeared briefly and disappeared just as fast. "Goodness - you should smile more often. It makes such a difference!" Not the most tactful thing to say, she knew, but she couldn't help it. It had taken about thirty years off his age. Good grief, Liz lived next door to a possible Man. She'd had no idea. She made the most of it though and shot through the opening. They were a bit close together, and he stepped hastily backwards.

"Yes. Do come in. Let's go through to the front room. I assume your house is the same as this only the other way around."

"Yes, indeed. Lovely houses aren't they?" Liz found herself in a room so crowded with books there was nowhere to sit. Books lined the walls, the floor, the mantelpiece. They covered the tables, the chairs and the piano. Liz loved books and always went out of her way to nose around other people's, but in here, where would she start? It was a treasury of the written word and they looked read, too. None of this smart binding and inside there's an empty box in which you could conveniently slide a DVD. She couldn't even see a television. Her opinion of Git-Next-Door underwent an instant transformation, especially as she spotted what looked like all the McGuigan mysteries ever written. He was a favourite crime writer of hers. Her neighbour was obviously a highly discerning reader.

"Mr Oliver, I must apologise for all the mean things I've thought about you. I'm so sorry, but tell me, why don't you let your cat stay in at night any more, not even at firework time?" Well, she didn't know how that slipped out when all she wanted was to be incredibly nice to him...

"I don't have a cat."

"You don't?" That explained that. "Oh. Well, why did you kick my car? I saw you do it. I even heard the 'thunk'." Some inner demon seemed determined to get all her grudges out into the open, just when she wanted nothing but to be diplomatic. And nosy.

He stood upright. He had been moving great piles of books off the chair. "That was when you had the flat tyre, right? It was me that put the note through your door about that."

"Oh. And I went and thanked the guy across the road… He accepted my thanks you know."

"My dear Mrs Houston - he's hardly going to refuse your thanks when he's been putting on the show ever since you moved in."

"He's what? 'Putting on the show'? For me?"

"You've never noticed?" He looked so surprised there seemed to be a danger of the flashing smile again. In fact, he laughed. Well, you could have knocked her down with a silk tie. What a difference! Liz wondered if her mouth was hanging open. She wondered if she was drooling.

"Oh, dear. The poor chap. All those spectacular pecs and tight short shorts and you've never noticed." By this time he'd cleared away a solid three years' worth of reading and lo and behold, there was a second chair. They both sat down.

"Anyway, Mrs Houston, how can I help you?"

"Do call me Liz and you are…?"

"Clive."

"Well, um, Clive, I was just wondering how, how you were…"

He gave her a wry look and said, "I'm fine, thanks. Why so concerned all of a sudden?"

"I noticed your, um, your hand…"

"Oh, yes, my hand." He looked at it in some surprise as though only just aware that it existed, let alone that it was attached to the end of his arm. By now Liz had decided that she was shouting up totally the wrong set of stairs here. How could such a nice man have anything at all to do with having his finger removed and put in her fridge? Here they were in a respectable neighbourhood, such things didn't happen. She must be losing it. And anyway, it was too much like coincidence if it turned out to be her neighbour's finger. Too neat by half.

Then he said, "I had an accident. With a power tool."

Her interest re-awakened briefly only to die again. That just explained the bandage.

But she tried for a kindly and sympathetic tone. "Ooh, nasty. I hope you've had it seen to."

"Yes. It was seen to all right."

"Oh, good. You'll be okay, then." But he didn't look okay at all. In fact, he looked as though he would burst into tears any moment.

"I won't be okay," he muttered, his head down as though studying his bandage for imperfections. "Never again will I be okay."

"It was serious then," Liz said feeling a little uncomfortable at witnessing the pain he was in, although she was beginning to feel he might be laying it on a bit thick. "I do wish you'd called for help. We are only next door."

"I don't think you could have helped."

"I wouldn't be too sure of that, you know. We're full of hidden talents next door. Some might be extremely well hidden, but they're there. Oh, yes indeedy." Liz was uncomfortably aware that his mood had changed dramatically. He was staring at her in what Liz could only describe as a calculating manner, opening his mouth and shutting it again as though undecided about saying more. Suddenly Liz didn't want to know any more, but it was too late.

"That was the finger I wore my ring on," he said. "I can't wear my ring anymore."

92

Ring? What ring? Liz couldn't even work out which finger he was referring to under the heap of bandage. Perhaps he meant a wedding ring?

Rather feebly Liz said, "Oh, surely when it's healed you can wear your ring again."

But he wasn't having any of it. "No," he said. "Never again."

And Liz suddenly knew that he hadn't just had an *accident* with a power tool. For some inexplicable reason, he *had* cut his finger off and put it in her fridge. Liz always knew there was something very, very strange about her neighbour and this just went to prove it. Liz just knew it was *his* finger lying out there in her back garden, masticated, digested and ejected by her best friend. She just knew it. She realised she'd make a great detective. She'd have the most incredible hunches and at the end of the story all her wonderful reasoning would take the last three chapters to explain.

In the meantime, her mouth was so dry she was afraid it had stuck irretrievably closed and would need a jemmy to get it open. He gave her another can-I-trust-you? look and came out with it. "It was cut off. Completely cut off."

Liz coughed, not sure quite how to react, feeling she should show surprise but unable to dredge any up.

She coughed again, wildly searching the book-filled corners of his front room for inspiration. "Your finger was cut off," she said. Great line, Liz!

"Yes, that's right. My finger was cut off, at the base."

Liz had to check what she thought were the facts. "Did you take the finger with you to the hospital in case they could sew it back on? I've heard that if you immediately pack it in ice, they can do amazing things, like re-attach it and it's as good as new."

"No, I couldn't find it."

Eek! It *was* his finger. Please God no one ever tells him that her dog ate his finger for breakfast. It *must* have been his finger. How many people in the neighbourhood had lost their fingers recently? But, hang on, how did it get onto a very pretty paper plate, wrapped in cling film in her fridge? That didn't fit. Even if he'd been in a delirious state of shock Liz couldn't imagine him fiddling about with pretty paper plates and cling film while his life-blood spurted from his finger's old home. Why her fridge? Why the plate? And then he'd have to mess about breaking into her house while he was bleeding to death. It didn't make sense.

"But what could have happened to it?" Liz could imagine some creature darting in to snatch up a fallen finger and darting out again - just about - but the rest of the presentation failed her.

"You ask a lot of questions, don't you?"

Liz flinched and stared at him. She hadn't even started to ask all the questions crowding into her mind.

"I'm sorry," he said. "I didn't mean to snap, but the memory is still rather painful and I'm afraid of what might happen next."

"I don't understand..."

"No, you don't, do you. I didn't do this to myself. Someone did it *to* me."

Liz's heart stopped. Her blood congealed. Or that's what it felt like. She struggled for breath and swapped Harrison Ford for Marlon Brando.

Although maybe one can't really compare a mere finger with a horse's head, but even so...

Finally she drew in enough breath to demand of him: "Why are you telling me this?"

"You asked."

Fair enough. Although she wished she hadn't now. That just went to show what can happen when you ask a few innocent questions. Liz didn't think she wanted to be a detective after all. She'd rather be an accountant. Cripes - what was she saying? It was all Hugh's fault, all this. If not for him she never would have tried the denial route, the distract-herself-with-something-else route.

"I did ask. You're right," Liz agreed. "Are you seriously telling me that someone else cut your finger off?"

"There were three of them. Two held me down and the other cut it off."

This couldn't be real. But he obviously thought it was. Best to humour him. You just couldn't tell about people could you? And for a while she'd been thinking he might, after all, be a nice neighbour to have.

"I'm sorry. It must have been very painful."

"Understatement."

She tried harder. "It must have been a nightmare."

"It was."

"But why would they want to do such a thing? Who were they?" It couldn't be helped. She was naturally interested in other human beings.

"They were trying to get information out of me."

Oh! "And did they succeed?" Liz wondered if she could leave without him noticing, but he was closer to the door than she was.

"No, certainly not. I haven't kept the secret all these years only to give it away now. I've watched and watched for years and they've only just found out where I am. It's what to do now that's the problem."

"You think they'll come back?"

"Undoubtedly."

"Ohmigod. What are you going to do?"

"I just can't decide. I think I'm still in shock."

"Why don't you call the police?"

"Don't be silly."

"I beg your pardon?"

"I can't call the police – that would really set the cat amongst the mice. My name's not really Clive Oliver."

Liz had a sudden premonition and sighed heavily and loudly before asking him: "The police are after you too?"

"Of course."

Of course. Naturally. Silly her. The feeling that she'd been transplanted to live her life in a cartoon just grew and grew.

"Well..." Liz was stumped. Unfortunate turn of phrase perhaps, but it explained her puzzlement perfectly – yes, Liz was stumped.

He was muttering away to himself, "Not exactly after me, but if they know then everyone will know..."

What on earth was he on about? Liz wished she'd left their relationship as it was, although his constant peering through his immaculately laundered net curtains was now explained. It had nothing to do with all the supposedly unwashed lodgers living next door to him, but rather to whoever it was he watched for. Liz supposed that was something although she was still suspicious of the eagerness with which he raced out of his house whenever one of them drove their car from outside of it. Seconds later, he'd be out there, haring down the road to get his car just so he could park it outside his own house. He *must* be watching them to do that so regularly. Anyway, this was all fairly pointless just at that moment...

She was saved by the bell. There was no mistaking it. It shrilled throughout the house. She looked expectantly at Clive. He looked at her. His face was grey. Sweat rolled down his cheeks and he was visibly shaking.

"Do you want me to get that?" Liz offered. "You don't look as though you're feeling very well yet. Perhaps it's still the shock of your accident."

"No! No, leave it. It might be them, back to get me."

"Oh, surely not. Not in broad daylight. Not in Malvern Road," Liz said, laughing, just a little hysterically. "I'll go and see." As Liz got up from her chair she heard her own door-knocker being enthusiastically exercised. "Look, whoever it is, is at my door now. It can't be them. It's probably someone selling dish cloths." And whoever it was had got fed up with ringing her bell and was now leaning on Clive's again. "All right, all right. I'm coming," Liz muttered as she left the front room, turned into the lobby and opened the door.

There were three men standing there. They all wore jeans and rather nice sweaters. They all looked pretty fit and wholesome. They looked like they could be fun. "Were you looking for me?" Liz asked. She batted her eyelashes a few times before remembering she'd given up all that.

"Are you Liz Houston?" asked the yummiest one. Fleetingly it crossed her mind to wonder why he assumed she was as she wasn't in her own house. But it was only fleeting. He was pretty yummy.

"Yes, I am. How could I help you?"

"We believe you have a man called Simon Medley living with you..."

She let out a big breath she hadn't realised she'd been holding. At least if they wanted Simon, it couldn't be the do-it-yourself surgeons who had pinched Clive's finger, although Liz was still having some difficulty believing in their existence. This *was* Malvern Road.

She was always cautious about other people's business, though. She didn't want to give away any information about Simon without asking him. On the other hand it might be to do with his work so neither did she want to put them off entirely. Liz couldn't think what to say so she said nothing. Was it possible that Simon was in trouble too? Was it possible that everyone she knew led secret lives about which she knew absolutely nothing? From this day forth she was never going to open her mouth again without, first, a great deal of thought.

Of course, by the time she'd come to this life-changing conclusion the three men were showing signs of impatience.

"Look, I don't know why I bothered to ask. We know Simon Medley lives with you and we want him. Tell us where he is." Liz must have looked startled. Yummy's tone had completely changed from a lovely warm toasty-brown to an icy bluey-green with frosting.

The middle one of the three chuckled. Liz hated people who chuckled for no known reason. Why do they do that?

She stood straighter. "Tell me who's asking and I'll leave a message."

"Don't mess with us, Liz," the shortest one said. "It could be painful."

Liz didn't like being threatened. It immediately made her do the opposite, but then, it was usually the likes of: "Don't eat that cake straight from the oven, Liz, you'll get stomach-ache". Mind you, cake straight from the oven was *worth* stomach-ache. Liz had by now decided, despite her earlier disbelief, that she knew who these three were and she was fond of all her fingers.

But what could they possibly want with an unassuming, pocket-burning man like Simon? Liz was certain the worst thing he'd ever done in his life would be on a par with going to work with no socks on. Sadly, however, it didn't seem that horrible things only happened to horrible people.

As if one being, Yummy, Shortass and Chuckler suddenly advanced on her, but she was ahead of them. She leapt back and slammed the door.

Chapter Ten

What now? Simon! She must warn Simon. Liz wasn't surprised he hadn't answered their door. He never did. He never answered the phone either. He was too humble to think it would be for him. Or, that's what she'd always thought. Perhaps she'd always been wrong and he was hiding from a colourful past, too. Even if he was, he was her friend and Liz wanted to warn him.

She dashed into Clive's front room, but it was empty. Oh, well, so much for him. She raced the length of his house, and bursting out of his already open back door, narrowly missed landing in a load of planted up patio tubs he had there - very pretty they would be later too. She turned the corner of Clive's house and ran across his neatly edged and shorn lawn, noticing while she did so, Clive himself leaping the garden wall four houses down. Boy, he could certainly move in a hurry and that was with one finger short. Liz vaulted, she liked to think in athletic fashion, his garden wall, scooted around the corner of her house and hurled herself at the dog flap.

She now had concussion she realised, as she found herself on her hands and knees slowly shaking her head side-to-side outside her own back door. Someone had locked the dog flap. Luckily the lock was only a plastic sheet inserted into the dog flap frame, otherwise she would have had a permanently flat head. That was when real panic set in. Moocher needed to be able to get out at will because of his age and because he was used to being able to get out at will and now he couldn't. Who the hell would lock his door? And what if whoever-it-was hurt him? Liz could imagine her lovely loving dog being tortured, held down while a claw was detached with a power tool.

She lost her head, what was left of it. She hauled herself from the ground and running full tilt crashed into the French windows. She'd always known they were old and ill fitting and now she was glad of it. They were the type made of many smaller panes of glass so she felt more confident than if they'd been made of single large panes. Sure enough the doors crashed inwards, without any glass breaking at all, and she was in. That took her into the old sitting room, now Tony's bedroom. She raced straight through. Tony could have been in bed with a netball team and a rugby team together for all she cared at that moment. She didn't think he was, though. She'd have noticed. She wrenched open his door, dashed into the hall and down to the back door expecting to see Moocher dancing about with crossed legs. No Moocher. He must be having a lie-in.

She pounded up the stairs shrieking her lungs out all the way for her dog. As she stepped onto the last flight of stairs leading to the attic, she was conscious that Simon had come out of his room and stood there looking startled. For someone with no range of expression at all, this completely changed his face. She had no time to ponder on it though. He was wearing a pair of jocks. Just jocks. Nothing else. "Get dressed," she

101

snarled at him in passing and continued on up the stairs.

When she'd searched under the bed and the desk and the pile of washing waiting to be done and found no Moocher, she raced down the stairs and, without knocking, crashed into Simon's room. He was crawling round the floor, no doubt looking for socks that weren't too stiff to wear.

"Where's Moocher?" she yelled. "Who locked the dog flap?" She took a quick look around Simon's room and stopped abruptly at the window.

She could see Moocher nosing about in the back garden. He must have been out there all that time. She knew exactly what had happened. Moocher was the real reason her back garden so closely resembled the plains of the Serengeti. He loved to stalk through the long grass pretending he was a great black lion. He would lope through his natural habitat blending in with the trees and the vines and the leaves and, single-pawed, he would cuff all opposition into submission. And then, exhausted from all the lion-like tension he would turn around in three magic circles and be asleep before he hit the ground. The grasses would lazily waltz and dip and wave above his nest.

He had been curled up in well-earned rest all the time. Her passing through the garden must have wakened him.

"Oh, thank God. He's okay." She collapsed suddenly on Simon's bed, the relief so great her bones felt like mush. She thought she was going to cry until she realised that although Moocher was locked out, and not in, it didn't solve the mystery of who had done the locking. Also, there were still three finger-obsessed perverts on the loose after Simon.

She did wonder for a second whether denial of the whole Hugh and some-person-called-Charity thing was having a very strange effect on her mental processes, but she didn't think she had imagined the visit next door, nor the locked dog flap.

She didn't think Simon would have locked the dog flap and, checking her watch, she realised no one else would be in at this time in the morning. Or would they?

"Simon, is anyone else in at the moment?"

"You know, I've been looking for you..."

"Simon, is anyone else in the house?"

"I wanted to tell you about..."

"Simon! Is anyone in?"

"No, Melanie's always out first thing and it's not first thing anymore. Julie went to Lydia's. Tony left at the same time. I've not heard the screechy bit on the door apart from when you came in a few minutes ago. I wanted to have a word with you..."

"Listen Simon! It wasn't me that came in the door. It must have been whoever locked the dog flap and it must have been someone who doesn't know about the screechy bit or they wouldn't have let it screech."

"Hang on, are you saying there's someone in the house with us, someone who locked Moocher outside and who is now keeping quiet somewhere?"

"Yes."

"Who?"

"Trophy collectors."

"Pardon?"

"I think there's three men in the house with us at the moment. And I think they're collecting fingers."

Simon had succeeded in finding a couple of socks pliable enough to get on his feet and was in the process of lacing up his shoes. He stopped his knotting and stared at her thoughtfully. "You know, I think that accounting doesn't really suit you."

"What the hell's that got to do with fingers on plates?" He came out with the dumbest things at the most inappropriate moments, he really did.

"Oh, nothing. Um, has this got anything to do with the finger that was in the fridge? The one Moocher ate?"

Liz went cold. "You talk about it as though there really *was* a finger in the fridge, Simon. I thought you didn't believe me. I thought no one believed me."

"I believed you. I put it there. That's what I wanted to have a word with you about, but you shut yourself away in the attic and I know you don't like people going up there and I haven't seen you until now."

"Tell me it wasn't a real finger, Simon. Tell me it was a fake finger for some crazy joke," she pleaded.

"No, it was real all right," he said, his concentration unwaveringly on the complicated knot he was creating in his tie. Simon always wore a tie. Always. Today's was maroon, the colour of old blood. Maybe the colour of blood from an old finger. Aargh. Chuckler, Shorty and Yummy were in the house and Liz and Simon were talking about old and long-eaten fingers when they needed to be more concerned about ones that were still attached.

She'd investigate Simon's admission about the fridge finger later.

Just now she really didn't want him to lose a finger. He played the violin. Although she wasn't sure you needed all your fingers to play the violin. Whatever.

"Simon, there are three men in the house and I think they want your fingers."

"How did they get in, then?" He had found his glasses and was looking at her closely.

"Through the front door – you heard it."

"Yes, but, how did they get it open?"

Ooh, that was a good question. And she knew the answer. She went hot all over. If anyone else had done what she'd done she would have thrown them naked into the street. In her hurry to catch Clive she must have pulled the door to, but not hard enough for it to catch. It probably would have looked shut until someone had pushed on it, or hammered on the knocker. She'd left her household wide open to the pernicious, opportunistic advantage of finger-thieves. Jeez, Simon was right – she really had to get out of accounting. Fast. Before *all* her brain cells went on permanent holiday.

Although, she knew in the deepest recesses of her being that it had nothing to do with accounting, and everything to do with Hugh's shock announcement. He'd unbalanced her. He'd got himself engaged to someone called Charity who didn't deserve him. It was obviously her that had made him all critical and horrible. She was changing him already. Her Hugh, her dearest friend – apart from Moocher – was not happy. She wasn't being bitch in the mangerish about it, but she was certain he was anything but happy and that made her feel really bad. Tears were near.

She gulped and twisted her hands into a pile of socks until she realised they were lacerating her palms. She dropped them like live snakes. "It was me. I left the door open."

Simon said nothing. That's the good thing about Simon. He often said nothing. Liz resolved to be like that in future.

"So where are they now? Where were they all the time you were thundering around the house shrieking for Moocher?"

Another good question. It did seem odd that they'd hide through all that if it really was the gruesome threesome. What were they doing? Perhaps it wasn't them after all. That would be nice.

She was getting a headache. She was yearning for the sight of a purchase ledger. It was all getting to be too much.

"Simon, are you in trouble with the police?"

"No, not unless they're after me for parking on the pavement again."

"Are you in trouble with any criminals from a past life that might be looking for you?"

"As far as I'm aware I don't know any criminals, except Tony, of course."

He really didn't seem to have taken to her newest lodger, but that was irrelevant just now. "So, no one's after you?"

"I don't think so." He stopped to adjust his collars as he'd now thrown on his 60s safari-type jacket-thing festooned with epaulettes and pockets. Then he looked up and she saw the blood leave his face. "Unless…"

Liz was fascinated. She'd never known Simon's expressions show so much emotion all in one day. He'd obviously had a truly horrifying thought. She sat up straight and awaited yet more startling revelations. Life was getting *so* interesting these days.

She wished it wouldn't.

He said, "Unless, it's Stella."

"Oh. Stella. Do you think your ex-wife would send three gorillas after you to collect a finger – does that make a pound of flesh?" Liz found that excruciatingly funny and nearly wet herself laughing. Simon looked hurt. She fought hard to bring herself under control, recognising that her sanity since Hugh's pronouncement, hung on a knife edge. "Nah, I don't think so, Simon. Can't be Stella, surely."

"Who do you think threw that brick through the window with the finger attached to it? It was a warning, Liz. I'm sure of it. She's after me. She'll never let me rest." The despair in his voice was painful to hear.

Just as Liz grappled with the surprise link between bricks and fingers, with no warning at all, Simon's door was flung open so hard it hit the chest of drawers behind it, toppling a rather ghastly bust of someone Liz always thought belonged in a Hammer movie, but was actually Beethoven. The door bounced back and slammed shut leaving three satisfied looking heavies on the inside of it. In with them.

At least they knew where they were now.

Simon and Liz both believed in mind over matter and working things out logically and in doing so the heavies who didn't appear to hold the same philosophy, had plenty of time to track them down and corner them in Simon's room. They advanced into the room, picked Simon up and stood there holding him, his feet dangling just above the floor.

Chapter Eleven

Simon was amazing. His face registered the exact same expression it would have if they'd offered him a slice of toast and marmite, his habitual form of sustenance. Liz took a quick glance out of the window for reassurance. Moocher was okay – she could see him doing his I'm-a-snow-plough bit where he lowers his snout to the ground and leaning on his chest he pushes his way through the long grass with his back legs. He always collapsed in a heap when he did that. Liz was sure he was laughing to himself.

She turned back to the little tableau in front of her. Yes, it was still there. She moved away from the window so they wouldn't realise that her weak spot was in the garden. They hadn't hurt Simon yet and she couldn't see any power tools. Perhaps they borrowed them as they went along rather than bringing their own? They were firing questions at Simon who still looked like he was about to tuck into a pile of warm and butter-dripping toast. Manohman, he was cool.

Yummy demanded: "Where is it then?"

Chuckler chuckled and added: "We know you know."

They completely ignored Liz. She wasn't too upset about that. She considered burrowing under Simon's duvet and pretending to be asleep, but as his bed seemed to be the repository of most of his discarded socks, that option was out. Not only that but she knew if she did that she'd never be able to look her lion-hearted dog in his beady eyes again. Bloody hell.

There was only one thing she could do. She inched casually along the bed in Moocher's snake-in-the-grass mode and then with what she was sure was an evil grace, she picked up old Beethoven, slightly chipped around the edges but otherwise good enough for her purposes, and in one athletic bound she was up and had smacked that old Beethoven down on Shorty's head. She'd gone for him because she wasn't sure she could reach the others. He dropped to the floor with a very realistic body-hitting-the-floor sound. Shorty himself didn't make any noise whatsoever. One minute he was there, being an outright ruffian, the next he was lying on the floor looking like a victim. Liz worried that the custard doughnut she'd had for breakfast was going to put in a reappearance. She'd never hit anyone in her life before and it felt very strange to have done so now.

Simon suddenly let out the most terrifying howl and, shucking off a life time of reserve, let loose with his feet and hands and, oh boy, Yummy and Chuckler didn't know what hit them. Liz didn't think they were hurt, but they were certainly surprised. So was she. In fact they were all pretty shocked. They stood around, carefully out of reach, watching with some apprehension as Simon did what could only be described as a fearsome war-dance, drumming his feet on the floor and shooting his hands out with lethal intent in every direction. Liz was afraid he might dislocate something, but he couldn't hear her pathetic cries of: "Be careful, Simon," above the cacophony of terrifying yowls and howls he produced from a face screwed up in manic and horrifyingly gargoyle fashion.

Liz's attention was distracted from this amazing spectacle by the sight of Hugh in the doorway. Her stomach lurched and she immediately dropped her gaze. She had no idea what he was doing here, but he looked just as unhappy, but at the same time disapproving, as he had the last time she'd seen him and she didn't want to see it. Nor did Yummy and Chuckler. They took off so fast they were a blur. They shouldered Hugh out of the way like he was a mere stripling instead of a six foot something chunky hunk of male and they were off, down the stairs and out. She heard the front door screech and then slam. You'd had thought they'd have learnt to lift that door by now.

And she was left with Shorty out cold on Simon's floor. Simon, thankfully, was taking a break from his demonstration of a short-circuited tap-dancing robot and stood there with a huge grin on his face. Liz had never seen that grin before either. Remarkable what it did for him.

She felt sick. She couldn't believe she'd knocked out a fellow human being. Liz had often wondered what she'd do if a burglar got in. She'd want to be absolutely sure he hadn't just made a mistake and got into the wrong house before she hit him with anything.

Maybe in this case it was all that denial venting itself on the nearest victim.

"Maybe you'd better sit on him, Hugh," she said, still not looking at him, but waving a delicately feminine but head-crushing hand at

Shorty's recumbent form. "Until we decide what to do with him."

Hugh didn't move. "Go on," she said. "You're much heavier than either of us." She trusted that would be true despite her biscuit-fest since he and she split up. Eek. Mustn't think of that. Mustn't think of Hugh in happier times. Tears hovered at the ready.

"No, I won't. What a ridiculous thing to do. We need to make sure he's not harmed before he brings action against you. What on earth possessed you?"

Unbelievable. This Charity person had a lot to answer for.

"Come on, Simon. Give us your weight." He and she crossed the room and sat on Shorty. Just in time too. Shorty was beginning to make the sort of noises one might expect from someone starting to come round after being smacked on the head with a bust of Beethoven. Liz felt cold and shivery. It was going to take a while for her to get used to the idea of hitting people. She much preferred arguing and shouting. It had a lot going for it that she never realised before she had the chance to compare it with getting physically violent. Or maybe it was the man-shaped glacier that had arrived in the room that was making her feel frozen from the inside out.

"Geroff," mumbled Shorty.

And, gosh, she thought Simon was going to. "Stay right where you are!" she glared at him.

She forced herself to move enough to grab Beethoven. Shuffling back on her knees she loomed over Shorty's head. He flinched and she grinned. Power was a terrible thing.

"Right then, Shorty. What were you lot after?"

"Go screw yourself."

"I beg your pardon."

"You heard. Go screw yourself."

"You're not in any position to be rude you know. I just want to know what the hell you lot were up to. It can't be that difficult. You must know."

"Not telling."

Sighing heavily in a you're-making-me-do-this-and-it'll-hurt-me-more-than-you kind of way, she held Beethoven threateningly, inches away from Shorty's face.

He laughed. For crying out loud – he laughed! And, of course, he was right. Sighing even more heavily, she placed Beethoven on the floor and looked at Shorty. What was she going to do with him?

Just thinking it made her look at Hugh at last. He had always had an answer to her little problems. But she was sorry that she'd given in to that impulse. Hugh's face at that moment could have made bread mouldy. It was too much. "Bloody hell, Hugh. I didn't ask you to come back. If all this just seems like too much trouble to you, then, please, feel free to leave. Go and get happy. Please be happy." She fancied her voice wobbled on that last bit.

He just glared at her as though he wanted to shake her. Then he left. Silence sank into the room for the time it took for him to go down the stairs and out the front door. She decided denial about all that would be a good thing, too.

It goes without saying that they went through all the palaver of why they couldn't get the police in and to be fair, she could just imagine it: "Oh, well, Officer, you see I left my front door open and three men walked in. They were coming to get Simon's finger you see and they picked him up off the ground and held him there threateningly. How did I know they were after his finger? Well because, well because..."

Liz felt she owed it to Clive not to mention him after what he'd told her and he *was* the one whose finger had been nicked and disposed of. He should be the one who made the decision about his own involvement. Although how that tied up with the finger Stella had apparently attached to a brick and chucked through the window was a complete mystery. In fact her brain was beginning to protest about all its unaccustomed exercise.

"Well, you see, Officer – I could tell just as soon as I clapped eyes on them that they were the type of people who removed other people's fingers with power tools. There's a lot of them about you know. Well, yes - you're right. Simon still has all his fingers. Why Mr Medley in particular? Why *his* fingers? Um, well, we don't know that. We were hoping you could find out. And, yes, I did hit Shorty with Beethoven, but I had good reason. No, he hadn't threatened me, but all the same he was threatening Simon. No, my dog didn't give any warning. He was outside being a Lion of the Serengeti. He'd been locked out though – you must admit that's suspicious. Oh, if it was you coming to take someone's finger you wouldn't want a great black hairy finger-eating lion in the house either, therefore you'd lock the dog flap too. Right... Thank you for all your help, Officer."

Yes, she could see it now.

"By the way, Shorty," she said. "Why *did* you lock the dog flap?" She waited expectantly for him to swallow his mouthful. They were in the breakfast room by then eating toast and drinking coffee. Shorty, it turned out, was as fanatical about marmite as Simon. That was nice. A common interest after all.

Shorty looked at her as though she was a foundation short of a house and said: "Why would we want to tangle with that ravening hound? Easiest thing to do was shut him out. Anyway, the chief's allergic."

Of course.

That was okay then – her near concussion had been worth it to save the thugs any hassle and 'the chief' a rash. The fact that she knew the 'ravening hound' would have been more likely to investigate their pockets than their motives was neither here nor there. It also meant that locking him out had saved him from getting hurt too.

On the other hand, how did they know there was a dog in the house at all, let alone a ravening hound and how did they know he was outside already, as if waiting to be locked out? She couldn't make any sense of it. In fact, she'd given up trying to make any sense of any of it by this time and still hadn't a clue what to do with Shorty. In all conscience she couldn't let a finger poacher run loose in society if she had him in her power and anyway, she still needed to get to the bottom of all the happenings. What to do, what to do?

The door bell rang. They all stiffened and looked at each other. This was ridiculous – cowering in her own house. Liz got up, marched down the hall, through the lobby and flung open the front door. She must have looked fierce because her client, poor old Mr my-mother-always-told-me-that-washing-up-liquid-would-taint-the-salad-so-I-use-just-bicarb, recoiled from her as though she'd slapped his face with a dead fish. Good grief - she'd completely forgotten her appointment. Tax implications. Jeez, fancy forgetting about Tax implications.

She bared her teeth at him. It was the closest she could get to a welcoming smile. She stood back for him to enter the hall, but he couldn't get past the lobby. Moocher, Simon, Tony and Shorty were all crowded around staring at the poor blighter.

"Get back," Liz ordered. "This isn't an exhibit. This is my client." But, as it turned out, her client had other ideas too.

"Brian," he squeaked, his face suffused pink with delight, his hands outstretched to the man recently hit with Beethoven and then pinned to the floor in a sea of stiff socks. Brian? He didn't look like a Brian to Liz.

A dawning look of recognition stole over Shorty's face. "Leslie," he shouted and launched himself into her client's arms. Leslie? He didn't look like a Leslie to her.

"Oh, this is so FAB - meeting you again," Leslie said. "Where've you been? Watcha bin doin'? We've all missed you so much since you stopped coming to the Tip of the Month Club. Why did ya stop coming?"

They'd stepped apart by then and were grinning uncontrollably at each other like a couple of hysterical wart-hogs. Liz shut the front door carefully, making sure that it was indeed shut. She'd seen a long low car outside with two men in it, looking very Yummy and Chucklerish. Why hadn't they gone home?

It was no good. She would have to ring the police.

She ignored the chorus of protest from the assembled party, marched down the hall and snatched up the telephone.

The police turned up. Eventually. She told them absolutely everything, held back nothing.

They turned out to be even more obstructive than she could possibly have anticipated in her wildest nightmares.

"Lion of the Serengeti?" PC Number One stared at Moocher. "That mutt?"

"Well, excuse me. 'That mutt' happens to be my best friend."

"What's he being now?"

She looked in Moocher's direction. He had no sense of timing, that dog. He was doing his I'm-a-very-clean-dog, I-wash-myself-thoroughly-no-matter-the-distractions-in-my-life thing that he did sometimes. Jeez.

Liz didn't like the leer on PC Number One's face, not at all.

"It's obvious what he's doing, isn't it," she said. "Just what all men do, all the time when they think people aren't looking. Checking it's still there."

Well, she was sorry, but she just couldn't take unnecessary insults to her best pal. It wiped the grin off PC One's face though. And he took his hand out of his pocket.

Liz had a feeling that little incident didn't help her case any.

"What's he doing now then?"

Oh, dear. She looked at Moocher, dreading what he might be up to now. But it was all right this time.

"Oh, he's doing his if-I-press-myself-close-enough-to-the-floor-everyone-will-think-I'm-a-plank-and-no-one-will-notice-that-I'm-inching-towards-that-bit-of-toast act. He's a bit of a thief, you see."

"He's a thief, ay? Well, that probably explains it. Perhaps he fancied a snack, thought he'd check out the fridge and had a spot of finger and that's why you can't prove your case." He thought that was hilarious and rolled about in his chair like a mad suet pudding.

Liz instantly suffered a severe case of sense-of-humour-loss, and didn't reply.

"Don't you get it?" PC One insisted on repeating.

Boy, he was thick.

He persevered. "Eaten the evidence, I mean. D'ya geddit? D'ya geddit?"

He'd choke on his own wit in a minute. It would be a quick death.

"Or was it too close to the bone for your liking? Hahaha."

Where was Beethoven when she needed him? Boyohboy, her celebrated patience was taking a real bashing today. She could have done with Simon there to back her up about the finger, but he'd disappeared, probably to smoke himself to death as fast as possible.

She could have done with the new Hugh there, actually. His sour-faced disapproval of everything that moved would have put this lot in their place in seconds. She nearly howled her head off at the very thought, but womanfully fought the urge back.

PC One persisted. She could tell he was the life and soul back at the station. "Perhaps he needed it to make a phone call. Couldn't get his claw to stay on the button and kept hitting the wrong digit. Hahaha. Digit, digit. Geddit, geddit? Hahaha."

Very bloody funny.

Liz was also picking up snatches of PC Number Two's thoroughly vicious interrogation of Shorty. It went like this:

"Oh, no, you should use lemon juice, that's the best bet for getting stains out of..."

Shorty: "No, no, no, bicarb – old standby I know, but old is best you know."

Leslie: "Brian's right, as always..."

PC Number Two: "As for carpets, especially for wine, salt's the best thing..."

Shorty: "Salt? Ah, yes, I'd agree with salt for wine, but not on carpets. Tablecloths, now..."

Leslie: "Brian's bound to be right. He's President of..."

PC Number Two: "Cat fur! Goodness me, yes, cat hair is just awful to get off..."

Shorty: "Simple though with a wet cloth, oh dearie me, yes."

He wouldn't say 'simple' in that lilting, carefree way if he'd ever experienced the Moocher Effect, that's for sure. The Moocher Effect could reduce a clean, well organised residence into a wasteland of tumbleweed-like hair-balls rolling about carpets that had mysteriously become all the same colour - overnight.

Leslie: "Tip of the Month Club. Meets on the third Thursday in the month..."

PC Number Two: "President? Proud to meet you, sir..."

Great manly shaking of hands all round. They all got out their diaries and there followed a great discussion as to where they would meet up and how best to use a taxi and not pay a tip. Oh, good. Liz was so pleased that satisfaction and beaming faces were the order of the day in her house.

After they'd kindly eaten every biscuit that could be found and used up all the milk and damn near all the coffee, they let her off with a warning about wasting *their* time and told her how lucky she was that Shorty, being the magnanimous chap he was, didn't want to press charges about her assault on him. Hugh *would* have been pleased.

Shorty made the most of it. He blushed and tried to twist his toe into her floor, the very picture of bashful oh-don't-embarrass-me stuff. She wished, oh how she wished, she hadn't rung the police. She would never ring them again. Everyone else had been right and she'd been wrong and she deserved every nasty pun and snide remark that came her way!

Shorty-Brian and Leslie, formerly known as her client, left together. It didn't seem right to let Shorty go after their traumatic experiences, and that wasn't even counting Clive's. As they were leaving, however, Shorty assured them, in a breathless voice that he'd seen the light and wouldn't be walking the dark path anymore. But although he had seen the light he couldn't possibly spill the beans on his erstwhile colleagues. Surely they could understand that? She supposed they could. In a we'll-stick-together-schoolyard kind of way.

"You needn't worry about me," he said. "I won't be troubling you again. It was only a part time job after I took early retirement, just to give me an interest and get me out the house."

"What was a part time job exactly?" Liz was mystified.

"You know, being a hoodlum."

"You can get a part time job as a hoodlum?" Was her mouth hanging open?

"Of course. That's what I did. But I've realised I have much more to offer by expanding the Tip of the Month Club. In fact I shall start producing a magazine and perhaps we'll meet fortnightly from now on. Much more my thing you know."

Leslie was overjoyed to hear this and capered around the front room clapping his hands. He stopped in front of Liz, puffing. "Sorry I turned up a bit early," he said. "But I'm glad I did or I wouldn't have met Brian again. Don't worry about the tax stuff. You just do whatever needs to be done and tell me how much. I have every faith in you. Well in terms of accounting, that is. Defamation of character's clearly not your thing. Lucky for you Brian is such a nice chap."

Yeah, right. Chortle, chortle.

"I expect the others are waiting for me," Shorty said. "We've made a good team, but now I'll tell them that it's over. Sad really, but every good thing must come to an end sometime." Shorty shook her hand and said: "Do give me a ring when you want to fit nets. I inspected next door's while we were in there - immaculate. Superb job. I'll be happy to help you with yours." He presented her with his card which read: 'Brian

Threadneedle at Your Service for all those little jobs you didn't know you needed doing.'

Short, concise and insulting.

Liz didn't actually throw them out, but neither did she lie down on the doorstep to prevent them leaving before they demanded sight of her stained cutlery and heaped unwanted advice on her. Why on earth had she ever felt badly about knocking him unconscious? She vaguely wondered if that was qualification enough for her to earn a bob or two at this hoodlum lark? She wondered how much it paid?

As the house went quiet Liz turned to Simon, who hadn't managed to smoke himself to death yet although he'd had a good go, and they stared blankly at each other.

They were still doing it when Julie burst into the room. Although the word, 'burst' with someone that frail isn't right. 'Dripped' might be a better word. Her already-pale face was paler than usual and tears poured down it. She ignored Liz entirely and fixing an impassioned stare on Simon she threw herself to her knees by his chair and laid her head on his lap, very reminiscent of Moocher laying his head on Tony's lap. How touching. However, Moocher's approval of Tony hadn't produced the terror that this incident did in Simon.

This was the first time Liz had ever seen him look frightened in all the time she'd known him, despite all the nasty little burning episodes, not to mention being threatened by three gruesome thugs. She watched in fascination as his hands, as if with a life of their own, levitated above the shiningly blonde head, hesitated and lowered to hang lifelessly once more down the sides of the chair. He stared imploringly at Liz.

122

She shrugged, heaved herself from her chair and left him to it. She was getting dead keen on things that weren't her business staying that way. Dead keen. Also, it served him right for not sticking up for her about the existence of the finger with the police. Then again, if he had, it might have got Stella in trouble and it would seem that, terrified of her though he might be, he didn't want that.

Curious though she was about what Simon and Julie were up to, Liz went up to the attic, got up her household finance spreadsheets on the computer and tried to pretend that fixing the French windows would cost nothing.

She did wonder where Clive was and felt a twinge of guilt that she no longer wanted to know anything about him either, but it was only a little twinge, and then she forgot him. Let them get on with it. She was sick of everybody and had a life of her own to get sorted. An early night seemed like a good plan all of a sudden. An early night and absolutely no thought of Hugh would do the trick. She'd just sleep that man right out of her head.

Chapter Twelve

In the morning she was back at the computer, trying to work out how one of her clients thought he could claim for his nanny's salary, when the telephone rang. She swore but picked it up anyway and a voice said, "Hello Liz."

The hairs on her arms, and on her legs and on her neck as well as hairs she didn't possess, shot upright. Oh, no! This couldn't be true. Why were they doing that? Oh, why, oh why? This was not right when the voice on the other end of the phone belonged to Hugh. She could have wailed, but she didn't. Instead she croaked: "Hello Hugh." Oh, so cold, so cold, so unlike the way they'd always been before all this.

His voice immediately changed to one of warm and husky, thrilling concern: "You've got a cold?"

"No, no. I just need to cough. Excuse me." Cough. Cough. Play for time. "There, that's better. Um, what can I do for you?"

"I heard you'd had a visit from the police. Not before time either, judging by bricks through windows and heavies at the door." This was the new Hugh all right! For one, wild ecstatic moment she thought the old Hugh had come back.

"How did you hear that? You got a mole in Malvern road?"

"Of course I have. I have to keep an eye on you. Can't have the family name dragged through the mud."

Ohmigod. Who was spying on her? She really needed that as well. She'd be eyeing up all the neighbours now, wondering who was the turncoat. How dare they? She lived here - they should be on *her* side!

"Who is it?"

"Who is what?"

"Your snake in the grass. Your mole."

"Now be reasonable Liz, if I told you that they would no longer be my mole would they? Where's the point of having an undercover agent in place and then telling who it is? Wouldn't work would it?"

He was being so very patient with her. She wasn't at all grateful.

"Male or female."

"Not sure."

"Not sure? You mean you've subverted one of my neighbours and didn't take time out to decide on their gender? Typical."

This was met with silence. He wasn't going to tell her.

"Do you need me to come over?"

"I thought you weren't supposed to do that anymore? I thought you weren't allowed to come over to this den of iniquity. And anyway, I've just realised what you meant about dragging the family name through the mud. I suppose I should give it up and revert to my maiden name now you're giving it to someone else?"

More silence. She supposed it wasn't very nice of her, but it was either get nasty or cry. He should know better than to ask whether to come over. He should have simply leapt on to his white stallion and galloped straight over without asking first. He was supposed to be her friend.

She realised how close to tears she was and how weak she felt and how lovely it would be just to lean back on him and let him sort it out. His powers of organisation were such that he would have all the answers before the kettle had boiled. How she wanted him to charge up Malvern Road on his war horse, yelling a challenge to her enemies, coming to her rescue. But she'd given all that up. Gladly. And not only had she given it up but someone else, someone with a name like *Charity* had taken it up instead. It was no longer hers to lean on.

"Everything's fine. Everything's hunky dory and under control. Thank you all the same. You're very kind, but no. Thank you. Thank you all the same."

Before Charity, he would have said something like, "Right, I'm on my way." He'd have thrown the phone down and she would have ranted and raved in her attic. Something like: Bloody nerve! How damn arrogant could you get? I've made it quite clear I didn't want him and he was coming anyway. She'd have leapt up from her chair and thrown herself down on to the carpet with Moocher. Nose to nose they'd stare into each others' eyes. His tail would thump the rug steadily like it did when he was laughing. She would laugh too.

But not now. No. This time, After Charity, she threw herself on the bed and cried in great, gulping, unattractive gasps of despair.

Because she finally realised that she did love him. Not as in love him for the person he was anyway. Anyone would do that. Anyone who met him Before Charity would love him. No, she loved him as her husband and she wanted him back. And she wanted him back when it was too late to have him. He'd moved on, put her in his past and found himself a new future. A new future that didn't have her in it. And she would do nothing to jeopardise that. Because she loved him.

She wore herself out crying. Moocher even hauled himself onto her bed – forbidden territory – just to keep her company, somehow knowing he was welcome this time.

Eventually, when she was all cried out and hating herself for her stupidity, she was dragged from the pit of despair by a diffident tap on her door. This was rare. Mostly, lodgers were too terrified to come up to the attic. She leapt from the bed, Moocher scrambled off, and she sat at her desk before saying "Enter" in a very cold voice.

It was Simon, looking, if possible even more frightened than before. He came straight out with what was on his mind. "I'm far too old for her."

"Yes, I think you are." she had to agree, her brain immediately swinging back into action in quite a heartening way considering it had been at death's door mere seconds ago. Thinking of Julie, she realised it wasn't the age thing so much, it was that Simon lived his life assuming it was still the swinging sixties. He wore lightweight jackets that made him look like he was going on safari any minute. Also, he was obsessed with his ex and frequently had imaginary conversations with her. On the other hand, another love interest might help him out of all that. But then, why should it be someone else that got him out of it, why couldn't it be him? Also, he might have been perfectly happy just the way he was and why should he get out of it at all?

"I agree," she said, faltering at the complexities of the situation.

His face relaxed.

A moment of inspiration came to her. "I think she may see you as a father figure type person, Simon, rather than as a lover."

He looked so relieved his face nearly slid off his head. He hadn't thought of that. His sudden urgency to beard Liz in her lair was forgotten. He nearly grinned. Good grief! He turned sharply and left. Gosh, that was an easy one. And then she remembered the finger.

"Simon!" she shouted. She listened and heard his footsteps come to a halt, turn and come back up again. His head appeared around the door, followed slowly by the rest of him.

"What was that about the finger? You did start to tell me."

He immediately looked sheepish. "I put the finger in the fridge," he said.

"Did you say it had something to do with the brick?"

"Yeah, it was attached to the brick with a rubber band. It was when Good-All-Rounder-Tony grabbed your arm and held you back and then you dashed out and he went off to get a vacuum cleaner – he's not human, that man – the first thing he thought of was an electrical appliance..."

That was the longest sentence she'd ever heard from Simon. She encouraged him to continue: "Go on, what happened then?"

"It meant that I was the first to see it and when I saw it was a finger I knew straight away it was a warning message for me and I didn't want to have to explain that publicly – not all the stuff about Stella. So I picked it up before anyone could see it. I didn't want Julie to see it either and get upset." He pinkened becomingly. "Of course, she did see it in the end, but I... Well... You know..."

"No, I don't know, Simon. Why should Stella throw a finger on a brick through my window?"

"It was a message for me. I've told you that. She's still trying to get money out of me. She was 'giving me the finger' in retaliation for my lawyer's success last week in court."

That startled Liz. She had no idea Simon lived in such interesting times. How could one tell when he slouched around the house the way he did, in odd shoes, spending all his time ironing his clothes and cleaning his teeth and doing the odd few moments of work on his computer? Oh, and sometimes playing the violin.

"I had no idea Stella was capable of being so, um, colourful."

"Oh, yes! This is only the start, I'm sure. You have no idea what she's capable of when she's not getting her own way."

"I just hope she doesn't take any more liberties with my house while she's at it then," Liz said. "In the meantime, perhaps you could sort out with her payment of the bill for the window and pay it back to Tony?"

He nodded.

"Simon. Why did you present that finger so tidily, on a plate and everything? Why, indeed, did you keep it? Why put it in the fridge? Why didn't you tell me about it? Especially when we were sitting around the table yesterday morning waiting to see what would happen when Tony or Julie opened the fridge. Why the hell didn't you tell me?"

"I didn't realise that's what that was all about," he said. "How was I supposed to know that's what that was about?"

Well, yes. He had a point. It might not have been obvious. Not to Simon.

"Anyway, I'd forgotten it when I first came down."

That was more like it. That sounded like Simon. Liz didn't believe there was anyone else in all of human history capable of picking up a finger from a brick through the window, putting it on a pretty paper plate, cling-filming it and putting it in to the fridge of a house with five people living in it and not tell one of them and go to bed and forget they'd put it there. It wasn't possible. Unless it was Simon Medley.

"The plate was one of Lydia's. It had ginger creams on it and I finished them and somehow must have put the plate in my pocket. So it was handy when I was wondering what to put the finger on. And of course I cling-wrapped it. You should cover things in the fridge especially if you're putting uncooked meat in with cooked. I thought it should go in the fridge because, whatever else it might be it's still meat isn't it?"

She couldn't deny it.

"But whose finger do you think it is?"

He shook his head, his hair flopping around his ears. "No idea. It won't be anyone special's. It's just to send me a message. You can buy anything, you know. If you know the right place to go to, you can order anything that exists, and get it if you're prepared to pay. Stella would know where to get body parts, I'm sure."

How morbidly fascinating, but she had this need to know: "Simon, just where would someone obtain a finger?"

His face brightened a little. He was always pleased when asked for information or conjecture. "Oh," he said. "It wouldn't surprise me if you couldn't go to a particular pub and speak to a particular person who would have a cousin once removed whose brother's wife's son worked in the crematorium and could probably get bits to order. After all, who's going to miss them at that point?" He gave her an approving nod as though she were a favoured pupil.

Liz wondered if that was possible. Did people do that?

"Why did you keep it?" she asked.

"It didn't seem right to throw someone's finger away and I thought if I left it until the morning I might think of something. You know – sleep on it."

That figured. Sleeping on it was always a good thing to do.

"But, it's more likely," he added. "That Stella gained access to the anatomy department or wherever it is that they cut them up at the university, because she can, you know. And I thought if she borrowed the finger in order to make a point, as it were, to me, with it – she might need to put it back. Well, it just serves her right that there's nothing to put back now."

Ohmigod. Liz could find nothing to say, so she nodded.

"You all right, Liz. You look a bit pale."

"Yes, I'm fine, thanks, Simon. I, er, I might as well tell you before anyone else does, that Hugh is engaged to be married."

The shock on Simon's face echoed the feeling Liz had of being kicked in her stomach because of actually saying it aloud. She'd given the notion life by uttering the words.

"*He's what?*"

"He's engaged to be married. To someone called Charity?"

"*Charity?*"

"Yes. Charity."

He seemed totally pole-axed. His eyes shifted from her as if suddenly embarrassed and flicked around the attic, not really seeing anything, she was sure. He stuffed his hands in his pockets, mumbled something and left.

Liz had absolutely no idea why Simon should be so stunned and she had absolutely no inclination to try and puzzle it out. She was quite pleased with herself, though, in a sad but noble way, that she'd told him. She had started the process of moving on. Life goes on even After Charity.

Also, the little interlude with Simon had answered those few, trifling queries of hers although it did seem odd that two severed-finger episodes could occur in two houses that happened to have been built next to each other. It could be coincidence. But that was stretching it a bit...

Hearing a car Liz stepped into her dormer window, her watchtower, and peered down at the road. She thought maybe she'd nightmared the last day or so and that Hugh would leap out of a stallion shaped car, swirl his cape and stride thrillingly to her front door, his chiselled features purposeful and lovely, come to sort everything out and make it all right again.

It wasn't him. It was Clive, last seen doing the marathon run, jump and hop obstacle course down the back gardens of Malvern Road at a truly remarkable speed. He parked across the road. Damn! She'd forgotten to issue the sacred writ to her lodgers not to park outside his house. He got out, crossed the road and kicked the car outside his house. It was quite clear, the 'thunk'. She heard it even up here through a double glazed dormer. Had he really put that note through telling her of her flat or had it been Superpecs all along? Superpecs! She'd forgotten him. All these men about and she kept forgetting them. That was a good sign. She was obviously developing well. Life was not just about men. She knew that and now she was proving it. She allowed herself a small, satisfied sigh, not exactly of contentment, but she'd work on it. She knew her place in life and it was here. With her dog.

The only trouble with the idea of Superpecs was that she knew he peed behind his hedge whilst waving to people in the street. Oh, well.

She was glad Clive and she were on better terms, but she had a feeling that, despite all the books in his house, he really was a Git-Next-Door. Nevertheless, although she'd tried hard, petty spitefulness wasn't really her thing. It was so wearing and you had to think about it all the time. He hadn't been watching for them anyway - he'd been watching for thugs coming for him. That was all right then. Mind you, he *had* just kicked that car. Perhaps he was her ex's mole? No, he couldn't be. She knew men tended to stick together, but an unholy alliance between those two didn't seem likely.

After kicking the car, Clive inspected his own gate, probably checking for scratches in the paintwork and thinking, excitedly, about touching it up. He scrutinised his miniscule, but obediently flat and forbiddingly neat lawn, and twitched away a damned cheeky chocolate wrapper that had blown in. He checked out the geometric flowerbeds surrounding the green square and pounced on something that dared to grow out of step. He wasn't acting like he was afraid of thugs coming back for more fingers at all. She looked more closely. In fact, he looked as relaxed and content as she knew she'd be feeling just as soon as she relegated all men in her life to exactly where they belonged. Having said that, she suddenly realised what a nice rear end he had. Not bad. Not bad at all. Out of place on a Git-Next-Door type, but a nice rear end all the same. Blimey – *another* nice rear end. They were everywhere just at the moment.

He disappeared up his path and she heard his door shut behind him. Her gaze wandered upwards, over the rooftops. Idly she watched a lone seagull sliding down an air current, swing round and back to do it all over again. A happy creature. She could see the floodlights for after-dark cricket at the grounds, intruding into the pastel sky. Further away she could see the mast thing for television reception. It wasn't a pretty sight.

Bringing her gaze closer to home she admired the façade of the house opposite. Three floors, red brick, dormer window in the roof-room. Handsome house. Just like hers. She shifted from foot to foot. She just knew something wasn't right. The passers-by continued passing by – a marvellously dexterous skate-boarder, a woman carrying far too much shopping in carrier bags the handles of which she knew would have reduced to the width of garrotte wire with the inevitable effect on her fingers, a chap in a turban…

And she had it! Clive had the same or a similar, massive bandage on his hand. The same arrangement of snowy white, carefully bound bandage. You'd have thought it might have got grubby by now, especially considering his recent gymnastics. He could have changed it of course, or perhaps he'd been out to have it changed. However, as she visualised the sight of him crossing the road and fiddling about in his garden, she just knew that he had a full set of fingers on both hands. She clearly remembered him moving piles of books one handed, using his right hand. The bandage was now on his right hand. Clive had not had a finger removed with a power tool or a rusty hatchet or nibbled away in his sleep by rats. Clive was a liar. So what the devil was that all about?

And, did she really want to know?

And where the hell was her ex? He wasn't coming. It really was all over. He really was engaged to someone called Charity. He really was beyond her reach forever. And it was all her fault. She was just stupid. Downright stupid. That bloody Charity had better sodding well appreciate him, that's all she could say, and make him happy. Or else.

Desperately trying to think of something heartening she realised that because she'd been fool enough to believe Clive, and to sympathise with him, at least she hadn't told the police about him losing a finger. She could just imagine the ensuing conversation when they went to check that one out and found it had miraculously grown back. Not much consolation, however, because she was in even more of a mental maze than before and getting fed up at being given the run-around. Maybe if she followed that up she could stop thinking about her lost love for a while.

She raced down the stairs with Moocher galloping behind her and shut the lobby door on him. He did his you-always-leave-me-behind, you-never-take-me-anywhere bit, which really creased her up and she had to go back and hug him several times before she could make herself leave him. She carefully shut her door, making sure it was as shut as she thought it was. She wouldn't make that mistake again. She leapt over the wall. Banging hell out of Clive's front door she saw his nets twitch and knew he was debating about letting her in, just knew it. If he didn't she would launch a back garden attack. Luckily for him he opened the door.

"Well, hello, um, Liz. Won't you come in?"

"Thank you Clive, I will." She didn't mess about this time. She marched straight in, removed the books and sat down in the front room. "How do you feel now?" she demanded. "How's your hand? I hope you're having it dressed properly. Don't want it to get infected do we? You could get gangrene and lose the whole arm. And then your shoulder. And then goodness knows where next.

136

Do you want me to help you out? Shall I make the coffee?"

Might as well make the most of it – there was no coffee left in her house after last night. The PCs had drunk it all, spent a happy hour mocking and scoffing her and her dog *and* eaten all the biscuits. Mmm, coffee. She rushed out to his kitchen and put his kettle on before he could refuse. She restrained herself from poking in his cupboards, but had a good look around while he hovered in the doorway. He didn't seem able to look directly at her. He inspected his nails and moved from foot to foot as though treading grapes.

His kitchen looked brand new. Perhaps it was, or perhaps it was never used, or perhaps it was that he was so immaculate, or perhaps it was in comparison to hers. Nothing interesting there, then. She looked through his tiny kitchen window and got a shock when she realised how much he could see through into hers. She'd never realised how one-way some of this funny glass was before, nor how two-way the glass she had previously assumed was one-way. She refused to dwell on either the state of her kitchen or the state of her sometimes when she inhabited it.

Although a chill swept over her when she remembered the odd occasions she would come down in the middle of the night when the rest of the house was asleep (even Sandra, despite her latest hot sex date). She wasn't always conscious of the need to get dressed to do that. At that time of night honest neighbours should be asleep too. She gave Clive a very nasty look. He shrank back against the door-frame and swallowed repeatedly, a faint but noticeable flush starting up his neck, gathering pace over his cheeks and disappearing darkly into his hairline.

Back in the front room and tucking into a load of chocolate biscuits she'd found in his bread bin, she fixed him with her most piercing stare. He looked like a caterpillar pinned to his chair. "So, Clive, tell me how your hand is doing. I'm really concerned." Yeah, really, really. She composed her face into an expression of genuine concern, but wasn't sure it was all that convincing.

"Um, well, it's okay. I'm a fast healer."

"Oh, good, I'm so pleased to hear it. Tell me, do you get phantom pains in that finger? I've heard of this – where someone loses a limb and then they still feel pain in it. Do you?"

"Ah, no, or not yet, I haven't. No, no, just a general discomfort as one might expect from having one's finger removed with a power tool."

"Was it a jig-saw? I've always fancied one of them, or was it more of a circular saw they used? Or perhaps a fret saw – that would be handy, wouldn't it – just think of all the things you could make with a fret saw – fret-type things, you know."

Sweat appeared on his forehead. He was easy prey. Oh, the power, the power of it all.

"It was… um… it was… I'm not sure. I didn't take note. I'm not a handy-man. It was a small sort of saw."

"Must had been I suppose or they wouldn't have been able to help cutting into the fingers on either side. Perhaps it was a sort of drill or a miniature road thumper type thingy. Did they drill it off, or just squash it a lot 'til it fell off or was it actually a cut type action? Or a hacking, axe-like motion?"

More sweat trickled down from the roots of his fair, floppy hair, remarkably like Simon Medley's now she looked at it. Simon's hair was very fine too, like a baby's, so it looked like he had millions of hairs on his head instead of the usual number, whatever that was.

With a suddenness that startled her into dropping her half eaten, seventh biscuit – you get into the habit of counting when you share a house – onto the floor, Clive leapt out of his chair and grasping his bandage, yanked it off in one smooth motion and hurled it at the wall. It thudded off and slid down to disappear behind a pile of books.

Liz had no qualms, in this house, of just picking up her dropped biscuit and finishing it off. In her house she would have ended up choking on fur balls for a week. She picked up another, the very picture of casual unconcern.

"There! See. Yes, I've got all my fingers. Are you satisfied now?" He fidgeted from foot to foot, his hands inches from her face.

She went for another biscuit. Might as well make the best of the situation. "I'm waiting for an explanation, you know, Clive, or whoever you are." She said it as coldly as she could considering she had a mouthful of chocolate crunch.

"We, the thugs and I, came to an agreement that they would pretend they'd sawn my finger off."

"Why?" She imagined it would be because part-time thugs didn't expect finger-severing to be part of the job. It seemed more of a full-time thug type activity.

"Because they didn't want to do it," he said.

"You're telling me the tiresome threesome got squeamish about it?"

"No, they forgot to bring the saw."

The world was full of incompetents these days.

"They could have used the bread knife."

He recoiled from her and dropped into his chair.

"I don't think they thought of that. They didn't seem awfully bright."

"Tell me, why were you so afraid when they came back then? Why did you run away?"

"I thought they'd changed their minds and come back with the saw."

Yes, that would explain it.

"You have no idea how worried I was that it was your finger that Moocher ate."

He froze and looked at her as though she'd just sprouted a waist length beard with rats and snakes nesting in it. "Your dog... Your dog ate someone's finger?"

"Yes. I didn't tell you because I thought it was yours. I thought it would be in bad taste."

"How very sensitive of you," he said.

Liz gave him the benefit of her coldest glare. "So, what about this big secret you've been keeping to yourself for years? Why aren't they still trying to get that from you?"

"They made a mistake. It's not me they want after all."

"As easy as that. One minute you're terrorised for a secret, the next it's all a big mistake and someone else was supposed to be terrorised for it instead. Oh, come on! Do you have a big secret or don't you?"

"We all have secrets. Some bigger than others."

Liz couldn't argue with that, but neither could she think of any secrets she had that someone would cut off her finger to get at. And anyway, they hadn't cut his finger off. She was getting that now-familiar feeling of frustration again.

"So, do you know whose finger was in our fridge?" She already knew since Simon explained it, but she wanted to see if she could get anything else out of Clive and couldn't think how else to keep the conversation going. Also, now she'd had some time for reflection she wasn't totally convinced by the Stella explanation. It could still be nothing to do with her.

"You had someone's finger in your fridge?"

"Yes."

"It was this someone's finger that Moocher ate?"

"Yes." She was a bit concerned now. At least if it *had* been Clive's finger she could have been certain it was clean. Still, Moocher didn't seem to have suffered from his first taste of finger food and maybe a bit of dirt was better for him than disinfectant.

"No."

"No, what?"

"No, I don't know whose finger it was in your fridge. That Moocher ate."

She knew that forever more she'd be acutely suspicious of anyone she met with a missing finger. She also would now spend her whole time assessing all her neighbours in Malvern Road both for missing digits and to see if

141

they looked like moles for her ex – ones she didn't already know about, that was. She already knew Melanie – who didn't know she knew - rang him up whenever she thought he ought to know something. Melanie was keen on the idea of them getting back together again. Sadly, Liz realised she'd need to let her know she'd have to stop. It wasn't fair to Hugh – or to that Charity person. She wrenched her mind back to matters at hand.

"So, none of the finger stuff or the part time thugs has got anything to do with you? It was all a mistake and we're none the wiser. You don't know why they wanted my lodger, Simon Medley?"

"No."

Perhaps it *was* all to do with Stella then. Deep in thought she reached for another biscuit. Her hand came back empty.

Biscuits all gone.

Might as well go home.

Chapter Thirteen

"If you have any inspiration, do let me know," she said, heading towards Clive's front door. As she opened it she saw her ex swirling his imaginary cape impatiently as he waited outside her house. He turned when he heard the door open and immediately frowned hugely at her.

Good grief! He'd turned up after all. For a man engaged to be married and not allowed round to his old, vice-ridden haunt, he was here a helluva lot. It was all she could do not to cast herself onto his manly chest and beg him to stay with her for the rest of their lives.

"Hello," she said trying desperately for the casual touch and hoping he couldn't read the burning love she still had for him in her eyes. "Been there long?" She also had to greet his darkling looks with light-hearted cheerfulness. It was none of his business what she was doing in Git-Next-Door's house. Especially now he was engaged to be married to the Charity person.

Gracefully she vaulted the wall, caught her foot on the top slab and fell in to his arms. Well, rats! How annoying. How graceless. Typical that he should be ready to catch her. How annoying that he expected to. How lovely that he did.

She could feel the tension in his body. Maybe he really couldn't stand her any more and couldn't bear to touch her. She should have disengaged herself and stood on her own two feet, but she just wanted his arms around her one last time before they were taken from her forever, leaving her cold.

He said, "Oh, long enough to help one of your lodgers move out. Not long enough to get bored." He was always such a polite man no matter what he might be thinking.

She could feel his words reverberating through his chest. His heart seemed awfully loud against her ear, but steady and reassuring, almost hypnotic. She felt an inconvenient stirring of lust so she forced her attention back to what he was saying in the hope it would douse any little embers thinking of fanning themselves to flame. She also, finally, made herself get down off his chest and move away a bit so they weren't touching.

"…you didn't tell me he was moving out. Not that you have to tell me anything about your business. Of course not."

Liz was glad he realised, finally. But, who was he talking about? Tony couldn't be going so soon, surely. She tuned in again to what he was saying.

"…just thought you might have, what with him being your longest standing lodger. Sorry to see him go."

Simon! He wasn't moving out last time she'd seen him but then, he might have decided to flee before Stella threw another, more telling, body-part through the window. Hugh carried on. If Liz didn't know him better she might have thought he was nervous the way he waffled on.

"Did Simon tell you why he was moving out?"

"I didn't see him," Hugh said. "The other chap told me. I just helped to get that enormous trunk of his into the pickup. Damned heavy it was too but, sensibly, he's hired some muscle to give him a hand, although why they couldn't have parked closer was a mystery. No, Simon's collecting other stuff from his room, I believe, so you'll still get to see him. Anyway, he wouldn't just leave without telling you..."

She would hope not! Bad enough that he'd sprung a surprise like this on her anyway, although it was probably more the case that he'd forgotten to tell her. She found herself dangerously close to tears again. It seemed too much to lose such an old friend as Simon at the same time that she'd lost her very best friend and lover of all time. Everyone was deserting her.

Pull yourself together, Liz, she admonished herself. As long as she had Moocher she'd be fine. She straightened up, pulling her shoulders back, sticking her chin in the air. Unfortunately, of course, her boobs came out rather sharply when she did that and she hastily rounded her shoulders and made them lie down, but not before noticing Hugh flush a little. She wondered if it was lust or embarrassment. The latter, probably. He had Charity to go home to. Aargh. She had to get her mind off this track. Thinking of Hugh all the time had become like getting a horrible tune stuck in your head until it drove you mad. There must be a word for that. In future the word would be 'Hugh'.

Luckily her front door swung open, screeching horribly. Hugh turned around. She stepped sideways so she'd have a view of whoever was coming out of her house. Hugh and Liz looked at the man. He stood in her doorway wearing all black clothing, with a cat mask completely obscuring his face. Obviously a burglar.

She was about to ask: "Excuse me, are you sure you're in the right house?" when the door slammed shut with enough force to convince her that as far as he was concerned, yes, he was in the right house and didn't want to see her just now. Hugh and Liz looked at each other and checked the number of the house. Yes, *they* were in the right place. She found her key, thrust it in the lock and hurled the door open.

She tried to keep her body in front of Hugh's. She was yelling: "Get out of my way!"

He was yelling: "Stay back, Liz. Stay there!" Just like she was a dog. Down, girl, down.

She shot in through the lobby, into the hall and raced down to the breakfast room dragging Hugh behind her. He had an unbreakable grip on the back of her sweater.

Wrong way. They clearly heard the anguished shriek of the front door as it was pulled ruthlessly across the tiles. He must had nipped into the front room and waited for them to pass before making his getaway. They skidded in a sharp U-turn. Hugh was ahead of her this time. He streaked down the hall, turned right at the end, left through the lobby door, and shot out of the front door, pulling her with him. She had an unbreakable grip on the back of his expensive leather jacket.

"Mind my bulbs!" Liz shouted, letting go of his jacket as he raced across her garden. But he was gone. Boyohboy, the power of that man, the strength in those thighs. Mmm… she ran after him on her stubby little legs. She must have been doing twice the work that he was and was miles behind, but she could see where he was headed so she

146

stopped in the middle of the road and stood there with her arms crossed. She adopted what she hoped was a determined and courageous expression to grace her femininely sculpted face. The wind playfully teased her hair into a halo around her noble features. A dog barked in the lonely distance.

Unless they reversed out, the baddies in their getaway vehicle were bound to come down this way and they wouldn't just run her over would they? Would they?

Her handsome-and-huggable ex-husband had reached the getaway vehicle. It was a very un-James Bond-like pickup truck and it was beginning to move fast. Hugh hurled himself onto the bonnet. What on earth had he been watching on telly recently? She cringed at the thought of the damage to his jacket. Not to mention the damage to all her neighbours' cars as the getaway driver couldn't see much through the windscreen with Hugh sliding about all over it and the pick-up consequently careered along bouncing off every other car on either side of the road.

Fairly late on, she realised that the driver probably couldn't see her either. She would have to abandon her Boadicea stance and get outta there. Quick.

She glanced around to see if anyone would see her utterly graceless and cowardly retreat, and leapt for it. The truck sped past her, Hugh slithering side-to-side on the bonnet. She could clearly hear him growling, or was it the engine, which never seemed to get out of second gear?

Unfortunately, Hugh's trousers decided to make a sudden descent. Must have been the unexpected workout they were getting. They hadn't deserted him altogether but were grouped about his knees. And he already had his hands full so could do nothing about it.

She was momentarily distracted when she noticed that one of the casualties of the wildly careering truck was Clive's car where he'd parked it across the road. Funnily enough, if he'd been parked outside his own house he would have been okay. Well, she thought it was funny anyway, in a gosh-isn't-life-strange kind of way.

Clive plainly wasn't amused. A very loud firework went off virtually in her ear. She staggered back clutching that side of her head, when another one went off. It must have frightened the life out of the pick-up because it shuddered and slowed right down. Hugh did some sort of athletic leap and clamber and suddenly he was in the back of the truck fighting off the chap in the cat mask and trying to do something to the huge trunk she could see in there. All this whilst battling with recalcitrant trousers.

The truck convulsed again and the tail-gate fell open, Hugh fell out still hanging on to the trunk, which also fell out with a dull 'phud'. With a roar of abused gears the pick-up shot off up the road and could be heard snarling and rattling into the distance. Why Hugh was so keen on getting the trunk she couldn't begin to imagine. Mysterious were the ways of her ex-husband's thought processes. Anyway, at least she could see that he was all right. She hadn't realised she'd been holding her breath in terror, until then. It expelled itself in such a rush of relief she nearly collapsed, but just managed to stay standing.

When the mist cleared from her vision she noticed Hugh's boxers. They were not boxers like

148

any she ever bought him. Not that she bought him many – he was the sort of chap who did his own shopping, but occasionally she might have bought him a pair with interlocking toucans on them or covered in what looked like black and white chequerboard but turned out to be packed with Border collies. Natch.

No – these were covered in golden teddy bears. On skateboards. Waving pink hankies to onlooking and adoring fluffy kittens. Good grief. Liz averted her eyes so as not to embarrass him.

She looked at Clive instead and saw that he had a gun in his hand. It must be one hell of a secret he was keeping and her impression of him underwent another instant transformation. He must be an underworld character of the first order. He not only had a gun but he had fired it, and all because someone had dented his car? Why hadn't he used it when he thought someone was going to chop off his finger? Perhaps his car was more important to him. Liz leapt into a handy bush before he thought of her.

He stooped down and picked up a couple of things that she could only assume from having been to the pictures a few times in her life, were bullet cases. They tinkled together in his hand. He then ran back into his house with the gun and almost immediately appeared again on his path with both his hands unmistakably empty. Not only that, but one of them had suddenly sprouted an outsize beehive of a bandage. He really should be more careful about keeping up that particular pretence. He rushed past her, putting a finger (one that was attached to his hand) to his lips as he did so, and tearfully inspected the damage to his car. She climbed out of the bush.

149

Then she spotted Superpecs or rather, Hedge-piddler out in the road with his digital camera getting a lensful of Hugh's teddies. Oh, dear...

She also thought she saw Tortoise-woman, basket swinging from her hand. But surely not...

"Liz, give me a hand here," Hugh shouted. She ran down to see what it was he wanted a hand with, exactly. If it was the trunk then he could jolly well wait for Simon to give him a hand as it was his stuff Hugh seemed so keen on rescuing. She became aware that Malvern Road was abuzz with irate neighbours all looking suspiciously at her.

Her! Why her?

Before she could reach Hugh, however, she was rudely pushed out of the way by a blonde gazelle, recently known as Julie. Strangely, she was shouting: "Dad! Dad!"

That brought Liz to a very sudden halt. She stared disbelievingly at Hugh, her Hugh (or rather, Charity's Hugh) and realised that their marriage had failed for many more reasons than she could ever have guessed at the time. He must have fathered her before they'd even celebrated their paper anniversary. Hugh gave her a strange look and frowned, but all the time he was busy trying to undo the belts around the trunk. Julie fell on the trunk, which wasn't at all helpful, and sobbed distractedly and appealingly. Her nose wasn't red. Her mascara didn't run. How annoying.

Liz made herself move again and saw Hugh pick Julie up and move her off the trunk so he could get it open. He did it in such a masterful but heart-breakingly gentle way, Liz wondered what would happen if she threw herself alluringly on the trunk. He would probably just curse her for being silly and she would crawl away consumed with embarrassment. Life was just so unfair.

At some point he must had pulled his trousers up and she hadn't noticed. Drat.

He got the trunk open despite the impediment of a lithe young body leaning over his arm, pressing up against his chest, breathing softly onto his cheek as Julie watched his every move with breathless wonder. Liz thought she was overdoing it a bit, but Hugh didn't seem to mind. Perhaps he didn't notice her as he was so intent on his task?

And there was Simon! In the trunk! Good grief! He looked like he was just waking up from a jolly nice nap, too. He sat up in the trunk, fished glasses from his shirt pocket, placed them on his face, yawned cavernously, riffled his already punk-looking hair, adjusted his tie and just sat there looking like Simon always looked.

"Dad! Dad." Julie threw herself onto Simon who promptly fell backwards into the trunk again, whether from the weight or shock was hard to tell.

Simon was Julie's Dad? Liz smiled broadly at Hugh, forgiving him. He scowled at her. He always could read her mind. Another reason they didn't work together very well.

But then, maybe their marriage failed because it never occurred to her to buy him boxers with skateboarding teddies on them. She had just neglected that man.

Back in the breakfast room, Simon seemed to be taking it all very calmly. Perhaps he didn't understand that he'd been kidnapped, thrown in a trunk, raced down Malvern Road (nearly ending Liz's life in her brave attempt to save him), and rescued by Hugh in a death defying bonnet manoeuvre, not to mention finding a daughter who at present was sitting on the floor staring up into his face with an adoring smile on her own.

"It's all right, Simon," Liz said, in case he was suffering from shock. "You can smoke. Just this once." He smiled gratefully and thrust a hand into his pocket. He produced an old stompie all of three centimetres long, and lighting it up with a magic pen that acted like a lighter, pulled in the evil cloud of smoke. It took years off him. Liz disappeared into the kitchen to make coffee. Of course they didn't have any, so she made squash instead.

Tony came in, carrying shopping bags and looking around him suspiciously. He said: "Someone seems to have trampled all over the front garden."

"That's right," Liz said as she carefully measured out equal portions of the squash. She could see she was going to have to make it last. "We have. It happened when we were in pursuit of some people who'd kidnapped Simon."

Tony looked at Simon. Then he looked at Julie. His mouth tightened. He put down the shopping and advanced on Hugh. "Hello, I'm Tony Armitage, lodger." He held out his hand. "And you are…?"

Hugh took his hand as though it was a rotting rat. "Hugh," he grunted, and dropped it immediately. Liz had never known him to be so very nearly rude.

Interesting that he hadn't said he was her ex. Verrrry interesting... He scowled at her. She smiled back. Hehehe. She didn't know why she found it amusing. She just did. Even amongst her heartbreak she found that amusing. She was a very sad person.

Tony and Hugh helped carry mismatched glasses of squash in. She didn't own a tray. And the police arrived. Who had called the police? Liz looked around in dismay, but obviously it was her wholly law-abiding ex who would do such a thing, not understanding their delicate situation.

Hearing the dog flap door being banged impatiently Liz found the lock had been slid back down into place again. Moocher was butting his head against it and didn't look pleased. He was missing out on the action. He was missing all the possible crumbs. He didn't know they were right out of biscuits. It didn't stop him from doing his, I'm-an-invisible-vacuum-cleaner bit though as soon as she released the lock and he leapt through and trotted into the breakfast room.

Liz was very pleased to note that these two PCs were not the same as the last two. What a relief. "Hello there," she said. "Do sit down. Squash?"

"Are you Liz Houston?"

"I am indeed. Where would you like me to start?"

"Is this your dog?"

Liz looked down at Moocher who was looking up with great interest, his lovely plumy tail slowing swaying from side to side.

"Is he the magic dog of Malvern Road who can open fridge doors with his mental powers alone and then snack a fridge finger?"

153

Liz froze. The PCs doubled up with misplaced mirth. One of them actually dropped to his knees, his legs unable to hold him, his face purple, gasping for breath. Liz wouldn't ring for an ambulance for him, that was for sure. That settled it – she wondered how many firelighters it would take to torch the police station. She was obviously the laughing stock, her credibility less than zero.

Hugh looked at her with an endearingly enquiring expression on his so caressable face. She scowled at him. Oddly, he didn't have his "Now, Liz..." look at the moment. In fact, he looked better, more alive and carefree than he had for the last several times she'd seen him. He was such a puzzle!

"We have a list in the station which is dependent on how many games of poker we win. We play poker far into the night for the privilege of being top of the list. Our marriages are going down the pan. Top of the list gets to come out in answer to any summons from Malvern Road. And today, it's us." PC One beamed at her. Fool. She would put slug death in his squash. She would put the slug in first and then the slug death and she would put his squash in a mug so he wouldn't see it until too late.

She let Hugh sort it all out while she sulked and answered any questions that came her way with eloquent grunts.

It was all a waste of time, predictably enough. No one had thought to get a registration number, least of all her. She wondered if chariots had registration numbers or if Boadicea just recognised them all by sight. No one could even be sure of the make and model of the truck, although Hugh could bear witness to the characteristic damage caused to the bonnet by a body sliding around on it. No one could explain the gun-shots and she wasn't going to. Fireworks were always going off round there so no one was sure anyway.

No one had a clue why anyone should want to kidnap Simon. And Simon, she noticed, didn't mention Stella. Consequently much was made of the possibility of mistaken identity playing a leading role in today's incident. Maybe it was all a practical joke. There were a lot of students in Bristol and what could you expect from a house full of unwashed lodgers anyway?

Mind you, Simon was so taken aback, and enchanted it must be said, to find he had a daughter where he least expected it, that the kidnapping part of the day seemed to have been reduced to a mere blur in his consciousness.

So no one got anywhere, except that Simon and Julie were wrapped up in each other, Hugh was the hero of the hour, the two PCs had visited this place of legend and made much of Moocher and were happy with that. So was Moocher. Tony had disappeared again and Liz spent the entire time sulking. By which time the window was fixed (again) and she had reaffirmed her intention of incarcerating herself in her attic and never coming out of it.

Nobody had said how brave she was for standing in the middle of the road, risking her life to stop the truck. In fact old Hero-Hugh had spent quite a long time telling her how silly she was, which was a bit irritating because she really wanted to tell him that she knew for certain that if he hadn't been doing his stuntman act, thereby preventing the driver from seeing her, then she would definitely have stopped that pick-up by doing her Boadicea act. Anyone who forgot his power tool on a job to forcibly relieve someone of a finger and then struck a bargain so that his bad memory was not found out, was not going to run someone down in cold blood. She was sure of this because she was sure it was the same lot of part-time thugs. The lock for the dog flap had been put in place again and there was no way your average burglar would even think of it, so it must be the same cowardly, allergic lot as before. Must be.

Chapter Fourteen

"Yes, all I know is that my biological mother died and my father was broken hearted. He knew he couldn't cope with a baby and that's why I was put up for adoption." Julie seemed to have developed a lisp in order to tell her story. She gazed deeply into Simon's eyes. Liz shifted her chair closer in order to hear these revelations. It didn't sound like Simon at all. The broken-hearted bit anyway. She didn't know he'd been married in the past, before Stella. They all knew *she* was very much alive.

Julie carried on: "I was adopted by a rather elderly couple. They had a son, but after him they'd been unable to have any more children. They were wonderful and I loved them dearly. But I always knew my father was there in the background, thinking of me. I always received presents at birthday and Christmas. Expensive presents, usually unsuitable, but nevertheless, the thought was there. It always upset my adoptive parents, but I suppose that was because they didn't want me reminded all the time that biologically, I wasn't theirs. Thank you, Dad." She looked expectantly at Simon. Everyone did.

He stuttered out something that sounded (to Liz, if not to anyone else) remarkably like a mumbled plea for a smoke. That seemed to satisfy everyone and a collective sigh went up. Liz moved closer. Hero-Hugh gave her a small, sad smile. He must have been caught up in the pathos of it all, or maybe he was reflecting on all kinds of past hopes.

"My parents both died last year. There was a break in, an attempt to kidnap me. Father tackled the intruders. He had a heart attack and died. Mother faded away after that and so I lost them both. In the space of a year.

"Shortly after that I received a piece of paper, just slipped under the door. All it said was, 'Malvern Road, Bristol'. I was so sure it was a clue as to where I could find my real Dad. He must have put it under the door knowing I was alone in the world by then."

It was no good. Liz couldn't contain herself any longer. "Why didn't he knock on the door, then? Why the mystery? Why didn't he just say hello instead of stuffing bits of paper under the door? And what about your brother?"

The assembled company threw a big, black look Liz's way. They obviously didn't want practical matters to get in the way of a good story. There was no disguising the impatience in the "Shhhh," directed at her. Hugh gripped her arm warningly and it made her cross. She snatched her arm away from him and his hand fell, empty, to his side. She sat there, alone, but independent, the very picture of a twenty-first century Boadicea, her trusty wolf hound by her side. Charity was welcome to him. Liz might still love him more than she'd realised, but he was still a pompous, irritating lunkhead sometimes.

Julie rattled on. "So I came here in disguise and got a room in this house and investigated all the men of about the right age in Malvern Road. I had thought it might be you, Dad, but the kidnap attempt made me certain. I am so happy."

"Hang on, hang on," Liz burst out. "Why the disguise? Why should the kidnap make you certain?" She did need things to be clear and straightforward.

But she didn't always get what she wanted.

Julie was very patient. "Because it was decided at the time that the attempted kidnap of me was to do with someone trying to get at my real father, rather than anything to do with me or my adoptive parents. So the attempted kidnap, using a trunk, of my Dad today seals my conviction that he is my Dad."

"Do you mean they tried to put you in a trunk, then?"

"Yes," Julie said.

To which Liz couldn't think of any argument. Simon simply *must* be her father. After all, they'd put him in a trunk. Now, if she'd stuck with the idea that they'd been trying to get to her father and they'd kidnapped Simon because they thought he was her father, then it might just have worked. Maybe that's what she meant. Though why they'd want to get at her father was unclear. It was beginning to sound like a Belvedere McGuigan thriller unfolding in her breakfast room. But with fewer guns. She'd had enough.

"Well, I'm very happy for you both," she said. "Now, I have work to do." She ignored Hugh's meaningful look and, getting wearily to her feet, she stomped off to her attic. She meant to get up her spreadsheets, but instead she climbed, fully dressed, into bed for an unaccustomed daylight snooze. She couldn't cope with this anymore. She even let Moocher get on the bed. Again.

159

Undoubtedly a mistake she would regret in the days and weeks to come as he tried to convince her that it wasn't a mistake at all.

She didn't have long to herself, but simply couldn't be bothered getting out of bed when a knock sounded on the attic door. Moocher didn't even lift his head. Poor dog – he must have been as exhausted as she was with all the excitement.

"Hello Liz, do you mind if I come in?"

"You're already in. Bit late to ask," she said and then felt mean.

Simon sidled in and sat on the chair in front of her desk. She levered herself up and leant against the headboard. "What is it?"

He fiddled with his watch-strap. He rolled up and unrolled his helpless tie until it resembled a lone red-splattered ringlet. Then he settled to undoing and doing up his cuff buttons, one of which broke in half as she watched. It must be hard to be childless one second and find you've got a grown daughter the next.

"Come on, what is it?"

"She's not my daughter."

"Oh." Why was she not surprised? She didn't think she'd ever be surprised at anything ever again. Imagine all the surprise ripped out of one's life. They sighed simultaneously.

"You didn't put up any arguments that I heard," she said.

"No."

"Why not?"

"She seemed so pleased. There are not many people... in fact, I can't think of *any* people, who have wanted to claim a relationship with me."

What could she possibly say to that? She peered over the edge of the abyss that must be

Simon's sheer, bone-aching loneliness and she drew back. She wouldn't want to explore it and she knew that if she attempted to say anything she would cry. Moocher, who was telepathic, heaved himself off the bed, padded over to the chair and laid his head on Simon's lap. Simon stared at him and, doubling himself up to do so, leant over and hugged her dog. She'd never seen him do that before. Come to think of it she had never seen Simon touch anyone before. An unruly tear itched her cheek. She smeared it away and called down silent curses on any others thinking of joining it. Her throat ached horribly.

Finally she creaked out, "Does it matter if she's not your daughter if she's so pleased at the idea that she is? Does it really matter? If it makes you both happy?"

He sat upright, and Moocher, released from the death grip he'd been in, turned around and casually climbed on the bed as though he was allowed to do it everyday. Liz knew it was a mistake. Give that dog a blanket and he'd take the four-poster.

Simon considered her idea. She could hear the cogs whirring inside his finely shaped head.

"It would matter if there really was a father waiting to hear from his daughter."

Liz hadn't thought of that. "On the other hand, if there was, why hasn't he taken steps to find her?"

"He did. He made sure he had that note delivered."

"It doesn't make sense though, Simon. Why did he have that note delivered? Why didn't he just deliver himself?"

"Perhaps he's a fugitive from justice?"

161

Ohmigod – not another one! "Why would you think that's a possibility?"

"Because of the kidnappings."

Startled, she sat up even further. "You think the kidnapping of you *has* got something to do with Julie? I thought you thought it was all to do with Stella."

"I did, but don't forget the attempt to kidnap Julie, too."

"What's that got to do with the price of fish?" She simply couldn't see the connection.

"It's too much of a coincidence."

"Is that the best you can do?"

"Yes, but you're forgetting the similarity of operation. You're forgetting the trunk."

"Right. Okay. But how do we know it was her father who had the note delivered? We don't know that do we? How do we really know that there was a kidnap attempt on Julie and she's not just making it up?"

"Her adoptive father died in that attempt."

"Oh. Yeah. Right. Well – do you mean that it was part of a gang war or something, if Julie's real father was a criminal?"

"It could be."

"What about the brother? The older brother. The son of the adopting parents. Where does he fit into all this?"

"Apparently he blames Julie for his parents' death because of the kidnap attempt and the consequent death of his father and then his mother dying shortly afterwards."

"Hmm. I can see that. However unfair. So that's why she's so desperate to find herself some family again I suppose."

"And I can understand that," he mumbled.

She was silenced again. Almost. "Simon, why are you so certain you're not her father? She must have some reason, other than today's farce, for saying you are."

He pinkened. Fascinating the way the blood slowly crept up his face. "I wasn't married to her mother."

Was he really as naive as he seemed? "You needn't be married to have offspring, Simon." God, she felt old all of a sudden.

The colour in his face darkened. He looked awfully hot. "I just know I'm not."

"You sound so sure."

He nodded his head vigorously, encouraging his floppy hair to cover most of his face. Where had she seen hair like that recently? It needed a cut, too. "I am sure," he said.

This was where her natural delicacy made her refrain from pursuing what was so clearly a sensitive issue. Except that her mouth was a separate part of her. Actually, it wasn't part of her at all. It belonged to another creature that occasionally inhabited her brain.

"Why so sure?" she asked. Yes, it was entirely beyond her control.

Simon was now purple. Quite alarmingly purple. "Because... Well, because..."

Even Moocher lifted his head to watch Simon flounder in the quicksand of his excruciating embarrassment.

"Because what?"

It all came out in a rush. "I took a vow when I was young to remain chaste until I married. And I've only ever married Stella."

Naturally, Liz was gob-smacked. But she recovered quickly. "You mean you never had it off until you married Stella?" She did like things to be clear and straightforward.

"That's what I mean."

At least he was recovering his normal complexion.

Liz stared at him. "I thought you only married Stella a couple of years ago."

"That's right," he said, studying his shirt cuff minutely, picking bits of thread from it.

"Right. Well then you can't be Julie's father, even if you *have* forgotten, um, knowing, her mother. Some chaps couldn't tell you all the people they'd had it off with, could they?"

"Quite so."

"So all we need to do is find Julie's father and make sure he doesn't really want to be her father and the way's clear for you to be an instant family. Have I got it right?"

"You have, but of course, he does want to be her father or he wouldn't have sent that note."

"I don't think he did. It doesn't make sense. If he had sent that note he would have gone himself. I'm sure of it."

A little gleam of hope appeared on his face and she decided then and there that Simon would be Julie's father come what may. But his optimism disappeared again as he had another thought, "What if we find her real father and she wants him and not me?"

"She'll be out of luck then, won't she, if he doesn't want to be her father. Beggars can't be choosers you know." Oh, dear, that was the wrong expression to use. "Um, what I meant was that I think she's so attached to you she'll probably be relieved if her real father doesn't want to be her father... If you see what she mean."

Basically, Simon was a nice person. He chose not to remind Liz that her foot was stuck in her mouth. "Okay. How do we go about finding her real father?"

"Leave it all to me, Simon. You go and cement relationships with Julie and I'll sort it out."

Simon looked so grateful it made her feel as tall as that radio mast out there. At least *someone* had some faith in her, apart from her dog and he, originally, was a stray, a beggar with no choice. Even if her ex, all her other lodgers, all her neighbours and the entire police force didn't have any faith in her, Simon did. And she wouldn't let him down. She knew exactly where she would find the answers.

After Simon got clear, she ran down the stairs, Moocher so close to her heels that one day she just knew it, he would trip her up. She would go flying down and break her neck and then what would happen to him? As he prepared to do his, you're-not-leaving-me-behind-*again* bit, she grabbed his lead and yelled back up the stairs: "Simon, it's your turn to walk Moocher." Moocher did his, I'm-going-for-a-wa-alk-nyah-nyah-nyah dance. This involved a few circles on the spot with his tongue stuck out and his ears up and then a leap onto the bottom stair where he jumped up to the next stair and back to the first one a couple of times and, if his lead hadn't been put on by then, he started again.

Julie appeared on the stairs so Liz put Moocher's lead in her hand. "And you can go with him. Learn where we go. You can carry the bags." Liz handed her a bunch of poo bags and Julie recoiled. Good grief. What do they learn in school these days? They were clean ones – Liz'd hardly hand her a bunch of used ones, would she? She bought them wholesale in a rather natty turquoise shade. To start with she bought patterned ones, but they were more expensive. She used to recycle supermarket bags but, disconcertingly, many of them had air holes in the bottom.

"Look, it's quite simple. You put one on your hand like it's a glove, pick it up with that and put it and the bag into another bag, tie the handles in a knot and then chuck it in the bin. Simple. Or you could pick it up and then sort-of turn the bag inside out and tie the handles."

Julie looked as though she was going to throw up. "It'll be… It'll be warm, won't it?" She looked at Liz piteously, but that act didn't go down with her. If it didn't work *for* her then it wasn't gonna work *against* her.

"Well, if it isn't warm that means Moocher's feeling extremely unwell. I wouldn't be happy about that. So be pleased that it's warm. Just do it quickly and you won't notice."

Julie looked at her hand as though it had turned into a decomposing pasty.

"Oh, for heaven's sake, I expect your Dad will do it for you." Julie brightened. "You could carry it though if he's got Moocher. And with any luck you'll have your bag snatched." She lost her brightness. Liz sighed in exasperation and spelt it out for her: "Just think how the thief will feel when he investigates his haul." Liz didn't think she'd got it even then but she could hear Simon coming down the stairs so she left them to it.

Leaping over the wall to see Clive, Liz realised this was becoming a habit and wondered, briefly, what the neighbours would make of it. Not that she was going to lose any sleep over that.

166

There was a lot of activity in the road. People were taking advantage of the fine day to give their front lawns their first spring haircut. Why was it usually the men who mowed and the women who weeded? Many neighbours were still mourning for the untouched glory of their cars' exteriors. Their wives busily vacuumed and dusted the interiors as though that would sort it out. She could only assume that Malvern Road featured heavily on this week's crop of insurance claim forms but wasn't about to ask.

Her attention was caught by the sight of a large van from a well-known store drawn up in the middle of the road. Men in natty aprons scurried around carrying heavily wrapped items into Lydia's house. She leapt back over the wall and went to investigate. Lydia had only just had her kitchen re-done for the fifty-fourth time since she'd moved in. What now?

Lydia was out there supervising, but took the time to turn to Liz and give her a filthy look. Liz jumped back in surprise. This was Lydia? Looking at her like that? Oh, what? She advanced on her neighbour. "Blimey, Lydia, why the dirty look?"

"How do you expect me to look when you take the phone off the hook to stop me ringing you up. I'm only trying to help."

"The phone's off the hook?"

"It's been engaged and now number unobtainable since I rang to tell you about the fridge door being open."

"Has it? I had no idea." Come to think of it, it had been remarkably peaceful with regard to the phone recently. She'd have thought, though, that in a house full of people, someone would have

167

noticed. Lydia looked slightly mollified but then must have thought of something else because her usually slightly vague and pleasant face hardened again.

"Not only that, but I'm tired of the way you treat Simon."

Well, strike me down with measles, Liz thought. What on earth was this all about and did she have time to find out and did she want to? Turned out she had no choice.

"You're obviously not looking after him properly. Fancy letting him be kidnapped like that!"

"I, um..."

A couple of rather nice wooden garden benches were carried past them.

"He's unhappy and lonely and I'm sure he's not eating properly."

A very nice double-seated swing arbour thing went by.

"Lydia, hang on a minute. He's a grown man. It's up to him how he eats."

A couple of smaller unidentifiable parcels were carried carefully up Lydia's path.

"It's up to him if he's kidnapped or not?"

The makings for a king sized bed were manoeuvred into the house and no doubt put together properly once inside. A king sized bed?

Lydia had a point Liz supposed, but that was the whole point about abduction – it wasn't up to the victim at all. But neither was it up to Liz.

A chest of drawers, a wardrobe - matching set - a desk, a few lamps and easy chairs went by as though with a life of their own.

"I can't run his life for him, Lydia. He's my lodger. That's all. My lodger."

Lydia's face tightened even more. "Not for long," she stated and turned from Liz in time to see Simon and Julie leaving the house to take Moocher for his walk. Well, more precisely, she saw Moocher leaving the house to take Simon and Julie for their walk. He was doing his I'm-the-leader-of-the-husky-team thing. "And as for that little slut," Lydia continued. "She's as bad." And she stalked into her house.

What was that all about? Liz didn't want to fall out with Lydia. She was a damned intrusive nuisance, but she was quite fond of her all the same. As Liz stared after her she reappeared in her doorway and shouted in a most un-Lydia-like fashion: "And your dog smells too."

That did it. She was happy to fall out with her now. She yelled: "Of course he smells. He's an uncut male. They all smell!"

An unusual and leaden silence fell over Malvern Road and she turned very, very slowly as she realised that millions of men, furniture men, car-owning men, lawn-mowing men, were looking at her as though she'd let a centuries old, forever unspoken secret out of the bag and they were about to burn her at the stake. Her nerve broke. She pelted up Clive's path and hammered urgently on his door, praying he would waste no time in letting her in.

Her prayer was answered. What a nice man!

Chapter Fifteen

So there they were again. This time she looked at the books before she moved them off the chair she intended sitting on. They were about crime, fiction and non-fiction. All about crime.

He looked apprehensive. As well he might.

"Are you going to get the coffee, or shall I?" She was keen. Her caffeine levels were perilously low since the PCs had finished it off – perhaps that was why she was being so slow on the uptake.

"We'll both get it."

Oh, dear. He didn't trust her. She jumped up. "Okay. Suits me."

So there she was, leaning on the back of his cooker, which was just the right height for leaning on. She couldn't do it on hers, it always being greasy, but Clive's was okay in that respect. He fiddled about with cups and saucers and cafetières and scoops and things. Great! Fresh coffee. This was getting better and better.

"Any biscuits?" Well, if you don't ask, you don't get. She would be just as gracious if the answer was no. Yes, she would.

"No," he said. "You ate them all yesterday."

Damn.

"Oh, all right," he relented. "I went out and got some more." He opened a cupboard and as if by magic, produced a regular feast on a very pretty cake stand thingy, all different sorts of biscuits already laid out and ready to stuff in mouth.

"You knew I was coming?"

"Yes." He gave her an impatient glare as if to say he wasn't as thick as she obviously thought he was. It just goes to show: never underestimate your neighbour if at first you think he's a Git.

"Okay. What do I want to know?" Why should she do all the work if her non-git neighbour wanted to show her he was so clever?

"Let's sit down first," he said. "Don't want to tire you out too much."

Liz laughed and considered tossing her sun-bleached hair in an appealing and coquettish manner. But it was dark brown and too short to toss.

She couldn't help thinking that Clive was improving in leaps and bounds. She carried the cake stand thingy to make sure it reached the front room safely.

So there they were, sitting prettily in his front room and it occurred to her to wonder how it was that someone as immaculate as Clive with his nets and his kitchen, could, at the same time, be so uncontrolled with his books. Didn't fit, did it? Perhaps he had a split personality. She regarded him with renewed interest. She also wondered whether she'd been too hasty in deciding not to take up private investigation as a career.

"Julie's father was a criminal wasn't he?" she said. "He did a job of some sort and got away with a lot of money, but in doing so he cut his criminal mates out of the game so they didn't get

171

any. Or perhaps they went to prison and now they're out. But he didn't. Go to prison, that is."

He looked fascinated. He looked admiring. He handed her the cake stand thingy again and looked vaguely shocked when she declined. How could she be expected to hold forth convincingly whilst also spitting biscuit crumbs? She'd come back to them. "Anyway, Julie's mother died, or didn't exist in the first place. Well, she must have, but perhaps she just had the child and made off, not interested in that kind of life. Julie's father was left holding the baby and couldn't cope. Babies don't really fit the criminal life style do they? I suppose they don't. So he put it, her, up for adoption." Liz looked at him for confirmation and the same admiration lit his eyes. She swelled up in importance. What a sleuth she was!

Hugh would be sorry he ever let her go. She nearly sidetracked herself at that, as a bottomless black hole opened up in front of her, but doggedly, she got herself back on track.

"Years later, Julie's father's criminal mates track the baby down. Perhaps they'd been released from prison by then. They try to kidnap her and that's when her adoptive father has a heart attack which was most unfortunate because that poor man was totally innocent. That misfortune spread when his wife, Julie's adopted mother, faded away and died because she was broken hearted at the loss of the love of her life." Liz wondered, briefly, if she might die through the loss of her love, but only briefly as she was really getting into the swing of it all now. She could see herself, a female Poirot, a Poirette maybe, holding forth in the last scene. As one does.

172

"What makes you think I know anything at all about any of this?" he asked.

She ignored him, carried away on the incoming tide of her theories. "The kidnap attempt failed. Come to think of it, I'm not sure why. Hardened criminals like that wouldn't have let someone having a heart attack stop them, surely. Anyway, it failed. Then Julie received a note that said: 'Malvern Road, Bristol' and she just knew it was an attempt to point her in the right direction towards her real family, or at least, that's what she wanted to believe. She was devastated by the loss of her adoptive family. She's only young. So she followed it up, came here in disguise, or perhaps it really was because it's easier to wear that many clothes than to carry them - to stop the criminals following her. But then again, how did she know they might? Did she know what the kidnap attempt was about? Did anyone know?"

Hmm. Too many questions, not enough answers. Losing sense of authority. Clive had relaxed back into his chair and was nibbling round the jam bit in the middle of a biscuit. She would rather he was sitting on the edge of his chair, alert and fascinated, but there you go.

"Julie checked out the males of a suitable age in Malvern Road and worked out that Simon Medley was her father. And they all lived happily ever after." She beamed at her host, who dragged his attention away from his biscuit. He'd reached the middle bit now and was holding it between his thumb and forefinger all ready to stuff the best bit in his mouth. Politeness, however, forced him to lower it as he looked at her.

"Got that all worked out then," he said. "So, why are you telling me all this?"

As an accolade in praise of her deductive powers, it was somewhat lacking.

"Because Simon isn't Julie's father. You are."

"What leads you to that conclusion?"

"Floppy hair. Right age. Continually looking through your windows. Thugs ready to cut your finger off even if they didn't. You're obviously well off enough not to need to go out to work. In other words you're living off your ill-gotten gains. Now that I think about it," she said, getting another wave of pure intuition. "It's obvious that those thugs were after your money, but you managed to fob them off. That's why they kidnapped Simon, because they think he's Julie's father and has all the money."

"And you're happy to have closeted yourself in here with a hardened criminal? And eat all his biscuits."

"You might be a hardened criminal but you're still my neighbour. You've got all these books. You must be all right now. You've probably changed over the years since the crime and all that. Look how you keep your nets." Proof positive. She couldn't imagine a hardened criminal keeping his nets in such pristine condition. "And besides, you must have retired from the hardened criminal bit, I'd had thought."

"Because you haven't seen me enter my house wearing a striped sweater, a black eye patch and carrying a loot bag over my shoulder?"

"You're being silly now. Because, well, because… have you?" When in doubt, attack. "Anyway, when they came for your finger thinking you were Julie's father, you then told them that Simon was Julie's father and that's why they made

174

the attempt to kidnap him. Which also probably means they'll try it again. Perhaps Julie and Simon should move out for a while, until we've caught the criminals."

"We?"

"It was your responsibility, you know. You started all this by keeping the loot to yourself. It's only fair." She helped herself to a handful of those particularly delicious shortbread type biscuits, very thin with their ends dunked in dark chocolate. Mmm.

"Anyway it shouldn't be that hard. They're not very good at it are they? Not only that, but one of them has given it up to concentrate on his Tip of the Month Club so there's only two to go. I'm sure they could manage that." She munched away happily. They'd soon have this sorted out and then she could get back to worrying about money. Not that she wasn't worrying about money right now, just that it didn't have that uncomfortable edge it usually did. It could also be that having discovered she suffered a terminal case of unrequited love for her ex, nothing else mattered very much any more. So she was being particularly brave and noble trying to interest herself in other people's concerns.

"Oh, by the way, do you *want* to claim Julie as your daughter?"

"Certainly not!"

"Criminy. No need to be quite that revolted by the whole idea. She's all right really. Bit wimpish for my liking but there's no harm in her I don't think."

"Nevertheless, I think I'll give it a miss, thanks."

"So Simon can be her father and they'll live happily ever after. That's good. He will be pleased."

He looked at her curiously. "Don't you think Julie should have the choice?"

"She hasn't got any choice, has she? You've made it quite clear you want nothing to do with being her father."

"That's not the point. You can't let her believe that Simon is her father if he isn't."

"Why ever not? If it makes her happy to think it."

"How well do you know Simon?"

"He was my first lodger," Liz announced proudly. Boy, had she learnt a lot about taking in lodgers since then. "He's the most mild and unassuming and gentle person you're ever likely to meet. So's Julie come to that. They suit each other." She moved on to the cream filled biscuits. A dainty custard cream found itself in her hand, unerringly heading for her mouth. She took a bite into its crispness, her nose taken over by the sweet smell of the delight to come, and the biscuit simply melted away until her tongue reached the creamy centre. The flavour woke her mouth up and forced her hand to reach for more.

"You don't really know him though do you?" Clive persisted. "Are you really such a good judge of character that you could know him, or her, inside out? How do you know you're not endangering that young girl? She's still a child."

Oh, so he did had some paternal feelings for her after all. Oddly, that was reassuring.

"Well, I… I suppose I'm not a great judge of character when I think about some of my lodgers, and my ex and my next door neighbour –

both of them." The biscuit suddenly lost all its charm. Carefully she laid it back on the cake stand thingy. Clive glanced at it with distaste. She looked at it and realised that putting the soggy remains of a half chewed custard cream back in the company of untouched Viennese crunches may not be in the best of taste, but she'd suddenly realised how right he was and the middle of her stomach had dropped out.

Liz caught his gaze and it came to her that he wasn't fascinated by her reasonings at all. No, it was a calculating and coldly intent look he bent upon her. She shifted uneasily in her chair. Once again he was closer to the door than she was – when would she ever learn? She sighed heavily.

She also remembered the extraordinary spectacle of Simon losing it with those thugs and wondered just how vicious and dangerous *he* could be if he wanted.

The world, she realised uncomfortably, was a very insecure place for one as unperceptive as her. She really should stay in her safe and homely attic and never leave it, no matter the temptation. She thought of Lydia and how horrible she'd been to her. Liz had always thought of her as being lonely and sad and soft hearted. Just a Poor Thing. The extremely well-hidden capacity she had to be really foul with no provocation whatsoever had come as a severe shock. She'd said her dog reeked with an awful stench of carrion. How uncalled for! How unkind! He just smelled like a dog. Her lovely loving dog – the only creature on the entire planet that she could really trust. Her sister and her mother didn't count. They were family, or they kept swearing they were, even though she found it difficult to believe. And she wouldn't trust them anyway, come to think of it.

"Also," Clive continued, as if her whole world disintegrating in messy chunks onto his front room carpet counted for nothing. "She should have a choice as a matter of principle. You believe that people should choose for themselves? You must do. It's the way you live."

What did he mean by that?

"Yes, I do. You're right. I'll have to tell her."

"Simon should tell her."

"Surely it's his choice whether he tells her or not."

"You've got me there. Have a biscuit."

But she didn't want one any more. She felt insecure and friendless. She felt stupid. She wanted to go home.

Back home the sound of someone beating hell out of something in the downstairs bedroom assailed her ears as she walked in. She peered around Tony's door and saw him, sleeves rolled up, concentrating on whatever it was he was doing to the French windows. She'd forgotten about them. She tiptoed away and left him to it. What a handy chap he was! Kept himself to himself too. Washed up. Cooked and cleaned. Just the sort of lodger she should have. But then again, what did she really know about him? Nothing.

She climbed the stairs, past Simon's room from which she could hear the soft murmur of voices – his and Julie's she presumed. Moocher greeted her in the attic. He was having a rest after towing Simon and Julie around the block, down to the park, around the block and back again. Being lead husky was hard work. So he was resting. On her bed. He feebly lifted his tail and let it drop back on the bed. That was it. That was her greeting after a hard hour's work deducing and then realising how unsafe her world actually was. Just one feeble tail thump. That was all she deserved.

She pulled up her domestic spreadsheet to see how broke she was and that was when she realised that her phone was not on the hook properly. That explained Lydia's accusation. She was tempted to leave it as it was. It had been peaceful on the phone front recently, but she might be missing clients' phone calls too. So she replaced it properly and the thing immediately rang. She remembered her injunction to herself to remember that no, she did not know for sure who was ringing before she picked up the phone. A virtuous feeling flooded through her as she answered: "AccountsRUs. Good Afternoon. How can I help you?"

"You do sound silly, Liz. Why don't you change it to something a bit more traditional?"

Her sister. Might have known. Just had to think about her and next minute she was in her ear again, being all superior and big sisterish. She was so annoying, Angela. Liz drew a deep breath. A very deep breath. "AccountsRUs is my trading name, Angela. My clients know me as such. It would be a bad move to change it now."

"You'd have more clients if you changed your name. It holds no credibility whatsoever. You've been on the telephone an awful lot lately. Whenever I've rung up you've been engaged. You'll have to watch your telephone bill."

"Thank you, Angela. Have you rung up with anything useful in mind or was it going to be more of your usual advice? I would like to remind you that I have asked you not to ring up in business hours. I *am* trying to work here."

Well, she was. Sort of.

"Well, that's nice, that is. I ring up to give you the benefit of my advice and you're rude to me!"

Her sister was unbelievable. She could be rude to Liz and call it advice. Liz could react to Angela's rudeness to her and it was rudeness. It was always a no-win situation for Liz.

Angela chuntered on, "Mind you, I can't think why I should expect anything different from you. Ever since you split up with poor old Hugh, you've been unreasonable and nasty."

Aargh – not this again. Liz couldn't think why Angela didn't marry Hugh herself. Always going on about how much better off Liz was married to him, how much better a person she was married to him. Blah, blah, blah.

"I'm waiting," Liz said. "With bated breath."

Angela fell for it. "That's better. Anyway, Betty's been round this morning."

Betty? Who's Betty? Liz didn't want to interrupt to ask because she'd be there for an hour getting the low-down on Betty's family and friends and whether she ironed her clothes correctly or not.

"Gave me the chance to show her my new kitchen."

What's with the new kitchen bit? What's the big deal about new kitchens?

"I gave her some of my ginger biscuits I'd made from that new recipe book I got from the author herself at the signing. She signed it specially to me."

Liz said nothing. Angela didn't need her around for this 'phone call.

"They're made with corn flour rather than ordinary flour. It makes them so much lighter and melt in the mouth."

"Wake me up when you get to the point please." Waste of breath of course.

"I must say, she sat there with a crumb on her chin the whole time she was with me. She must have been mortified when she got home and found it there knowing she'd sat in my kitchen, with me, the whole time with a crumb on her chin."

Mortified! Must have been. She must have rushed to the mirror when she got home and seen that offending crumb. Bet she cringed with embarrassment and swore she'd never go out in public again without a veil. Poor old Betty. Ruined, she was, ruined for life. How could anyone live it down? How could anyone ever live down the painful and ruinous experience of sitting in Angela Rowbottom's brand new kitchen, eating melt in the mouth, made with corn flour, you know, ginger biscuits, from a recipe book signed to the owner personally and not next door's cat, with a crumb on her chin. Good grief, the shame, the shame.

"… and said she'd seen you standing in the middle of the road in front of an oncoming car, but she didn't think it could be you – even you're not *that* stupid…"

Certainly not! Boadicea might be, but not her. Oh, no, no, no.

"But what she wanted to tell you about because you won't have seen it, always buried in your attic playing at your accounting stuff was that Hugh, good old Hugh, went to the rescue. He was superb apparently. He dived onto the bonnet and brought the truck to a skidding halt. The criminals were so frightened at his appearance they gave themselves up and released their prisoner."

Liz woke up with a start. "They weren't so frightened that they didn't get away though."

"Oh, that. Yes, but the point was that Hugh was magnificent. All the females in Malvern Road must have been swooning at his feet."

Liz noticed she made no mention of skateboarding teddies, but then, Angela wouldn't. She'd ignore something like that so successfully that for her it might as well not have existed.

Angela was still blabbing on about Hero Hugh. "You really need to grab him before anyone else does. You can't manage without him. Look at all this silly stuff about having lodgers in your house. You don't know where they've been. Not only that, but I can't begin to imagine having to share my kitchen with a load of unwashed and un-house-trained lodgers."

Horror of horrors.

Liz wondered whether to tell her about Charity.

"Betty was particularly interested because she noticed that Kevin's vehicle, which was stolen the previous night, presumably for this criminal activity, had a back light out and he could get in trouble so of course, she's round there now to tell him. You don't always know if it's a back light do you, so it's not your fault, but the law doesn't always make allowances does it?"

"Do you think she's recovered enough, then, to go out in public so soon after her awful faux pas round at your place"

"What are you talking about now?"

"The crumb on her chin."

"Oh dear. You do talk a load a drivel sometimes, Liz. In fact that's been the case ever since you split up with..."

"Yes, Angela. I know. Talking of which, by the way, you might like to know that your Hero Hugh is engaged to be married," Liz said, before she realised she was going to.

A silence greeted her, which went on so long she wondered if Moocher had chewed through the telephone wire while she wasn't looking, but it seemed intact when she checked.

Pity he hadn't. When Angela got her voice back she said, "So you've lost your chance to get him back. You shouldn't have messed him around so much."

"I didn't want him back, Angela," she said. "We'd already tried all that and it wouldn't have worked." She tried to make it sound as convincing as it had been for the last couple of years whenever she'd had need to say it, regardless that now she no longer wanted it to be true. Too late.

"Her name's Charity," she added hastily before the silence got too long.

"Charity? I'm sure she's very suitable. What else do you know about her?"

"Well, she's made Hugh stop having milk in his coffee, and she doesn't want him coming round to see us, and she doesn't like him seeing Moocher..." Liz trailed off miserably, conscious that if she continued her voice might wobble.

"Yes, well. See how cold the world feels," Angela said, "...when you lose someone who loved you. It's like when someone dies and you know there's one less person to love you, one less person to make you feel special. It's very hard."

Liz couldn't speak. If she'd tried she'd have howled her head off. Angela sounded as though she was the one who'd lost the love of her life, not her. But Liz couldn't think who she could have lost to make her feel like that. As far as Liz was aware she'd married her first love and was happy.

So they both sat in silence for quite a lengthy period of time. Liz spent the whole time trying to stop her eyes from melting.

Eventually, Liz coughed. "Yeah, yeah." Just to get Angela off the subject, she asked: "Who's Kevin anyway?"

Angela cleared her throat. "Her nephew. You haven't been listening have you?"

And just like that things were back to normal.

"Kevin's the one who won that cup for table tennis and then got in trouble because he swapped it for an old skateboard which he took down to College Green to learn how to jump the steps down there. He's the son of Roger, her brother, or rather her half brother because her mother married again after finding her husband in flagrente delecto, you know, (giggle giggle) with the girl at the cricket ground and then finding that she couldn't even cook, let alone iron a shirt properly..." On and on and on. "...so when she realised that Hugh was scratching Kevin's bonnet, not that she holds it against him, of course. He was so brave and courageous..."

"Hang on a minute. Are you saying the truck that Hugh was reclining on in male model fashion belonged to Kevin, Betty's nephew?"

"You don't listen do you? Of course that's what I'm saying. But anyway, Hugh…"

A lead! A lead! "Must go," Liz said, trying to keep the excitement out of her voice. "There's someone at the door."

"Somebody else can get it. Yes, Hugh looked particularly fetching, I gather, not that Betty's got any taste whatsoever in the clothes department. Did I tell you she was wearing…"

"There's no one else in. I must get the door. It might be a client."

"…and a checked blouse with it. Well, really. How unsuitable for someone her age, especially with green shoes. Those shoes didn't come from…"

"I'm sorry Angela. I must insist on going. I have to take a cake out of the oven. It'll be burning by now."

"Oh. Why didn't you say before you silly girl? I'll call back later." And she was gone, the phone burring in Liz's ear.

She had a lead! Kevin's truck, it appeared, while it was stolen, was the getaway vehicle. This was something substantial she could follow up. Magnificent! She leapt out of her chair and suddenly stopped. Who the hell was Betty? Dohh! She smacked her forehead and dialled Angela's number. Of course it was picked up immediately: "The Rowbottom Residence. Good Day."

And she had the nerve to say Liz's greeting sounded stupid!

"Oh, Angela. It's me again. Just before I take the cake out of the oven – who's Betty?"

"You haven't taken the cake out yet? Good Lord, you never did get your priorities right! Betty Needles and I ran the tombola together for the church fete when that nice vicar was there, not that she was Needles then. No, she was Podger. She was always trying to get one up on me, but there's no chance of that. After all, look who she married. She lives at number two hundred Malvern Road. Fancy not knowing that! You'd better get the cake out. Talk to you later."

Fancy Angela falling for the cake in the oven routine. She was not very bright.

Number two hundred, eh? Liz could feel the thrill of the chase coursing through her veins. She really was on to something. Nothing could stop this fearless crusader pursuing justice now! The day had brightened. Even Moocher wagged his tail more enthusiastically. He stayed where he was, though, as if to say that having found the bed, his rightful place in life, he wasn't ever losing it again.

Maybe she wouldn't miss Hugh so much if she spent her life dedicated to crusading, selflessly and nobly, on other people's behalf. Yeah, it was the only thing to do when one was going to die young of unrequited love.

Chapter Sixteen

On second thoughts, all that talk about kitchens and cake had made her hungry. She couldn't do a decent job of sleuthing on an empty stomach so she rushed around to the friendly local store and bought a quiche. Got it home and ripped its box off. Well, drat: it wasn't cooked! Or maybe it just needed heating. She wasn't sure, but although now starving, she thought she'd better play safe and so she struggled to light the oven.

How come other people's ovens light themselves at the touch of a button, whereas she had to struggle with a match in the back of hers and then have a bath to get rid of all the grease she'd collected? She hated cooking.

Then she read the box and it said to take the foil plate off it first and put it on another oven-proof plate. Why? And, of course, it didn't want to come off. By the time she'd removed the foil plate the quiche was decidedly out of shape. She hated cooking.

Then she had to wait for it. She glanced out of the window and was immediately transfixed by the sight of Lydia's new furnishings. The swing arbour thingy was not in her back garden. It was round the side of her back extension, facing Liz's breakfast room window. How blatant! At least until now they'd been able to pretend that she really didn't sit and stare into her neighbour's house all day.

Lydia and Simon were cosily ensconced on its stripy, brocade seat. To the side, on one of the wooden benches she'd seen earlier, sat a sulky-looking Julie. Quite the family party. What a shame for them no amputations and police comedies were appearing in the window opposite. There weren't even any potential lodgers doing a getting-in-without-keys test.

Then she spotted Tony and Melanie through Lydia's breakfast room window. They were putting things on trays and she could smell their barbecue hotting up. And then she realised none of them were looking over here, but she was peering out of her window, into Lydia's, living *her* life.

How ironic.

No one had invited her, or Moocher, to the barbecue. They were obviously persona and canina non grata.

Well then, she'd have to change her plans a bit and take Moocher with her to number two hundred. She didn't want him looking out of the breakfast room window and realising he'd been scorned and rejected all because he smelt like a hold full of rotting mackerel.

She raced to the bottom of the stairs and yelled: "Moocher, oh, Moocher. Come for a walk."

That must have surprised him. He'd just been for a walk. It didn't take him long to recover, though. Liz identified the particular thud that meant he'd fallen off the bed. Then came the thunder of his feet as he ran down the stairs, gathering speed as he came. He appeared on the first landing and, tongue flapping behind him with

188

his speed, he flew down to her, hitting her squarely in the chest. She fell over like a rotten log.

Her boobs would never be the same again. They would never recover and rise again from where they'd been driven between her ribs. Moocher thought it was hilarious. It wasn't often she was sport enough to lie full length on the floor and let him jump up and down on her stomach.

"Get off!" she yelled when she was able to draw breath. Crestfallen, he immediately stopped and merely stared deeply and sadly into her eyes, breathing dog-breath into her face. Gack! "Lovely dog, I didn't mean to shout." His ears perked up and he flung himself full length onto her again. Oomph! His mouth was inches from her face. As the full charm of his nature inescapably claimed her nose she realised Lydia might have had a point. Moocher smelt like a bog rat. Perhaps he needed a bath. Horrible thought. He didn't like having baths. But, that was for later.

They made it, finally, out of the house and down the road in pursuit of their investigation. They presented themselves to the inevitable net-curtain-twitching inspection before the door to number two hundred was thrown open by a tiny woman with a large wart on her chin. Angela really should get herself some glasses.

"Do come in, dear," the woman said, obviously recognising Liz whereas Liz was sure she'd never seen Betty Needles in her life before. She wasn't a near neighbour. Her house was right the other end of the street from Liz's. Could this woman possibly be Hugh's new mole?

"And you've brought your lovely doggie to visit me, too."

Liz instantly warmed to this discerning and tasteful woman. She could see nothing wrong with lime green shoes, a ruggedly checked skirt in violet and yellow, topped off with a fluorescent pink wraparound blouse. Nothing wrong at all. The woman was obviously very bright. Very bright indeed.

It took several weak teas and a mountain of ginger nuts, custard creams, chocolate digestives and lemon cream wafers before getting round to Kevin. Plus two trips out to Betty's back garden for Moocher, and a bowl of water for him to top up his reservoirs again. He couldn't be expected to walk back up the street empty-bladdered when the time came for them to leave.

Finally, Liz got her chance: "Oh, Kev," she said, "I'm sure I remember him from, um, from table tennis club. I expect he remembers me too." He'd need a brain transplant from someone who had actually met her to do that, but never mind. She thought she'd caught just the right note of familiarity.

"Really, dear. I don't remember him playing table tennis, but I'm sure you must be right."

"How is the dear fellow these days? What's he up to?"

Liz wouldn't have thought it possible, but Betty brightened even more. "He's just got himself a new job. I'm so relieved. He's been sitting around doing nothing much for far too long. And he's got a head on his shoulders, that one."

Well, that's a relief. Could have been sticking out of his knee. Where would he get trousers to fit?

"You mark my words. He'll go far, that one. He's a fine catch for any sensible woman."

Liz ignored that. Betty couldn't possibly mean her. "Oh, what kind of job is it?"

"Driving. It's a driving job."

This was promising. Liz asked, "Is it the kind of job where he drives his own car or someone else's?"

"When it hasn't been stolen, he drives his own."

"Oh, yes. I heard about that."

"I thought you might," Betty said and smiled. She obviously knew Angela well enough to know she'd be straight on the phone passing on this bit of gossip. Liz smiled back at her.

"Just as well he hadn't had it signwritten yet," Liz said, hoping that would spark off more information. "Has he got it back yet?"

"Haven't heard from him today, but I'm sure he's got it sorted out by now."

Liz didn't want to embarrass her with searching questions about yesterday's little incident, as she hadn't offered the info. So she settled for a more indirect question: "Who does he work for?"

"Himself. He couldn't get a job so he's set up his own business. Here's a card you could have. Perhaps you could put a little business his way. Oh, and he'll need an accountant. You could be good for each other. You're about the same age, too."

Liz did not like the way Betty looked at her when she said that. She pressed a small rectangle of cardboard into Liz's hand. The card read: 'Kev Speedwell for all your Driving Needs'. And there was his telephone number. She could see at the bottom, unsuccessfully obscured by a thick, black line, another phrase that said; 'For that Once in a Lifetime Occasion'. He must have realised that 'Once in a Lifetime' wasn't that diplomatic these days if he wanted wedding work.

Liz clipped Moocher's lead on to his collar and got up to leave. She thought the best part of three hours was enough to give for this information. She sidled towards the door. "Thank you so much, Betty. I'll see what I can do."

"Will you get in touch with him soon?"

"Yes I will. I promise."

Betty beamed at her, and Liz beamed back from outside her front door. Moocher patiently waited for his opportunity to leave messages all up the street for his pals.

"Good Day," she said and shut the door.

Liz and Moocher didn't move off straightaway. Liz had glanced up the road and was wondering what it was about the Bettys and Angelas of this world that they used the expression, 'Good Day', when it so obviously wasn't. She could see fire engines outside her house and could clearly visualise that bloody quiche going in to the oven and her carefully putting the timer on for twenty-five minutes. No way she'd hear it from Betty's house. Should she just walk in the opposite direction and leave her shoes, socks and Moocher's collar on some deserted beach somewhere? Or should she go home and find out what damage had been done? Oh, what to do, what to do…

She could also see a police car. Obviously they'd used the excuse of a call to the fire station for the next top-of-the-list privileged person to visit Malvern Road. As Moocher and she were the main characters in their very own little soap, she wanted to spoil their anticipation by not turning up for the curtain call. But it was her house and she wanted to know how it had suffered. Drat.

Her writhing thoughts were rudely interrupted by the impatient blaring of a car horn. She turned and there was Hugh looking more than ordinarily like a patronising, bad-tempered Superman. However, he had turned up too late to rescue a house in distress. He should be sacked. She looked at him. He looked at her. He said, "I'll see you up the road. Okay?"

Oh, well, there was no disappearing off a lonesome beach for them, then. And no lift up the road either. He must have heard about Moocher's current aroma.

Moocher and she slogged home, to find, oh joy, Angela waiting for them. She launched straight in: "This is what comes of having all kinds of people sharing your house. When will you learn?"

Tony said, "Sorry, Liz, but hers was the only number we could find on the board." Liz approved of his immediately picking up on the situation with reference to her sister. She also approved of the way he pretended not to see when Angela batted her eyelashes at him. All of a sudden Liz liked him a lot.

"What's Hugh doing here then?" she asked. She thought he was supposed to be ignoring her these days, regardless of whether a mole had apprised him of recent developments concerning fire engines.

"No idea. He just arrived."

"Just as well he is here." Angela just had to say it. "You need someone to sort this mess out."

She couldn't help it. She was naturally obnoxious. Born like it. She was well past the age of growing out of it, too.

In some trepidation Liz went into her house and ventured down the hall to the kitchen. What a relief! It was only the kitchen that had been gutted. She'd been meaning to have a whole new one for a long time. When she was filthy rich that was. In the meantime, who needs kitchens when there are biscuits to be had in just about any shop you care to enter? She would need something to cook Moocher's food on though. She'd get one of those little ring things. All the lodgers seemed to be quite happy to take their meals in Lydia's. They could get on with it. She was a teeny bit fed up one way and another. She would just lower their rents a little to allow for no kitchen.

Her audience had followed her in. Angela let out a sob and holding her arms out to her cried: "I know it's a tragedy, but Hugh will help. Your kitchen…"

Liz stared at her with what she sincerely hoped was a freezing glare. "Angela, it's a kitchen. Just a kitchen. There are no corpses, human or otherwise in here. A kitchen – you know, cooking and washing things, pots, pans and cupboards. A kitchen."

Hugh said: "Calm down, Liz. I'll sort it out. Don't worry."

"Thank you, Hugh," she said. "I know you mean well, but I'm not worried, and it's not your business. I'll sort it." Liz didn't have the nerve to ask him how Charity would feel if she let him sort it, but she certainly didn't want to cause any trouble in that quarter. She really wanted him to be happy.

Tony said: "I'll give you a hand, Liz. If you want."

"Thank you, Tony. I might take you up on that."

Hugh frowned.

Ha!

Melanie said: "I'll bring down the little electric oven I've got in my room."

She had an electric oven in her room? "Thank you, Melanie. You're very kind."

Julie said: "You don't need to worry about us. Dad and I are moving into Lydia's. She's asked us to lodge with her."

Liz contented herself with a glare because she could think of nothing to say. The betrayal by her neighbour deprived her of words. Criminy, a kitchen down the pan and now two rents gone as well, one of them someone she'd thought she could rely on.

"Suit yourself," Liz said, determined to be nonchalant, although she couldn't help but cast an icy glance at Lydia. She at least had the grace to drop her gaze. Liz also noted, with some satisfaction, that Lydia was tearing a lace handkerchief to shreds, as though she wasn't aware of what she was doing.

Simon mumbled something that sounded like he was dying for a smoke, despite there being plenty in the kitchen, flicked her a petrified look that could have meant anything, and scuttled outside, fumbling in his pocket, no doubt for an old stogie two centimetres long. Liz had to confess that she felt hurt by Simon's betrayal, but she ought to know by now that you could never tell about people.

The two new PCs craned to see over the crowd in her kitchen. They were probably waiting for Moocher to whip out his tambourine and do a rendition of 'I'd like to teach the world to sing, in finger harmony'. They suddenly whirled around at the sound of breaking glass. Everyone galloped off to the front room. Liz didn't bother. She really didn't want to see another broken window, her home under attack yet again. It was getting tedious and upsetting. The only thing more upsetting was going to be the state of her spreadsheets when she added in this little lot. That was going to be very tiresome indeed.

Moocher licked her hand. He knew everything, that dog. PC Number One, or should that be Number Five, came in and, instead of giving her the note from off the new, just-arrived brick, insisted on reading it to her, no doubt to add dramatic flavour to the proceedings. It said: 'This time just the kitchen. Next time the whole house if you don't give us what we want.' PC One was very excited about this. He must have been a very junior PC, that's all she could say. She was sure that after a slightly longer spell of duty, the advent of note covered bricks through people's front room windows would become old hat.

He stood there hopping from foot to foot in his excitement, speculating on the deep and profound meanings of the note.

"What could they want?" he demanded.

"I don't know what they want," she said.

"You must have some idea."

Simon had come back in to the kitchen surrounded by a more peaceful aura than he'd had when he left it. He must have been chain-smoking

196

furiously to gain this much tranquillity in such a short space of time. Liz envied him.

"Well, come to think of it," she said. "Simon here is an arch criminal. He did a big job years ago and didn't share the loot with his mates. They've come back to get it."

Simon looked startled. As well he might.

"No, seriously," PC Number One said, glancing with a tolerant smile at Simon. "You must have some idea."

Liz sighed. Hopeless case. He must be very good at poker because he sure as hell couldn't tell when someone was telling the truth. He continued: "Aren't you worried about your house? About them coming back and torching your whole house?" He thought she was a very odd specimen. She thought him a very odd policeman – relishing his job a tad too much.

She couldn't tell him that she found it impossible to take seriously the threats of a bunch of part-time thugs who couldn't even remember their power tools. They weren't even capable of successfully kidnapping someone as static as Simon Medley!

"Look, they're just opportunistic. They didn't set fire to my kitchen. I did. They've just used the opportunity to throw a brick through my window. Probably makes them feel big. That's all."

"You set fire to your own kitchen?"

"Yes."

"Insurance fraud I suppose?"

"Quiche and a greasy oven."

"Yeah, right. You had a finger in your fridge too. A one digit snack for your dog." He fell about laughing.

The PCs, after questioning everyone in sight, left. They took the note with them and said they'd be back.

Everyone else left, too, without too much ear-bashing from her sister and her ex, for which Liz was very grateful, although also extremely puzzled. Hugh had said nothing about the brick through the window or anything. Not even a, "Now, Liz..." How very odd. In fact, thinking about it, he'd been very low-key the whole time he'd been there, almost as though he hadn't really been there at all.

Then she heard a commotion and went to investigate. In the front room Tony and Julie shouted at each other. Tony yelled, "I still say it's ludicrous that you're moving into Lydia's."

"Mind your own business, Tony."

"It is my business. As well you know."

"I *am* over eighteen. And anyway, now I've got Dad to look after me."

Liz's uncontrollable mirth at the idea of Simon looking after anybody gave her away, but she was beyond embarrassment at being caught eavesdropping.

"Come on then. Explain," she said.

Julie looked her up and down as though she was something from the bottommost regions of Moocher's basket. "Tony's my adoptive brother of course."

Of course. Silly me, Liz thought.

Tony, who, of course, was Julie's adoptive brother, said he'd sort out the window. Again. Liz felt she should attempt to find out what was going on. At least it explained the lack of embarrassment when he unclothed her to get her out of the dog flap. But, why was Tony so willing to fix everything all the time? Why were these two lodging in her house? And why did they omit to mention their relationship? But she didn't have the energy for any more sleuthing that day.

She went to bed. It was time she went to bed, even if it was only seven-thirty.

Chapter Seventeen

The morning dawned bright and clear and invigorating. Despite it Liz decided she was going to stay in bed all day and the following day too and probably the next week as well. After all, no one would notice. No one would care. However, Moocher had other ideas. He wanted his breakfast.

Liz slogged downstairs and hurled herself to the floor to crawl under the breakfast room window. Not that Lydia needed to look this way anymore. She had a life of her own now.

Melanie, it turned out, had been as good as her word and her electric oven stood there in solitary splendour on a table someone had dragged in from somewhere. Someone or several someones had cleaned and scrubbed the kitchen as much as possible. It made her feel quite teary. How lovely. Perhaps someone did care after all.

There was also a huge bouquet on the floor from Hugh. The card said: 'Fancy some dinner tonight?'

Liz's heart jumped. She'd love to go out with Hugh. She could pretend they were on a date. She'd have to be very careful he didn't realise that was what she was doing of course. But it seemed jolly odd. What would the sainted Charity think? Ooh – what if she was there too? He didn't say she wouldn't be, but the note didn't say she would be either. She must be. This must be his way of them getting to know each other. What other reason could he have for inviting her out for dinner?

Liz wasn't sure she could handle that just yet. Her feelings for Hugh were too new to her even if they had been around forever, and she had enough hassle and mystery in her life without deliberately rubbing her face in that particular mess she'd got herself into.

Perhaps she would refuse the invitation. On the other hand, she ought to check Charity out. Make sure Hugh wasn't making too bad a mistake. She'd accept. That sorted out her nutritional requirements for the day, too.

Moocher settled for an oven-baked omelette. She cut it up for him after he'd grabbed one edge of it and slapped his face a few times shaking it around his head. Funny dog. He was very happy with his new style breakfast – food and toy rolled into one. Given all those eggs, though, she would have to make sure she didn't find herself enclosed in a small space with him for the rest of the day.

Something would have to be done about the kitchen. There wasn't even a kettle. To hell with it, she would get someone in to sort it and simply adjust her spreadsheet. That's what she would do.

In fact, she'd adjust her spreadsheet now for an exorbitant amount and then she'd be used to the idea when the bill came in. She went up to the attic to do just that and, joy of joys found a custard doughnut she hadn't got round to eating whenever it was. She surveyed it with pleasure. She held it up to the light and the sun struck little rays of gold from each speckle of sugar.

The phone rang. Damn! She picked it up anyway. "AccountsRUs, Good Morning!"

It was Angela. Oh, happy day. She was ringing her up before even the birds realised the day had started, to give her the latest news-break on potty training.

"Okay, so it's not exactly business hours," Liz said. "But you still wouldn't have rung me when I was going out to work in an office and was breaking my neck to get ready to go to work, would you?" If Angela had ever rung her when she was hopping around trying to find a matching stocking without reducing her drying nail varnish to the consistency of weeks old rice pudding and trying not to let melted peanut butter drip onto her just-ironed blouse she would have torn her limb from limb. Verbally. That must be it! Since her redundancy she must have been far too patient. That was her problem – too patient.

"What's the magic about working in an office, Angela? I'm still working you know, just at home instead, and I think you should respect that." In her heart Liz knew this was wasted effort. Also, the doughnut was calling out and her mouth watered in response. She just wanted Angela to go away so she could sink her teeth into it.

"Since I was kicked out, Angela, I've been trying really hard to set up this business from home - constant interruptions are not helping." Rising temper tightened her grip on the phone and on the doughnut. She tried to relax a little, unsuccessfully.

"No! I don't want to hear about little Johnny using his little potty." Liz took a swipe with her tongue at the custard oozing out of her doughnut before it fell on to the sales ledger wide

202

open on her desk. It was difficult to stop Angela in full flow especially when one's mouth was crammed with custard doughnut at the time. The worst thing was when someone made you laugh and you had a mouth full. Cleaning sprayed custard off the monitor and out of the keyboard was not easy. At least with Angela, there was no danger of that.

"I *am* interested, but it could wait until this evening. No, I don't want to hear about the little darling missing a little, quite accidentally, of course, and it squashing out of the..." Ohmigod, she was seeing her doughnut in a whole new light now. She put it down. Her stomach had turned against it.

"No! I don't want to know! I refuse to hear! Don't ring me again during the working day!" Liz slammed the phone down and dropped her head onto her arms on the desk, sighing heavily. This meant she didn't have to look for her doughnut again when she wanted it because she unexpectedly found it. It had now spread its contents all over the sales ledger, and her face, and somehow insinuated custard all through her hair. Aargh, the day was not shaping up well and it had barely started. Perhaps she should go back to bed and get up again in the hope of a new day. As she considered this option the phone rang again. This was seriously asking for trouble!

She snatched up the phone and gulping in plenty of air and temper mixture she released it down the receiver. "You can take your poo and stuff it back where it came from," she shouted. That would teach her. It would also teach Liz. She should have learnt by now - whatever the provocation – to never answer the phone assuming she knew who it was. Dohh!

"Um, yes – I have finished your accounts and would like to set up a meeting with you to discuss the tax implications - poo - did I say poo? No, not really. But I did say, tax implications. No, I really didn't say poo - no, no, it was 'pool' - with an 'l' on the end. 'L'. Poollll. No! *Not*_tool - oh, God - you're right it was poo - I thought it was my sister on the phone and her bear - I wasn't shouting at you. Tuesday all right - 11am? See you then. You have a bear? Bring it with you - erm, yes, feel free. He's good at accounts and understands them better than you do – oh really? He's paying the fee?"

She put down the phone and groaned long and loud. Moocher lifted his head attentively. Sometimes life just seemed to go on and on.

The phone rang again. With great restraint she answered: "AccountsRUs, good morning!"

"Mrs Elizabeth Houston?"

"Yes. Who's speaking please?"

"My name's James Conway. Sergeant. Police. I've been standing on your doorstep for the last ten minutes trying to get an answer from you. It would appear that your door bell isn't working."

"Oh. Right. How can I help you?"

"Would you be kind enough to let me in?"

"Well, um… I dunno…"

"It's in your best interests to do so."

She was too tired to argue about whose idea of her best interests they were interested in here. "Okay."

She didn't hurry down the stairs. She wondered what source of amusement had brought them around now. She also stopped off in the bathroom and attempted to lose the custard she was wearing. When she finally made it to the lobby she was just too weary to lift the door. It shrieked piercingly. Sergeant James Conway winced. Behind him was another PC. He hadn't mentioned two of them, but maybe they went around in pairs for protection from ravening finger-snatching hounds. Liz stood back and let them in. They went straight into the front room almost as though they'd been here before which they hadn't. Perhaps there was a floor plan pinned next to the list on their entertainment board.

He got straight down to it. "We're here because we ran that note from the brick past our hand writing expert and we're pretty certain that we are, in fact, dealing with a dangerous criminal. We need more information from you Mrs Houston, than you're giving us."

Well, well, well. What had they got here then?

Of course, she couldn't give them any more information than she already had. Not only that, but the fridge-finger episode had lost its legendary appeal. In an effort to distract them she regaled them with the incident in the hope of raising a laugh and knew what it must feel like to bomb as a stand up comic. She'd knock that off her list of potential careers, then. It was odd, but for the first time, she really felt as though she was impeding the law. It didn't seem right to let them go on thinking they were dealing with a dangerous criminal when in fact they were dealing with a bunch of part time amateurs, but whatever she said they wouldn't believe her. They even refused her offer of squash.

Nothing she said would shake them from their conviction that she was living in deep waters and about to drown. No doubt her water logged and purpled body would float to the surface at some point. Still, it was nice to know they were concerned. Sergeant James Conway was quite cute really. Not ohmigod-I've-lost-my-breath-cute, but cute, nevertheless.

It was only after they'd gone she realised that if they hadn't been real policeman, she wouldn't have known. She must find out how to check. Her house was becoming more and more reminiscent of the town centre on the Saturday before Christmas, except that around Malvern Road you could usually park fairly easily and people seldom indulged in trolley rage. It was all getting too silly for words. Come to that she supposed it was possible that the firemen who'd been all over her house could also have been fake firemen. Any of them might have been the criminals trying to scare her for some reason. But then again, they might not.

She was fed up with staring at her spreadsheet. Nothing ever changed on it except the deficit. Instead, she thought she'd check her e-mails. She hadn't looked at them for some time. There were a few from friends that she'd have to answer, one of two about business, one enquiry about a room. That was encouraging. Perhaps things would pick up a bit. She worked her way through them. It was so satisfying to deal with them in order and see the pile diminish. She reached the last one which was apparently from MrNoName – not someone she knew. It bore the enigmatic title of 'Moocher accessories'. It had only just come in judging by the time clocked up on it. She clicked her cursor on it and the email opened up on her screen in big red letters. And then what she read sank in and she froze.

It said: 'Remember when people had a rabbit's foot on their key ring for luck? We're offering you a Once in a Lifetime Chance to have a dog's paw on yours. Or Two. Dogs can be okay on three legs, but they fall over with only two. You'd better give us what we want. We'll be in touch. Don't call anyone in or it'll go bad for him.' It wasn't signed.

Moocher. Liz's heart stopped. Her lungs turned to glass. But she made herself print out the email before closing down the computer.

As she stumbled down the stairs she knew she wouldn't find him. It was a sunny day. The kind of day when he would sleep in the long grass. A tired out lion. She just knew he wouldn't be there.

He wasn't.

She searched the whole garden, shouting his name all the while, her voice wobbling with fear. The garden wasn't that big, but it was a cross between the Serengeti on the lawn bit and a rain forest around the edges. She forced her body between overgrown bushes to check under their lower branches and around the back of the pampas grass that had well over grown its welcome. She even lifted great flat leaves off the pond to stare in to its black depths, knowing all the time that he wasn't there. She checked in places impossible for him to get into. She checked in places impossible for a newt to get into. He was not outside. She slowly walked back into the house. Her eyes felt as though they were so wide open they would never be able to close again. He would be in his basket. He had to be in his basket.

His basket under the stairs had never been so empty. It was located under the coat pegs which meant that if anyone left their coat unused on a peg for more than a couple of days it would develop a hem of Moocher-hair which would have to be wrestled off with every trick known to humankind, including the wet cloths that Shorty-Brian recommended for cat fur. Moocher would lie in his king-sized basket with his head resting at a seemingly impossible angle on the edge of it in order to keep an eye on everyone going by. From that basket he could also check up on happenings in the breakfast room.

She checked under the blanket. He wasn't there.

They would leave the breakfast room door open so he could see them, despite the howling gale that swept from the dog flap in the back door, through the kitchen where it gathered extra momentum, before pouncing into the breakfast room to freezingly stab at the unprotected flesh of unwary diners. The jubilant stream of cold air, unimpeded, would yowl straight down the hall and slam shut the lobby door if anyone had left it open, before blasting into the front door and escaping through the gaps around the door frame. This was an exceedingly well ventilated house.

If when the weather got really cold they shut the breakfast room door in self-defence, that dog would be out of his basket in a flash, immediately scratching at the door to come in, upset that they would shut him out. He would then collapse with a great groaning sigh under the table and they would know how uncomfortable it was for him to have to give up his basket to lie on the cold, cold floor. In that draft.

They might sit it out in strained silence for a few seconds, but then someone's nerve would break and they would leap up and open the door again. He would drag himself out from under the table, give the door-opener a pathetic lick on their hand and, suddenly revived, he would trot out of the breakfast room and hop into his basket. He would hurl himself down into his blankets and, propping his head up into a suitable position, his supervision of them would resume, accompanied by a slow thumping of his tail. He'd got what he wanted.

Again.

But perhaps never again.

Chapter Eighteen

He was a Once in a Lifetime dog that one.

She checked again. No, he definitely wasn't under that blanket.

Liz had never been so conscious of her body. She could feel every part of it as though all the bits of it were independent of each other – they just happened to have been assembled into her for the time being. All the parts were made of cold steel. She as a person existed as an entirely separate entity somewhere within that machinery. And she knew that she was capable of killing. And she would kill these bastards with no thought. They might chicken out of hacking off someone's finger and think it was easier to cut off a paw, but they would find out that the cost to them of the one would be in no way similar to the cost of the other.

Once in a Lifetime. A phrase she'd seen before. On the card Betty had given her for Kevin's new business. The coincidence was too great to ignore.

As she headed towards the front door, she heard its familiar screech. It was Simon. When he saw her he started to mumble something incomprehensible. She wasn't interested enough to disentangle any meaning from it. "Not now, Simon," she snapped as she swept past him and out of the house.

"But Liz," he said. "I need your help."

She stopped on the path and turned to him. "Not now was what I said. Not now was what I meant." She turned away from him and started to run. Down the path, turn right, smack into a solid body. It was Hugh.

"Don't get in my way," she yelled, dodging to the side of him and racing down the road. To number two hundred. She hammered on Betty's door. If the woman's nets had twitched for a fraction too long Liz would have thrown herself through her window. She was lucky. She opened the door quickly. "Goodness, Liz..."

"I have no time for the social niceties. I need to know where Kevin is. Now. Where is he?"

She looked all coy and gave Liz what she no doubt considered a sly wink. "Well, my, my. You are keen aren't you?"

"Yes, and I'm in a hurry. So, where is he? He's taken my dog and I'm going to kill him. So tell me where he is."

Liz heard someone breathe, "Moocher," and she spun around. It was Simon. He'd followed her down the road. She was conscious Hugh stood there, too. She turned back to Betty. "Don't waste my time. He's probably torturing him already."

"Oh, I'm sure he wouldn't do such a thing..."

That was it. That was enough. Liz shouted: "Tell me where he is! Now!" She trembled violently and had some difficulty making all the bits of her body work together properly. Her limbs and face felt as though they wanted to shoot off in different directions and start killing people. Betty by this time was shaking visibly and tears had started to her eyes. So what! Liz's own eyes were fixed so wide open they felt as though they'd dried out and the lids had disappeared into her head. That would be just as well because she knew she would never be able to shut them again without seeing her lovely loving dog in pain and torment and wondering why she wasn't there for him.

Finally, Betty Needles whispered, "Cakehole..." and sagged against her door frame.

That was enough. Liz was off, a tiny spark of hope igniting in her stomach. Cakehole was a newish caff on the Gloucester Road. Just a few houses away. She might be in time.

She had never run so fast and probably never would again. She could feel the cold wind slicing into her body, cutting her heart to ribbons. Terror was not hot. It was very definitely cold. Pictures tumbled through her mind as she threw people out of her way, conscious of Simon and Hugh keeping pace, saying nothing, helping her make her way. Because she wasn't going round. She was going through. Nothing would stand in her way. Nothing.

Moocher, raising his face to the sun, worshipping in its light, his old bones comfortable in its warmth. Moocher, asleep with one front leg over his nose as though shy of his dreams. Moocher, alert, bright-eyed and interested in everything that moved and everything that didn't if it bore any resemblance whatsoever to possible food. Moocher whose love for her was unconditional, life-giving and beyond price.

Moocher.

The times he would find a basket of washing straight out of the machine, still warm and steaming and fragrant. He would sniff all around it and without warning would gracefully leap into it, do his three magic circles and settle contentedly into its damp embrace. Another basket of washing to do again. The time Simon played gypsy violin in the garden and found Moocher sitting on his feet, hypnotised by the music. She had a photo of that. The time he commented on Angela's driving by throwing up down her neck, in her new car. The time he interrupted one of her monologues about Liz never taking anything seriously by audibly farting when Angela drew breath. They collapsed in snuffly giggles and low, pleased woofs as Angela, highly offended, stalked out muttering about wasting her time and energy on ingrates.

Moocher.

Her friend. Her lovely, loving dog. He had taught her a lot.

The way he completely ignored next door's cat even though it invaded his house every night. Live and let live. The way he would fling himself with such enthusiasm into the chase. Everything's interesting if you are interested. The way he would always be there for her when she was down, licking her hand but at the same time, written all over his furry face would be the message, 'You can do it. You can deal with it.' Everything had its positive side. Whatever it was, however awful it seemed.

Except this.

It was as though her life, as they say it does, passed before her eyes, in the time before she died. It was exactly like that. They speak truth. She couldn't imagine a life without Moocher in it. It would be forever an empty basket, a mown lawn, a house of desolation. Not a life at all.

A car hooted its horn as it screeched to a halt. Cakehole was on the other side of the main road and she had simply run across, not realising until now, that she was towing behind her, with invisible threads, a whole rabble of neighbours, Simon and Hugh, and others besides who must have got wind of something. Not surprising she supposed. She must have looked like a mad woman. She felt like a mad woman.

There was a 'Closed' sign dangling crookedly in the glass door of the caff. Cakehole was shut. Next to it was a greengrocer, their wares spread out colourfully onto the pavement. It was the kind of greengrocer that sold cut flowers and plants as well to pad out their living. Liz grabbed the nearest, biggest object to hand – a conifer - and hurled it at the window of the caff. It bounced off.

Ignoring the cries from the proprietor's wife she snatched up a metal bucket full of long stemmed freesias and swung it at the window, water and bunches of flowers dropping at her feet. It hit with a satisfying 'thunk' but still no glass fell. What the hell was it made of?

She was conscious of Moocher's name being passed around in the crowd, but it was as though no one else really existed in this cold world in which she moved and acted. Frustrated, she pounded the bucket again and again at the window. She thought she might have been yelling all the time. She wasn't sure and didn't care.

Becoming aware that someone was shouting at her, she turned to them and concentrated as though swimming up through muddy water to clarity. She recognised a neighbour, but could find no name for him. Wordlessly he pointed at Simon. She looked at her erstwhile lodger and realised he had a cordless drill with him and was approaching the door in a business-like manner with the drill suddenly buzzing and stopping, buzzing and stopping, as though he dared the door to give him trouble. To steady himself he reached out and grasped the handle – and the door obediently opened. She'd feel sheepish later, probably.

For now she raced through the entrance, ran between the tables, their chairs upturned on them. Nothing in there. She ran out the back, through the kitchen and into the store beyond. There was nothing there. She tore all the boxes and tins off the shelves in case bits of Moocher had been hidden behind them. Other people opened cupboards and hauled out the contents. They wrecked the place. But there was nothing there, apart from loads of dry provisions. Hugh came in through the back apparently having gone round in the first place, but there was no sign of Moocher. No dog. Just a thoroughly despoiled caff.

She had to think. She had to work this out. It was not possible that she couldn't. It was unthinkable that she wouldn't be able to. She walked back through the caff and stood on the pavement staring at its frontage. She ignored the crowd, the protesting horns of cars at a standstill and the curses of their drivers. A young girl, positively twittering with excitement came up to her and put her hand on her arm. Liz stared at the white fingers stark against her black sweatshirt and they suddenly dropped off her like a salted slug. "What's this all ab…" the girl started, but Hugh pulled her away.

Liz stared at her, noting just one feature as the girl slowly receded away from her, question unfinished. She had long floppy blonde hair. And Liz was off. Back across the road, down the

Gloucester Road, left up the little road, left and immediately right onto Malvern Road. The wind couldn't keep up with her, nor could the streaming crowd. But they tried and were there, stamping down the new shrubs in Lydia's front garden as Liz hammered on her neighbour's door.

Lydia opened it and, uselessly, held up her hand to stop Liz entering. "Get out of my way, Lydia. This has nothing to do with you." Liz brushed by her and headed down the hall-way. There, in the extended breakfast room-come-kitchen were Julie and Tony seated at the table obviously enjoying a home cooked meal. How very cosy. Liz swept in, round the table and grabbed a fistful of Julie's floppy blonde hair. She screamed. Good! Liz hoped it hurt.

She turned her hand in the hair, momentarily surprised that it didn't all pull out of Julie's scalp with little bleeding roots on the end. Julie screamed some more. Liz pulled her from her chair which fell and hit her in the shin, but she felt no pain. She forced Julie to her knees on the floor and turned to the yelling crowd. She noticed Lydia with both fists pressed against her cheeks. Simon just stood there looking vaguely protesting, his mouth opening and closing but no sound coming out. Tony looked like he was ready to spring at her. Hugh was the one she was conscious of most of all. He merely looked at her and she knew that she could do anything and he would be behind her all the way, however pompous he sounded sometimes. Tony moved towards her.

"Stay there," she shrieked, grabbing up a gravy smeared knife and holding it threateningly above Julie's face. "Or the cow gets it."

Abruptly silence fell. A falling feather would have made more noise. They'd got the message then. Don't mess with Liz when her dog's been kidnapped.

For good measure, to make sure Julie wasn't missing out on her meaning, she shook her head. Julie yelped. "Ok, Julie, or whoever you are. All this crap only started when you turned up. Where's Moocher?"

"I don't know," she wailed.

"You'd better think of something pretty damn quick then," Liz said, raising the knife to make sure she could see it properly.

Vaguely she wondered what the spectacle looked like because there was a collective indrawn breath at this.

Liz shook her head again and tightened her grip even more. Julie screamed again.

"I'm losing patience," Liz snapped. The icy cold grip of fear tightened around her guts. "You're at the root of all this. I'm sure of it. There's just too much coincidence going about. You knew about my dog before you even came to see the room. I remember the so-called coincidence that allowed you to share a house with that sort of dog but not any other."

Julie's eyes were shut now and tears coursed down her face. She looked awfully young. A sudden pang of remorse forced its way through the glacier that used to be Liz's chest. What if she was wrong? But she could think of no other options. She couldn't be wrong. If she was, Moocher was dead.

Feeling as though she was going to spoil the whole effect by throwing up, she deliberately brought the knife down so it threatened Julie's eyeball. Jeez, how do people do that for a living?

Julie stopped sniffling and stiffened. "Attic," she said in a defeated voice. Liz didn't have to do anything. The sound of feet thudding up the stairs told her she wouldn't stand an earthly of getting up there anyway. She hung on to the cow in case she needed her again. She now knew what was meant when people said: 'their heart stood still.' She thought hers would never beat again until she heard the unmistakeable acceleration of, surely four, paws as they raced down the stairs, the crowd standing back to let him have his head. He turned the corner at the bottom of the stairs, spotted her ahead of him and thundered along the hall, launching himself into the air, the feathery bits on the back of his legs floating out behind him.

Moocher. Her lovely, loving dog, galloping along with all his feet in action.

She dropped the cow and the knife, held out her arms and collapsed on the floor under the weight of his I'm-really-a-rocket impersonation. Strange for a dog, he loved fireworks.

He probably couldn't work out what the game had been. He probably wanted his supper. He hadn't had his walk yet.

Liz noticed Lydia shaking Julie by the shoulder and shouting at her, but she had more important things on her mind now.

All the ice making up her body melted in one go and she bawled her eyes out much to Moocher's surprise and consternation although he enjoyed the salt. She was alive again. The neighbours, after a rousing round of applause, handed out hankies and someone found a

218

celebratory crate of wine. But Moocher and Liz, they left the house without looking back. They couldn't take any more.

What a mess. The PCs no longer laughed at her. She'd become a liability to society. She'd maligned good old 'Once in a Lifetime' Kevin and busted up his caff. She'd caused traffic jams and threatened righteous citizens. She'd held riotous meetings in the street. This time, although she had no idea why he was there again, she was glad to see Hugh, towering above the crowds, threading his way through to her side and then turning to face them, as if to keep the others at bay while she escaped. How had he known she needed him? She would let him sort it out. She knew when she was beaten. Moocher looked back once or twice, maybe wistfully, at the impromptu party, but they went home.

Chapter Nineteen

So what was she going to do about Julie? Why did she abduct Moocher and threaten such foul things? She couldn't be allowed to get away with it. Who was she, really? If only Liz knew just what the hell was going on. If only life could go back to being the way it was before that fateful day when, due to her desire to pay her bills, she took in two new, unknown lodgers. That would teach her a lesson. She'd never pay her bills again! That would sort it.

Even then, she didn't have much to pay her bills with had she wanted to. There were only two lodgers in residence now. Liz was still upset about Simon. He'd been there for a long time and to up and leave just like that was quite a rejection. She'd thought they were friends. She could imagine the allure of finding a family when he thought he was on his own forever, but even so… she leapt up and ran upstairs to his room.

Flinging open his door she saw that his room looked much the same as it always did. In other words she was still in danger of being mobbed by a load of old socks gone bad. What did this mean? Perhaps he was coming back later to get his gear. Perhaps he was going to rent two places at once in case one didn't work out. She chased along to Julie's room and saw that it was completely clean and clear, as though she'd never been there. Actually it was cleaner than it had been before she took it, and all ready for another lodger.

Even so, Julie couldn't be allowed to roam the world abducting innocent dogs and, possibly, torturing them for her own ends. But what could Liz do about her? Perhaps she should call the police? As soon as she thought of it she went cold at the very idea – they'd turn up eager to take her away she suspected and lock her up in their deepest, darkest and dampest dungeon. After all, she'd wrecked property and threatened someone with a knife. Then who would there be to protect Moocher? She flung her arms around his neck and buried her nose in his fur. He stank! He really, really stank. She tried not to hurt his feelings by recoiling too violently. He ought to have a bath, but considering what he'd already been through she didn't want to expose him to more stress. She'd leave it until tomorrow, until things had settled a bit.

In the meantime there was still the problem of Julie, not to mention a load of unanswered questions. Sighing, she made her way out to the kitchen, if it could still be called that, but she didn't make it as the door bell went just as she was in the vicinity so, breaking the habit of a lifetime, even though she wasn't expecting anyone, she answered it.

It was Hugh and the look he gave her was so loving and kind she immediately burst into tears and threw herself onto him. To hell with Charity. She needed her ex just now. Charity could have him later.

They sort-of shuffled into the front room and sagged onto the sofa until she was all cried out. She felt a lot better but could only imagine she looked a lot worse.

Drained, she pulled away from him and finally looked at him properly. He didn't look too good himself. "What is it?" she demanded.

"Charity's broken off our engagement."

There. He just said it. The wild uprush of elation that immediately overcame her had to be ruthlessly crammed back down again. He looked so miserable and stunned.

"Why would she do a thing like that?"

He shifted slightly in his seat. "You haven't seen the Evening Post, then?"

"No."

Sighing he pulled it from his inside pocket where it had got tangled with his wallet, and opened it to the offending page. It was a very nice picture, she thought. Hugh looked very hero-ish on the bonnet of that car, tackling crime, not flinching from his social duty. The teddy bears had turned out quite well too.

She slid her hand over his wallet where he'd absently placed it on the sofa.

"She already had doubts because I'm always around here."

"How does she know that?"

He stopped and frowned. "I'm not sure. But then with this as well... She said it just showed I didn't respect her enough. She said it would make her a laughing stock."

If Charity really loved Hugh that wouldn't stop her, but Liz wasn't going to say that. He really did look pole-axed. At first, Liz had thought: he's free now. He's free for me. But then she realised, sinkingly, that he was probably further from her now than when he was engaged. Anything she could get out of him would only be on the rebound.

But then – who cared? She'd take him any way she could get him. She leant forward, unobtrusively pushed his wallet under the cushion, and edged herself over it as she did so, grabbed his hand and stared thrillingly into his eyes. "I love you, Hugh," she said, putting all of herself into the proclamation.

He patted her hand. "I know you do," he said soothingly and pulling away he stood up. "Now that we're caught up I'd better be off. I'm due in at the office."

And he was gone.

So much for that! She'd declared herself to him and it seemed that although he believed her, it had no future. After all, she'd been telling him for years they had no future. What would be different now?

Dazed, she wandered out into the kitchen and switched on the new kettle. Then she meandered out into the breakfast room to see if there were any biscuits she could filch when she became aware of a strange and unsettling incident being acted out next door.

In her breakfast room Lydia stood facing Julie who held a gun and waved it about in a very disconcerting manner. Julie appeared to be saying something with a great deal of passion. Outside their window, Simon lounged in the swinger thingy, his eyes shut, smoking a cigarette. It seemed he had no idea of what was going on behind him. Liz tapped on her window to get his attention. She couldn't think what he could do, but somehow it didn't seem right that he was out there enjoying a smoke whilst directly behind him, their dear old neighbour, Lydia, was being threatened by a gun-toting dog-torturer.

However, he didn't hear her frantic taps. Nicotine heaven was too enticing for him to pay attention to what was going on. Julie heard, though. She swung around, saw Liz, brought the gun up, and pointing the business end of it at her, she pulled the trigger. There was no thunderous roar though, so perhaps she didn't. Moocher suddenly barked and ran up and down the hall in a frenzy of excitement. Liz had fallen to the floor just like in the films. But surely Julie couldn't have pulled the trigger or the windows would be broken. There was nothing to stop her doing so, though, if she hadn't already, so it wasn't necessarily safe yet.

Liz gradually raised her head above the level of the window and saw that Lydia and Julie had gone. She looked some more and realised that Simon had disappeared from sight, too. She immediately convinced herself that she'd been mistaken. Perhaps it had been a cigarette lighter or something. After all, she didn't see guns that often. She wouldn't necessarily know the difference on sight between a gun and a cigarette lighter.

On the other hand, for all she knew, Lydia was lying mortally wounded on her floor. And even if she wasn't, Liz still had to do something before she was harmed by that innocent-looking little girl who was turning out to be the worst thing to hit Malvern Road since the fish and chip shop stopped using newspaper and started using polystyrene containers.

But she was torn as to what to do with Moocher. She didn't want to take him with her in case he got hurt and she didn't want to leave him in case someone got in again. Her dilemma was resolved when she heard the front door screech and Melanie advancing down the hall shouting: "What are you doing grovelling around on the floor? Lost something?"

"Nah," Liz said. She scrambled to her feet trying to brush off great drifts of dog hair as she did so. It was time she hoovered before someone collected up all the dog hair scattered around the house and made a Moochenstein out of it. Ooh – a Moocher-dog with a bolt through his neck.

"Actually, Melanie, could you keep an eye on Moocher for me please? I just want to rush in next door. I won't be long. How about taking him up to your room? That would be best." Melanie nodded and Liz ran out of the house, down the path, along the pavement and up Lydia's path. Of course, the front door was shut and did she really think some trigger-happy cow was going to answer it just because Liz might happen to ring the bell?

She wondered where Hugh was. She could do with him now, but realised he was probably sorting out a crazed café owner, although he'd said he was off to work.

"Silly Billy," she admonished herself as she turned around and, running, retraced her steps, through her own house and out through the back, over the wall and in through Lydia's back door. She dashed through her very nice, very elegant, extended kitchen and through her breakfast room and down her hall and into and out of her sitting room and front room and upstairs and all around and everywhere else as well. No one there. No one home. They'd disappeared fast! Where on earth had they all gone, and did it mean that Lydia had been abducted now?

It was all getting to be too much for her brain. It felt decidedly limp and she sagged into a chair in Lydia's front room and stared at the floor wondering what she should do next. Which was how she came to completely overlook the entrance of a man with greying hair cut close to his head and an evil-looking scar across his face. She finally spotted him when his hand-made shoes came into her view. Slowly she lifted her head to behold Lydia's brother. It had to be Lydia's brother. The resemblance was uncanny. Liz didn't know she had a brother, but then, there was no reason why she should had told her *everything* about herself. She just *thought* she had told her everything in all those interminable conversations over multitudinous cups of tea.

"Hello there," Liz said with great originality. "I take it you're Lydia's brother." She stood up and held out her hand for his. "I'm Liz Houston from next door and I do have a good reason for being here."

He looked very surprised, which she thought was odd. Their resemblance must have been remarked upon many times over the years. "Yes," he said eventually. "Yes. My name's Vincent Banton."

They shook hands in a very civilized manner considering neither of them were in their own home and maybe both of them were trespassing. But Liz was now incapable of being surprised.

"I expect you're looking for her. Lydia, that is. Well, I'm very pleased you're here. You might be able to help. I'm looking for her as well. I think she may have been kidnapped."

Vincent stepped back from Liz and eyed her strangely.

"Sorry," she said. "I should have given you some warning. There have been some peculiar goings on here recently. Mind you," she added, as another thought struck her, "It's also odd that you've turned up just now considering you haven't been here in all the time I've known Lydia. Which is quite a long time." She stared hard at him wondering what foul deed had resulted in the scar that spoilt an otherwise good-looking face. He might be Lydia's brother, but that didn't necessarily make him a good guy. He might be one of the baddies for all she knew. Here she went again – diving in without enough caution. When would she learn? It was her turn to step back. As she did so she looked around, rather wildly, for a possible weapon in case he went for her.

"What do you mean, kidnapped?" he asked, with every appearance of horror. He even looked a little pale. He couldn't be that good an actor. Perhaps he was okay after all.

"I have a feeling that she's been kidnapped by one of her new lodgers." Liz really couldn't imagine Simon being in on abduction. She didn't think it was his thing at all. "Namely, a girl called Julie Carrington-Smythe who kidnapped my dog and was going to cut his paws off. I still have no idea why she did that. She probably cut off the finger that was in my fridge too, so she's a nasty piece of work, but, to be fair, that might have been Stella..."

"A finger in your fridge... Stella?"

Oh, dear, her new accomplice seemed to be faltering at the first fence. People simply didn't have the stamina these days. Where the hell was

Hugh? He should have known she needed him like he always used to know.

"Yes, that's right," she snapped. "But we don't have time for that. We must find Lydia. Now. Come on." She dived out of the house and ran down the path with Vincent in hot pursuit, and lo and behold, for once, just when she really wanted them, there were two PCs waiting for her on the pavement.

"Oh, wow! Hello," she exclaimed. She didn't know why she bothered. They completely ignored her. They were concentrating on what they could see over her shoulder, or rather, *who* they could see over her shoulder. There was a yell and Vincent took off as though chased by a bad-tempered leopard. The two policemen ran off after him but not nearly so convincingly. There was no chance they would catch him.

Well, what was *that* all about?

She didn't have to wait too long to find out. Another couple of PCs suddenly appeared as though they'd been hiding in the bushes, which she had to assume they had been, and she recognised one of them. So. They *weren't* taking proper turns after all. He'd been here before. And he immediately started rabbiting on about how that letter found around the brick *had* indeed been written by a known and wanted dangerous criminal. A drug dealer. This PC was positively preening himself as he informed her that this drug dealer, this dangerous criminal, was the chap that she'd just come out of Lydia's house with - a certain Mark Scotter who had stolen a load of money years and years ago.

"Nah," Liz said. "You must have it wrong. That chap's name is Vincent Banton, and although my next door neighbour hasn't exactly been herself recently, she's a model citizen and Vincent Banton is her brother."

But he wasn't convinced. "Sorry about your neighbour, Ms Houston, but that chap's definitely our man."

"How you can possibly tell from that glimpse of him I don't know," she said, and hurried on before he could tell her. "But, anyway, you must help me find Lydia. She's missing and I'm afraid she's been kidnapped by her lodger and she's got a gun. The lodger, I mean. Not Lydia."

He coughed and looked everywhere except at her. Then he got out his notebook and pretended to look for something in it and then he put it away again. The other PC started to whistle and wandered nonchalantly off to peer in the flowerbeds as though they contained opium poppies in profusion and he'd only just spotted them.

"What is it?" she asked. She had one of those sinking feelings she got occasionally. She'd been getting them more and more just recently.

"It was Lydia, um, Mrs, um... herself, who telephoned us to say there was a burglar in her house who had broken through from your house. Not only that, but she recognised him and named him as our man – this Mark Scotter. I can't tell you how she knows who it is. That would be giving away a confidence."

He blushed though, so Liz could imagine. Except that Lydia didn't strike her as someone whose life would have been in any way different before now as it was now, except that she would have been younger, of course. Now, it turned out, she was some gangster's moll! Not only that, but some gangster that looked exactly like her brother!

"Oh, maybe that means she's not been kidnapped. Good. Although where Julie fits in is anybody's guess," she said. "That also means she must be the connection with the person who's been breaking my windows – or at least the last time because it might not all have been the same person, might it?"

He whipped out his notebook again. "You've had your windows broken before?" he asked, giving her a very dark look. Very dark. She remembered, then, that the other breakages hadn't been reported for what seemed like good reasons at the time. She was heading for deep water if she wasn't careful. She scrutinised her nails and decided to chew the corner of one of them whilst casually looking around for a diversion. And she spotted one. Hallelujah! There was a diversion just waiting to divert.

There was a car with opaque windows racing up Malvern Road, closely followed by Kevin's truck, last seen at close quarters when Liz was being Boadicea. The first vehicle tore into the side of the road, mounted the pavement and just missed her PC who still stared at his notebook as though that would protect him. The car came to a rocking halt. Liz and PC stood, as though turned to gravestones, as the driver's door slowly opened and smoke mushroomed out of the interior. The windows weren't opaque at all. It was just Simon with his own special aura. He appeared out of the smokescreen and stood there looking as though he wasn't sure why he was standing there. He probably wasn't. The other vehicle screeched to a halt in the middle of the road, three men jumped out and ran over to Simon.

"Ooh, look, if it isn't Yummy and Chuckler and someone else," Liz said. "I wonder if the other one is Kevin."

Her PC said, "You know these people?"

"Yeah, sure. The first one is my supposedly loyal lodger who has now defected to next door. The two guys with the handsome sweaters on are Yummy and Chuckler. Their job is to remove people's fingers with a power tool, if they remember to bring it. And if I'm not mistaken, the other guy actually owns that vehicle and is known as Once-in-a-lifetime Kevin. His Aunt Betty lives down the road and has a wart on her chin. There you go. Quite clear isn't it?"

By this time the three in the second vehicle had realised there were two hulking great policemen standing on the pavement. They stopped to carefully consider this clearly unforeseen development. They slowly drifted backwards as though no one would notice. They'd obviously been practicing the Michael Jackson moon walk.

Simon looked positively harassed as well he might if he'd been chased all over town by three men intent on his kidnap. He fumbled around his pockets looking for a cigarette end and in the process found his glasses. Placing them on his nose he also realised there were two policemen present. He immediately yelled: "Arrest them – they keep trying to kidnap me – and that other one is a drug dealer."

"Blimey, Simon, that's a pretty serious accusation to throw around," Liz said. It's one thing to go around kidnapping old lodgers and swapping tips with people, quite another to be accused of being a drug dealer.

"He is," Simon shouted. "The café's been his cover. I know it. His name's Mark Scotter."

Yummy and Chuckler looked at each other and looked at Kevin. Yummy said: "We're not into that sort of thing, mate. You been leading us on?"

"Stuff you," Kevin said and leapt for his pickup.

Liz's two PCs looked at each other and simultaneously said: "The café?"

"The Cakehole Café," Simon said.

"Oh, shit! It's not that other one, it's this one," shouted one of the PCs and they both jumped into action. They wrenched open the doors on their car and took off after Kevin in a welter of exhaust fumes and streaks of rubber left on the road. As far as she could see when Kevin braked to take the junction at the end of Malvern Road, his back-light was still out, so they could get him for that if nothing else.

"Right, that does it for me," Yummy said. "I can't handle it when it gets into that sort of thing. I'm retiring."

"Yeah. And me," said Chuckler, and chuckled. "It was only part time anyway and it hasn't been the same since Brian left."

"How we gonna get home?" Yummy enquired, looking hard at Simon.

"Catch a bus?" Simon suggested, fumbling around for another dog end, only this time there were none and he had to light a whole new cigarette. He sucked down that smoke like it was the elixir of life. Liz almost wished she was a smoker.

"I reckon the least you can do is give us a lift home now we ain't gonna kidnap you no more," Yummy said, with every appearance of sincerity.

Amazing the processes of some people's logic. Simon obviously thought so too and gave them what she could only describe as a glacial stare.

"Well," huffed Yummy. "There's no need for that attitude. We was only doing our job when all's said and done."

Amazing.

Apparently not so amazing. Simon took them home. "Just to get rid of them," he said to her later, somewhat sheepishly.

Chapter Twenty

When she got back, followed shortly by Simon, Melanie very kindly made coffee and the three them sat around the front room trying to work out what the hell was going on.

Melanie said, "You know, I'm awfully confused still."

"We've been over it and over it," Liz said. "We should have the picture by now for Pete's sake!"

"Let's try again."

Liz sighed. "Okay. Here they go. The Vincent Banton person was Lydia's brother – don't know where he fits in yet. Lydia, who we now think is fine and dandy and making phone calls to the police quite happily, used to have Mark Scotter as her toy boy, hard though that is to imagine. Mark Scotter just happens to be Betty Needles' nephew, the Once in a Lifetime Kevin. Somehow Lydia knew that Mark Scotter was about to call on her place so she rang the police to shop him."

She scratched behind Moocher's ears and turned them inside out so he looked like a hairy model with a new style hat on. He shook his head so they bounced the right way out, and begged her to do it again. "Mark Scotter did a job of some sort that resulted in a lot of missing money. He's also a

234

drug dealer and stashed his stuff at the Cakehole Caff. Which wasn't a very bright thing to do when you come to think of it and it also explains all those 'dry' provisions we spotted the other day when we raided it. It doesn't explain why the caff wasn't even locked, which I still find very odd. Anyway, his fingerprints were on the note on that last brick through the window..."

"Do you think this Mark Scotter could tie up with Julie's father?" Melanie suggested. "Do you think he's Julie's father?"

Liz stared at her in amazement. Why hadn't she thought of that? Then she remembered Simon's yearning for a family, although why he should want to be associated with Miss Poison she couldn't imagine. As for Clive, she didn't feel she could give him away until she knew more than she did at that time.

So she said, "Trouble with that is that Simon's her father."

"Thanks, Liz, but not any more," he said. "Not since the whole thing with Moocher. She's just not my type of daughter."

Oh! So much for that. Liz wondered, briefly, if one could throw off one's sister as easily if they weren't one's type. "Um, okay, so we have Mark Scotter as Julie's father – although he must had sired her when he was three. I've never been very good at guessing age, though. But maybe that's why Simon was kidnapped. They think he's the robber and maybe that's what they want – the money he's supposed to have stolen. By the way, why did Julie kidnap Moocher and threaten dismemberment?" She looked around for enlightenment, but none came her way. "What about the gun? Where did she get that? And where is she now anyway? Okay, Tony's her adoptive brother – where's he?"

She almost choked on a mouthful of coffee when a voice said, "I'm here. What do you want to know?" Tony strolled into the room and lowered himself onto the sofa.

Liz was pleased to see him. "We're trying to work out what's going on," she explained. She wiped her mouth with the back of her hand to get shot of the coffee moustache that must have appeared. The way Tony watched her do that made her feel suddenly shy. But there was definitely no room in her life at the moment for anything of *that* nature. Well, not with anyone other than Hugh, anyway. "So, why are you here, Tony? Why were you so desperate to get into this house?" It felt like years since he'd arrived.

He leant forward, his elbows on his thighs and his hands clasped loosely together, a slight frown wrinkling his forehead. "My idea, originally, was simply to try and keep Julie out of trouble," he said. "But then, I'd always been a bit suspicious of her. I know she's not the sweet little thing that her parents seemed to think she was. Take, for example, the ill-advised business of kidnapping Moocher. But even so, she is my sister. However, when I realised there was a lot of money at stake, I decided there was no reason why I shouldn't help things along a little. After all, who wouldn't?"

"I wouldn't, not if it meant forcibly relieving people of their fingers and paws," she snapped. "Anyway, what do you mean? How did you help things along a little?"

"I employed the part-time thugs," he said.

Simple. He employed the part-time thugs. Just an ordinary, everyday activity. Why should her eyebrows be half way down the back of her head? How does one go about doing such a thing anyway? Does part-time thuggery enjoy its own section in the yellow pages?

"What, to get Clive's finger? To kidnap Simon?"

Simon got up and sat on the other side of the room. He fished a large not-so-white handkerchief from his pocket and feverishly polished his glasses, shooting sorrowful glances at Tony as he did so. The top of Liz's head started to warm up. She wasn't going to have someone make her oldest lodger's life a misery. It wasn't on. She assumed Simon wanted to be her lodger again, given his sudden antipathy to his long-lost daughter who wasn't his daughter at all.

At least Tony had the grace to look uncomfortable. He lost his relaxed air and attempted to sit upright on the sofa. "Well, they didn't succeed in kidnapping Simon, so what's the harm?"

"What's the harm?" Liz stared at him. She was constantly amazed at how it was that people could walk the same earth that she did, breathe the same air she breathed and yet think in such a completely different way. They might as well be a different species. Was it her, or was it them? "You petrified Clive next door – he's still living in fear, for all I know, of your lot coming back to get his finger…"

"What do you mean, 'coming back to get his finger'?"

Well, it was take-your-breath-away-time. She'd forgotten Clive had entered into an agreement with the part time thugs about that particular item of information. "You mean you still don't know that they didn't get his finger? That makes you even worse. You're a lodger in my house, you're sitting in my front room, you're stroking my dog... Moocher! Come here!" She leapt up and examined Moocher's ears. Yes, he still had two. "And yet you're capable of paying someone to cut off someone else's finger with a power tool! And you can sit there being so casual about it..." She was seriously running out of breath, unable to get to grips with the enormity of it.

"Now, calm down, Liz," he said. "I'm bound to be interested aren't I? For one thing, that means that I paid them for nothing. Now I know, I shall set about getting my money back. And for another thing, that means that the finger in the fridge didn't belong to the person I thought it did. So who does it belong to?"

"I don't know," Liz said. What else could she say? "I don't even know how it got in there." She crossed her fingers behind Moocher's head and hoped Simon would stay silent. Maybe they'd learn something.

"Simon put it in there," Tony said, very patiently, as though she was being particularly slow to pick up the obvious.

"Give me strength," she muttered, resisting an almost overwhelming urge to bury her face in Moocher's neck. She remembered how he smelt. "How do you know that?"

"I saw him do it."

"Why would he do such a thing?" asked Melanie.

"I haven't the faintest idea," Tony said. "Simon lives to his own plan, don't you old chap?"

Simon flushed slightly and raised a hand, briefly, as if in acknowledgement.

"But if you saw him put it in there, why did you let your poor little sister open the fridge the following morning. You must have known she would pass out." (Yeah. Poor Julie. What a shame. What a cow.)

"Ah, well. That was a bit awkward, I'll admit. As she assumed, obviously, that it was Clive's, she couldn't very well take responsibility for it at that stage. And, anyway, I can assure you there was no guarantee that Julie would pass out. She really isn't the passing-out type, believe it or not. I had no idea what she would do."

"Where did you think it came from, then? The finger."

"It was on the brick. The brick that came through the window. I thought it was a novel delivery method employed by the thugs. I wasn't that impressed, tell you the truth. But that was one reason why I got the window fixed – to save too much thought on anyone else's part. I was going to deduct the cost from their wages."

"Why would anyone, even a bunch of amateur thugs, chuck a finger on a brick through my window? And where did it come from if it wasn't Clive's?"

"I have no idea why they would do that. I don't know them at all. I only hired them. Maybe they could think of no other way of proving they'd done the job. But we're going to have words about it. One of them dropped out early on and now the other two have packed it in. And I'm just left with the new one who seems to be several planks short of a floor. He's probably now being picked up for having a broken brake light. It's hopeless trying to get staff these days."

"Yeah. You have my sympathy. It's much the same trying to get decent, straightforward, you-are-what-you-seem lodgers, too."

"There's no need to be like that," he said. He seemed quite affronted, but she couldn't be bothered with him anymore. She was much more interested in what she didn't know. "So we still don't know where the finger came from," she said. Well, Simon had given her a theory, but she didn't want to involve Stella either.

"Doesn't matter now, does it?" Tony said. "Moocher's kindly disposed of it for us, so its presence won't make life awkward for any of us. And even if it did, it's nothing to do with me anymore as Simon claimed it as his own and wrapped it and put it in the fridge. So I'm in the clear anyway." He beamed at them. Melanie uncrossed her lovely long legs and shifted away from him. "And," he continued. "Simon did the right thing with regard to fridge hygiene. No one's suffered any unfortunate after effects. No, it's not a problem any longer."

He sat there with a silly smile on what she'd previously thought was a good-looking face. He wore the air of one expecting praise for his thoughtfulness, but it was beyond her. It was apparently beyond Simon and Melanie too, who both stared at Tony as though he were something Moocher had dragged in. He really was way outside their experience of life, which, up until now had obviously been far too narrow.

"Do you know why Julie kidnapped Moocher and threatened maiming?"

He smiled at her. "I think it was just to put some pressure on you. You would have shopped Simon and told everyone his secrets before you'd let something happen to that dog."

I glanced at Simon. He said, "Don't worry about it. It didn't come to it, so it doesn't matter."

What a hero! She still felt ashamed though. Just in case Tony was right, which he probably was… Not that she knew any of Simon's secrets to tell, but if she did then she probably would if that was the alternative to hurting her Mooch.

"No," Tony said. "I fancy you ruined Julie's plan by finding Moocher so soon."

"Hmmm. I think I'm going to bath the dog," Liz said. She was fresh out of patience with it all and wasn't much further on with getting things sorted. And Moocher still stank enough to make any woodworm in the vicinity crawl out of their planks in surrender. First things first and to hell with severed fingers, abductions and all these dodgy people she suddenly found herself surrounded by. "And by the time I've finished I want you out of here, Tony. I don't care where you go, I don't want to know, just go. Good bye." She supposed people can't really be locked up for *intending* to do something, if they were actually prevented from doing it. Pity.

"Don't I get any brownie points for telling you everything I know?"

"Just exactly why have you told us everything you know?"

"Why not?"

He was incredible, but she'd thought of something that would deflate him. "Did you know that the latest thug you've hired is a well-known and much wanted drug dealer, Tony? You're going to be in the sticky brown stuff when your part in his employment comes to light."

But he shrugged it off. "That's his problem, not mine. I don't know anything about his business."

Liz heaved herself out of her chair and made a dignified exit, only slightly marred by tripping over the mug she'd left on the floor and spilling the dregs over the carpet. She didn't look back. Moocher followed her out with no thought in his head at all as to what was in store for him. If he'd had the slightest inkling he would have been out there packing his bags in company with Tony. He would have left without leaving a forwarding address, too. Moocher did not like having a bath.

Chapter Twenty-one

But she chickened out of doing it straightaway when she remembered she'd nicked Hugh's wallet to make him come back. Liz telephoned him and sure enough, he said he'd come round straightaway as it contained the office swipe cards.

She met him at the door and grabbing his arm, she walked hastily away from the house. "Hugh, would you come with me for a coffee to that new café? Not Cakehole – the other one. I'm just waiting for Tony to move out and I'd rather not be in the house, but I'd rather you were there when I get back just in case he hasn't gone."

Of course, he fell for it. It wouldn't occur to him she'd been underhand, and she wasn't usually, but she felt the need to see him again soon. If he thought someone needed help he was a bit of a sucker. She'd bet a new kitchen that was how Charity got him in the first place. Damn, Liz didn't want to think of her when she was about to try the alluring thing. He must have found her alluring once. Maybe he would again.

So they went off down the café and settled themselves in its noisy, trendy depths. It had an awful lot of children in it, but then, mothers with small children made up the bulk of their trade. For a moment she became quite misty-eyed to think that when she managed to get Hugh to see sense it could be her in here with a chic three-wheeler this time next year, dunking her marshmallows in her cappuccino, gossiping with others who were doing the same, her terribly well-behaved, clean and quiet child patiently waiting in its conveyance. Oh, yes, she could see it all now.

The coffee arrived and dragged her out of her daydream. Hugh had ordered a freshly baked chocolate and pear muffin. She had declined because being in love takes it out of you so you don't have enough energy left to have an appetite – that was one good thing about it – it would help with the weight loss, not that she needed to lose that much, but she thought just maybe there was something in Melanie's assertion that she'd been comfort-eating for a couple of years in unconscious bereavement from losing Hugh. She knew she'd chucked him out, but we all make mistakes.

His chocolate confection did look scrummy. And she wasn't back with him yet. Maybe she needed just a little more comfort-eating. He started in on it with every appearance of huge enjoyment. He didn't look at all like a man mangled beneath the shredding blades of lost love. She wondered just how Charity had entangled him. She thought he'd just found himself in that position and it hadn't really sunk in and then suddenly it'd been broken off. Maybe it hadn't really registered at all, although she knew he'd have gone through with it if he'd given his word and she'd have ended up with all his worldly goods and disillusioned him, too. It didn't bear thinking of.

And then Liz saw Tortoise-woman. And Pink and Fluffy. They sat in a corner by the window in deep conversation. There was even a pet basket on the bench next to Tortoise-woman. She looked up as Liz stared, and smirked at her. Liz hoped it was her poker face in place as she gazed blankly back, trying to pretend she hadn't seen her.

It occurred to her to wonder how come the tortoise got out so much. They must be very careless with it.

"Do you know, Tortoise-woman, Hugh?" she asked, suddenly struck with an odd idea. "She's sitting over there with her two little girls."

He didn't even turn around to look. "Oh, yes. I discovered she's Charity's cousin and has been spying on me, especially when I came round to see you, which was how Charity knew so much. I wasn't best pleased. We had words. Why would she spy on her fiancé? I found it quite distasteful."

He seemed genuinely puzzled and savagely squashed a chocolate sponge crumb on his plate before continuing: "She kept the tortoise in the basket. She could go anywhere and then produce him as though she'd just found him. The two little girls aren't hers, either. They're borrowed from a friend and earn pocket money pretending to be hers as extra cover. Why would someone feel the need to do something as underhand as that?"

Another crumb got mashed. "I was going to stop coming round so much, too, because she'd already said it made her feel insecure. I thought she'd get used to it later. We all have friends, don't we? She'd have got used to it."

Bit naive Liz thought, but sweet.

"Charity's got men friends," he said. "Her last fiancée was still a good friend of hers, always round there cooking up schemes and laughing together. I didn't begrudge her any friends."

This was information Liz wasn't sure she wanted. He'd said it innocently enough, but she wondered if he'd thought they were in league together to fleece him, which was immediately what she thought when he painted a picture of Charity and her previous love being quite so friendly.

Liz realised he was watching her, and having caught his eye she found it difficult to pull her gaze away. His eyes were dark and warm and tender and lovely. He *must* be wondering if they could make a go of it. She consciously made her own gaze more melting, more alluring. She narrowed her eyes a little so her eyelashes fanned out more sexily, subtly changing into a temptress, a siren, indeed a regular honeypot.

So she wasn't surprised when in the middle of this loud, aromatic and busy café Hugh lowered his voice to a throbbing murmur and said, "Liz…"

"Yes?" she said, leaning forward slightly and placing her hand close enough to his hand - the one that didn't have a half eaten muffin in it - for him to take it in his moment of revelation. Her heart knew something was about to happen and started to skip with excitement making her blood leap about her veins with eager anticipation.

"I wonder if you need glasses?" he said.

"What?" she asked, rudely snatched from her delicious fantasy.

"Glasses," he said in a tone of voice that suggested that maybe she needed a hearing aid as well. "I wonder if you need glasses." He paused. "Spectacles, Liz. Glasses to see things with…"

"I know what you mean," she snapped, trying very hard not to sound as sulky as she suddenly felt. "What makes you say that?"

"It's the way you keep looking at me as though you can't really make out my face," he said, thus shattering, for all eternity, any idea that she might make a successful sex kitten.

In what she hoped was a completely natural, accidental way she found herself looking at her watch. "Ohmigod! I have a client turning up. How could I have forgotten? I must go. I'm so sorry." She stood up and grabbed her jacket. "I'll be in touch."

"I thought you wanted me to come back with you to see to Tony," he said, but she pretended she hadn't heard and gave him a cheery wave from the doorway before disappearing out of his line of sight and stopping to wipe the sweat of embarrassment from her brow.

It was some time later before she realised she'd left him to pay for their coffees, too. The coffees she had invited him to share. Oh, great – blind, deaf and running out on the bill as well.

Chapter Twenty-two

It occurred to her as she sat on the floor in the bathroom that it was a bit strange that she could just carry on as normal despite all the weird things that were happening. But what else could she do? Normality had to be allowed to reign supreme or she'd lose her mind. And what could possibly be more normal than the happy pursuit of bathing a dog that simply refused to be bathed?

Anyway, the police were on to it now so she could take a back seat. With the other stuff she meant, not bathing Moocher.

And of course, the other thing, the thing she'd been trying very hard not to think about, was the whole situation with Hugh. There must be a way she could let him know how much she truly loved him and how much she'd like for them to have another go at being a couple. Knowing what they knew now that they didn't know back then, surely, if they established the ground rules up front, they could make a success of it this time.

She'd got the distinct impression he'd been engaged to Charity for a little while before he'd finally told her, and she wondered why he'd found it so difficult to tell her. Maybe there was hope for her in that, for a start. Or maybe it was just that he felt a bit of a pratt – after all, the whole engagement with Charity sounded a bit suspicious

- as though he'd been taken advantage of, but that could have been her over-protective mind at work. Hugh was an astute businessman, just a bit gullible when dealing with women. She didn't think he really believed how foul and mercenary they could be sometimes.

Uncharitable Charity... That was it! She and her previous boyfriend cooked up some scheme between them to fleece Hugh when he was vulnerable. Did this mean he'd lost a chunk of money to them? Or had they realised they'd get nowhere, fabricated an excuse and dumped him before he caught on and sorted them out? She realised she might never know as, strictly speaking, it wasn't her business and she wouldn't want to embarrass him

And if she ever did meet Charity she wouldn't puree her limbs in revenge. No, she would thank the woman for making her, Liz, see sense.

Thinking about the last couple of years of him steadfastly trying to get them back together again, and her, kindly, turning him down made her feel awful. He'd been right all along. They *did* belong together. On the other hand, if not for those couple of years they neither of them would have the understanding they had now. Maybe it would be *because* of those years that this time it would work.

If only she could convince him of that.

She was sitting on the floor because she was taking a rest. It was exhausting work trying to get a stubborn dog into a bath. Moocher lay on the bathroom floor, his nose between his paws, his eyes rolled up looking at her, his tail twitching. It was very annoying. It was like someone who wants to laugh at you, but was determined they wouldn't because of how insulting it would be. But they're unable to control the corners of their mouth and those corners twitch upwards as if they have a life of their own. That was how Moocher's tail was going. He was trying not to laugh at her.

Dogs have this amazing ability to make themselves really, really heavy. Just as soon as you want to pick them up, if they don't want to be picked up, they make themselves as heavy as a train. It's almost as though they've glued themselves to the floor. Moocher was perfectly happy for her to lift each of his legs from the floor, his tail also came away easily, his head would come up. No, he wasn't stuck to the floor. He had just made himself impossibly heavy. All the muscles in her body ached from the time they had spent, her trying to lift him from the floor, him just lying there, laughing to himself. Being heavy.

She forced herself to her knees and leaning over the bath tub, checked the water. It had cooled significantly in the time it had taken for their first round of tussles. She added some hot water. She didn't want to give him a chill. Ha! Give him a chill... The number of times he had leapt into the sea, or a river, or just any old puddle or ditch, regardless of the warmth or otherwise of the day, and then, of course, wanted to get in the car... she was beginning to get suspicious about Moocher's supposed dislike of baths considering the enthusiasm with which he submerged himself in liquid of virtually any description anywhere else but here.

His tail twitched. He was probably wondering what Liz'd do next. She was wondering what she'd do next, too. Then, just as she was forcing herself to do something, anything, Melanie and Simon appeared in the doorway.

Melanie said, "Tony's gone, but not far."

"Let me guess," Liz said. "He's gone next door."

Melanie nodded her head, her hair bouncing with the movement. "Yup, you've got it. Strange, isn't it, the way Lydia's suddenly started to take in lodgers? It's not as if she needs the money."

"I think it's mainly for her loneliness," Liz said, somewhat absent-mindedly. She was thinking about the gun Julie had. Regardless of what anyone said, she still felt uneasy about Lydia. She couldn't explain the phone call from Lydia and the story about a burglar, unless it was her trying to shop Mark Scotter because he'd found someone closer to his own age. Liz still wasn't as convinced as she'd like to be that Lydia was okay. But she didn't know what to do about it.

On the other hand, Lydia's brother was there now and he would probably take care of things.

Liz was beginning to feel more generous towards Julie, too. After all, she hadn't actually harmed Moocher. Also, the revelation of how immoral and unfeeling her adoptive brother actually was made her see Julie in a different light. Living with him must have made her hard - if only to survive.

"Yeah, but I thought we were all friends," Melanie said, breaking into Liz's train of thought. "So what's with her taking in lodgers who've fallen out with us and why's she getting all funny with us?"

"I think she may have had the hots for Simon, you know…"

Simon swallowed hard and audibly. A red tide of embarrassment crept from under his collar to disappear into his hair.

"Ah, gotcha. She's a 'woman scorned' is she?" Melanie said with her usual delicacy, looking at Simon as though waiting for him to spill all his sordid secrets.

"Look, I'll tell you what," Liz whispered. "While the black furry animal over there thinks we're all engrossed talking about Lydia and Simon and Lydia's thwarted attempts to get Simon for her next toy boy, let's all get ready to pounce on him and get him in the bath. Okay? Moocher, that is, not Simon."

"Oh," Melanie said. "I wondered why you were whispering then."

"Well, let's stop whispering now or he'll realise something's going on. Don't look at him!"

"Oh, sorry. Okay, where were we? Um, oh, yeah, talking about Lydia, um…" Melanie casually rolled up her sleeves in readiness. Clever girl. She'd got the drift. Whereas Simon just stood there still looking startled, still a deep pink.

"Okay, Simon, ready to grab black furry animal?"

He nodded, too frightened to look around.

I said, "Okay, now listen, I'll grab him around the head and shoulders, you two get his rear end. Actually it's best if one of you, Melanie you do it, get his rear end especially making sure you have one leg and Simon you just make sure you keep his other hind leg close in to his body, whilst supporting his middle. We'll just lift him straight up, move over a little and then straight

252

down into the bath. Okay, I won't count because Moocher can count, you know. He's sooo clever, that dog. I'll just say, 'here we go', Okay?"

Her co-conspirators nodded, looking grim. There was a short uneasy silence in the bathroom. They could hear a car pulling up, handbrake going on, door opening and slamming. They could hear a fly thud into the window and start to whine about it. They could hear an aeroplane in the distance flying off to some white sanded shore where people wouldn't dream of cutting off other people's fingers or kidnapping dogs and terrorising them with threats of torture.

Very quietly, she said, "Here we go." And they all pounced on that poor, unsuspecting dog who'd been nodding off into a doze. He didn't stand a chance, not against the combined deviousness of three human beings. Ha!

All that happened was that after they got him airborne, all four of his legs suddenly, as though responding to some mechanical instruction, stuck out at the corners of his body and effectively stopped him from being lowered into the bath. He became as rigid as a Victorian wardrobe – he wasn't going anywhere. However, in the ensuing struggle through which Moocher whiffled and snuffled, occasionally letting out a single delighted 'woof', Simon fell into the end of the bath; Melanie skinned her elbow on the wall and Liz managed to smack into the bathroom cabinet so hard it threw itself, plus all its contents, into the bath to join Simon. To add insult to injury Liz also managed to snag herself in the shower curtain which, with a gigantic unzipping sound, ripped itself from its restraints and landed in the bath too.

Enough was enough. She helped Simon out, produced some antiseptic cream and a plaster for Melanie, scooped out various chemistry products from the bath, rather unwisely tore the shower curtain out which seemed to bring with it half the water, put on the taps to top it up and got in the bath herself.

"Moocher, come here. Good dog," she said in a wheedling, let's-have-fun voice.

He looked all around as if to say, "Well, why didn't we do it like this from the start? If only I'd known what you wanted." And he jumped in to join her. Easy. Any dog was only too delighted to join their owner in the bath if they're asked in the right way. She reached for the very expensive special dog shampoo and, removing the cap, poured a good handful in to her palm.

That was when the front door bell rang and Moocher, who always felt obliged to welcome people into the house properly, if he was awake, leapt out of the bath. The shampoo landed on the bathroom floor and proceeded to leak away into the carpet. Liz was left, fully clothed, sitting in a rapidly cooling bath with no dog to wash. This wasn't quite the plan.

She could hear Moocher thundering down the stairs closely followed by the clack of Melanie's sandal shod feet. The front door opened and there was a sharp, very irritating scream. Liz might have known that Angela would call round now. There was also the low rumble of an accompanying man, but she couldn't think why she should have dragged her hubby round with her. He, to give him his due, simply wasn't interested in poking around in Liz's business, not in the same way that Angela was. Then she heard footsteps on the stairs and her sister appeared in the doorway.

Liz noticed that Melanie and Simon, very wisely, didn't accompany her.

"How nice to see you," Liz said. Well, what else could she say?

She sniffed. "Sarcastic to the end, aren't you?"

Hugh appeared behind her. Ooh, it wasn't Angela's hubby, it was Hugh. Liz felt herself go hot. "Getting ready for our dinner date, Liz?" he asked.

Good grief! She'd forgotten! She couldn't believe she'd forgotten. Too much had happened in too short a space of time. "Er, well yes, of course," she said, enthusiastically rubbing dog shampoo into her scalp in a fair imitation, she thought, of someone getting ready for a dinner date. She noticed that dogs' flea shampoo didn't smell very romantic. "So, to what do I owe the pleasure of a visit from you, Angela?" she enquired. Very reasonably, she thought.

Angela ignored her. "Why are you in the bath with all your clothes on?" she asked.

"Well, I wouldn't be entertaining all and sundry in the nude would I?"

"I know what it is – your washing machine's broken isn't it?"

Amazing. She's amazing. Moocher chose that moment to shoulder his way back into the bathroom producing little shrieks from Angela as she tried to stay out of his reach. He jumped into the bath. He knew his place. His place was by his mistress, wherever she may be.

"Just tell me why you're here, Angela." Liz was fresh out of polite social niceties by then.

Hugh raised an eyebrow. He's the only man Liz knew who could do that with his eyebrow and not look like a right poser who thinks he should be the next Sean Connery. He then gave her an orchid all ready to be pinned to her bosom when she was ready, with some leaves nicely taped on to it as a suitable backdrop to its lush petals. Actually, he thought better of handing it to her and laid it tenderly on the back of the sink. Angela stared at it and stared meaningfully at Liz and her look was unmistakable. It said, 'What an unbelievably stupid person you are to turn this man away.' May be, for once in her life, she was right.

Liz was beginning to think she needed someone to get some order back in her life, and if it just happened to be the man she was madly in love with, then so be it. Mind you, it was horrible to admit Angela was right, but Hugh was too important to let that get in the way, although Liz would burn with resentment about it for a while.

But then again, she didn't like orchids. She would much rather have a freesia corsage or just a rose from the garden and Hugh would know that. But he would consider an orchid much more the thing. In the face of knowing that he knew that she knew that he knew she would rather not have an orchid but he still felt he knew better, then she knew she could cope very well on her own, much as she loved him. Hmm, maybe she would be better off on her own after all.

And she wouldn't be on her own. She would have her trusty, clean and sweet-smelling, dog by her side. On the other hand, she no longer wanted to be on her own, despite a couple of years of enjoyable singledom. Maybe they could be a couple but not live together? Hmm – that had possibilities. But she still had to convince him...

Angela snorted. Not a very lady-like habit that one, but she just wouldn't be told. "I came round to tell you about Betty," she announced, looking very important. Liz just knew something nasty had happened to Betty. Angela looked too pleased for it to be otherwise.

"Don't tell me," Liz said. "She's discovered she was sitting in your kitchen for three hours with a crumb on her chin and she's committed hari kiri only it's not a crumb, it's a wart, but she didn't put her glasses on either..."

Angela was oblivious. Angela was triumphant, and beaming, in her role as news bearer extraordinaire. "Betty's nephew, Kevin has been arrested for drug dealing," she said. "But it's actually Betty's operation. She's been dealing in drugs all these years under the name of Mark Scotter."

Well! You could have struck her down with a blade of grass. All Liz could manage was a strangled, "What?"

"Yes," Angela continued. "Kevin has been the brawn, she's been the brain and the café's been a cover. Kevin reported you to the police for breaking and entering and when they went there they found all these drugs hidden away in bags of sugar and bags of flour. He's not very bright."

Angela stopped to gulp in a breath and look important and then carried on, "She was absolutely livid and tried to shoot him but missed. It seems that he took a part-time job, too, because she never gave him enough money and the police were on to him already through that. And, to think, she and I ran the tombola together for the church fete when that nice vicar was there, when she was plain Betty Podger. Do you think they'll want to interview me?"

Liz massaged more shampoo into Moocher's back as he lay across her lap in the bath. He was ecstatic. Her mind buzzed and looped, trying to sort out what she already knew from the new stuff and trying to work out the extra convolutions this added to the picture. She still couldn't believe Betty was a drug dealer, though, whatever she called herself.

"Why would they want to interview you?" she asked.

"So that they can build a profile of her as a wanted criminal, of course," she said. "Profiles are all the rage. I know. I read all the right books."

"Why would they want to build a profile?" One must exercise a lot of patience with Angela.

"You haven't been listening," she snapped. "They've got Kevin, but Betty got away."

"You mean they had no trouble apprehending a strapping, muscle-bound young man, but a dear little old lady fought her way clear and made a successful dash for freedom against all the odds and half the police force from the West country?"

"She's not a dear little old lady. We did a tombola together. She's barely middle aged."

"So how come she got away?"

"Apparently she retreated into her house and simply vanished. She must have had this manoeuvre worked out for a long time just in case she needed to be able to disappear. It was live on the local news. That's where I heard about it and I came over straight away. The police are still looking for her. If you weren't so wrapped up in yourself all the time you'd have noticed the carryings on in the street."

"So this vicious criminal is on the loose and possibly wanting revenge from the family that, quite accidentally, exposed her life of crime, and my sister is wondering what to wear for the interview. If I were you I would be at home right now battening down the hatches, stocking up on tinned foods and bottled water, and getting ready for a siege, not prancing about looking for cameras to be coy at and microphones to lisp down."

"Don't be so melodramatic, Liz. Betty won't come after us. We did a tombola together, don't forget."

"Dearie me," Liz sighed. She turned away from Angela and, holding the shower head, fumbled with the dial-thing to get it on. It would need to be on full blast to rinse the shampoo from Moocher's exceedingly thick coat. He loved this bit. He was definitely a shower dog and definitely not a bath dog. Sometimes, in the summer she would chase him around the garden with the hose at full power and when she was exhausted he would bark, 'More, more,' at her. When she couldn't get it turned on from where she was sitting, she turned back only to find Betty in the doorway, brandishing a gun.

Why was she not surprised? She was beyond it by then. Never again to feel that refreshing edge of astonishment - what a sad state of affairs. Hugh sat on the edge of the bath and Angela sat, quivering, on the loo. They both had their hands in the air. Very sensible, she thought. She put hers up too so there'd be no mistake about who was in charge here.

"I know you're not as thick as some," Betty said to Liz. "So for Chrissake put your hands down and stop that animal of yours coming anywhere near me or I'll be forced to shoot it."

"Him," Liz said as she whipped her hands down and gripped Moocher hard. "He's a him not an it." She couldn't seem to help it.

"Liz, just shut up," Hugh said.

"No!" Betty shouted. They all flinched and watched the gun with unwilling fascination. "*You* shut up!" Betty continued. "No one asked you, Hugh. Don't let a man ruin your life, whatever you do, Liz."

"I won't, don't worry," Liz assured her and risked a grin. Just now, she didn't really want to grin at a drug dealer, but she did want to get out of this situation alive and they seemed to have found, unexpectedly, some common ground. Betty's marriage couldn't have been a happy one by the sounds of it. Liz wondered where Melanie and Simon were and looked behind Betty, worried that they might appear at the wrong moment.

She saw the look. "The other two are out in the street enjoying the fuss. Everyone's looking for me. I doubt they'll look here just yet. I only want a moment to clear something up anyway. I'm not interested in you lot or in revenge, despite what you might think. I want to know about Simon Medley. Is he Julie's father or not?"

Liz couldn't begin to imagine why she would want to know, but she was happy that in the face of that gun this was one question she could answer with utter certainty. "No," she said. "He is definitely not Julie's father."

"Shit! Are you absolutely positive?"

260

"Yes, I'm afraid so," Liz said sadly, her illusions of dear little ol' ladies shattered by the curse. But then, she hadn't really got used to the idea of her being a drug-runner yet. She supposed it might be all right for a drug-runner to swear like that.

"Who else could it be? I was sure it had to be him."

"Who, Julie's father?"

"Of course, Julie's father."

"Why do you want to know who Julie's father is?" Liz thought she might as well get as much information as she could under the circumstances. But Betty raised the gun even higher and pointed it more menacingly at her.

Hugh said, "Shut up, Liz!"

Whereupon the gun swung around to him and she said, "No! *You* shut up!" and thanks to Hugh's timely admonition to Liz, Betty proceeded to tell her: "Julie's father and my sodding husband were in cahoots together when that job was done. Julie's father got away with all the money. I know he did the time for it, but he came out to a very nice early retirement pension. Very nice indeed. If I'd had that I wouldn't have been forced into the burglary game. But I had to keep body and soul together somehow."

"Burglary?" Liz said.

"No need to look at me like that," Betty said to her. "We all do what we have to. I'm not sure I believe you anyway – it has to be him – if it isn't him, who else is there? I know he's here in Malvern Road – I know this from some papers of Tom's that I found. He was my husband – useless sod that he was. I thought if I lured the daughter here she would lead me to him and she led me to

Simon Medley so why should I believe you? I even got Kevin to get it together with the girl, but she was only leading him on as it turns out. By the way, the thing with the dog – I didn't approve of that. She just took an opportunity and overplayed her hand. She thought you knew about the money as you were such good friends with Simon Medley."

Liz felt her mouth must have been hanging open. The torture of not knowing whether Moocher had been maimed or was even dead was just "an opportunity" Julie took to get at her. Betty cracked a mirthless laugh as she took in her expression.

Abruptly she turned to Angela, but was unable to get in the first word. "I don't know how you could do it," she said. "How could a woman be a burglar?" Angela stared at the gun defiantly. Liz was quite pleased with her sister actually, much as it pained her to admit it.

"Oh, don't be so boringly sexist, Angela," Betty said. "Do you know who Julie's father is?"

"I haven't the faintest idea. This is my sister's house and nothing to do with me." She shuddered delicately at the very idea. "I always knew she shouldn't take in lodgers. Who knows where they've been? On the other hand, I would find it difficult to believe of that particular lodger that he was capable of planning, and carrying out successfully, anything more complicated than getting matching shoes on at the same time. I certainly can't imagine him doing the job, surviving gaol and then keeping hidden all this time."

"Hmmm…" Betty said.

Liz was in a quandary. She wanted Simon out of Betty's frame, but should she drop Clive in it? Shouldn't he take responsibility for his actions, including those that produced a daughter, especially one as nasty as his? And what about this Mark Scotter person? She just didn't know enough.

"We thought you were a drug dealer, not a burglar," she said.

"I wouldn't stoop that low," Betty said. "It's because I discovered Kevin's nasty little habits in that direction and the name he was using, that I shopped him to Angela. I knew she wouldn't be able to help herself. I knew she would tell you and I expected you to do something about it. But you did nothing." She looked at Liz in disgust. "Well, you did come to see me, I suppose, so that I could make it even easier for you. But you still did nothing."

"Angela didn't tell me he was a drug dealer," Liz said, glancing at Angela.

She dropped her gaze. "I think I forgot to tell you that bit," she whispered.

"Anyway," Liz said, strangely unsettled to see Angela look hangdog, "When I came to see you Betty, you thought his van had been stolen for that job."

Betty smiled at her. "Well, of course that was the impression I was going to give. You'd have smelled a rat if you'd realised I was dropping my own nephew in it. Even you're bright enough to think that would be suspicious. Or I thought you were. I had second thoughts when I realised you were trying to break into a café I'd already left unlocked for you…"

Gee, thanks, Betty. Liz opened her mouth to make some scathing retort when Betty jumped around at the sound of footsteps on the stairs. Liz heard Melanie shout, "Simon, your pocket!"

Liz sniffed the air. Yes, above the smell of dog shampoo spreading throughout the bathroom carpet, could clearly be smelt the peculiar and characteristic odour of a pocket on fire. Then she heard a yell and a series of thuds. Simon must have fallen down the stairs.

Suddenly, Hugh pounced, with an athletic grace that took Liz's breath away. He was like a bounding lion, like a swooping eagle. Like a speeding shark he was on to Betty. There was a shout, a scream, a grunt, a clatter, racing footsteps, a thud as a body hit the floor, muffled moans and then a taut and waiting silence.

It was all so quick.

Liz looked at Angela. She was stiff with shock and appeared to be glued to the loo seat. Liz had released Moocher and he was out of the bath in one leap, spraying soap suds everywhere. She slowly stood up, unable to move any faster. She'd been sitting in a hard bath with her legs crossed all that time and was afraid of permanent disfigurement, not to mention everlasting wrinkles and water-logging.

Hugh was on the floor, clutching himself where men always clutch themselves whether they've been kicked in that area or not. In this case, he *had* been kicked, or kneed, in that area, and he was being a very brave boy and not making too much noise about it.

Betty was gone. The gun was on the floor. Liz felt she should pick it up just in case Betty came back intending to use it or just in case some other baddie got in and decided it was too good an opportunity to miss. But somehow she couldn't bring herself to touch it. It seemed to give off an aura of badness, of dank and chilly memories, of pain. She kicked it behind the loo and dropped to her knees beside Hugh who seemed to be recovering rapidly. He smiled, a valiant but somewhat strained smile. He had never looked so appealing to her and she leaned over and kissed him on his mouth. That wiped off the smile and a look of extreme puzzlement took its place, quickly followed by annoyance and she leant away from him, confused.

"Don't," he hissed. "Not even in pity. Don't do that."

Pity? He thought she kissed him because she pitied him for being kicked in the goolies? Or maybe, her mind took a leap – maybe he meant pity for him being dumped by old Uncharitable. He was never going to believe she loved him. Despair hit her and she had to bite her lips to stop them quivering.

"What about Betty?" he said, as though they hadn't just exchanged life-changing words.

But Liz wasn't worried about Betty getting away. After all, there were two fit and healthy people between her and the ground floor and then the area outside the house was crawling with policemen, media people and nosy neighbours.

Chapter Twenty-three

The speakers on her radio buzzed with more than their usual excitement as the message they carried percolated through to her. "The sad, the mad and the bad were to be found in Malvern Road today," it said.

She would have to get onto that radio station and offer to write their headlines for them. She couldn't do worse than they had, surely.

"Reports are coming in of the attempted abduction of a petite, frail old lady who kept her attackers, who consisted of five people and a rabid dog, at bay with an empty gun, before making good her escape. Allegedly, a drugs haul of considerable street value came to light when local people ransacked a nearby café known as the Cakehole. Our reporter was on the scene and we'll go over to him for clarification. Bob?"

There was the sound of sirens, some excited barking from the rabid dog, and a confused gabble, no doubt from the crowd of Malvern Road inmates, all blended artistically together the way radio reporters do to start their reports with a local flavour. "And here's the householder in whose house this incident has taken place, Liz Houston. Can you tell us what happened, Mrs Houston?"

"I wish she could," she heard herself say from the speakers of her radio. Why did her voice always sound so hellishly squeaky when it was recorded?

Liz cringed. She knew what was coming. If only she'd had a bit of warning... But, no. She didn't. Just a microphone stuck in her face as soon as she risked looking outside her front door to find out what on earth was going on.

She switched the radio off and hoped that everyone else in Bristol did the same. Fat chance. Luckily the complete dialogue and scene in which it took place didn't *all* get broadcast she discovered later.

"Are you Liz Houston," the tall chap with the crinkly eyes had asked her when she peered out onto Malvern Road from behind her front door.

"I'm not sure," she had said. She was learning fast. "Do I want to be her at the moment?"

He had laughed, showing lots of lovely white teeth. Then, all of a sudden, without even a 'goodbye', he leapt over the wall into next door's garden. Moocher had come hurtling through the door, barging her out of the way and barking as only a rabid dog can bark if he knows he's appearing on local radio.

She fully understood the immediate panic exhibited by the reporter and the surrounding crowd. Moocher *was* foaming at the mouth. And at various other parts of his anatomy as well. But so would anyone who'd just had an entire bottle of shampoo lavished on them and then not had it rinsed off. He thought it was a great game – all these people screaming and running away. He was having a hard job deciding which lucky person he should chase. Liz could tell he was undecided by the way he started to run up and down, snapping at the air, barking frantically all the while. Obviously the signs of a mad dog to them. Thankfully Melanie caught him before he'd terrorised too many of the onlookers, and dragged him back inside.

Liz had looked around expecting to see Betty shackled to a policeman, but there was no sign of any such thing. Perhaps she'd already been taken away, no doubt closely guarded by a contingent of husky officers of the law. She was a pretty slippery character.

Bob appeared again from the other side of Clive's wall. "You seem to be rather wet," he said. He was sharply observant for a media man.

"So would you be if you'd been trying to bathe a rabid dog," she said, already fed up with this conversation. "So, has Betty been taken away?" she asked.

"Betty?" Bob said. "There was some confusion when a man came running out of the house with his trousers on fire. He was being chased by a young woman. The crowd was fairly stunned and before anyone could go to his aid he'd ripped his trousers off and thrown them in the wheelie bin. He then started patting himself, obviously looking for something. He didn't find it and he opened the wheelie bin. The flames reached out and set light to his hair, but the girl quickly slapped that fire out. Somebody rushed up with a bucket of water and threw it in the bin and the fire went out immediately so the wheelie bin's okay. The man then leant in to reach his trousers, but the bin was quite big and he tipped over and fell in. The water-guy and the girl hauled him out. They had a few words. The man gave him a cigarette and lit it. The man thanked him and wandered off. He got in that car over there, finished his cigarette, refused to speak to anyone who rapped on the windscreen and now he's having a nap. The young woman went back indoors. Was she Betty?"

"No," she said. "Betty is middle-aged."

"I'm a bit confused," Bob said. "After the man came out of the house with his trousers on fire there was a little old lady, all hunched up and hysterical, who told a tale of having been dragged into your house and set upon by all these people and a rabid dog, who seemed to think she was someone else. The people that is, she didn't know what the dog thought."

Liz took another look at Bob. He seemed pleasant enough, but he must have been some turf short of a lawn to think the dog thought she was anyone but who she actually was. The dog wasn't stupid.

He continued. "She was in a helluva state and some man gave her a lift to somewhere or other. And then, shortly after that – this all happened very quickly - there was uproar because, apparently, she wasn't a dear little old lady, at all. She was a notorious drug dealer and she'd got away right under our noses. So all the police have gone off after her apart from those two over there who've stayed around in case she makes her way back here."

Bob scratched his scalp, his brow screwed up so much in puzzlement he looked like his head had been ploughed. "The odd thing was that there was a bit of a row about who was to stay here. Between the policemen, I mean. Something about whose turn it was to visit Malvern Road this time. I didn't understand what that was about either. Do you know?" He looked appealingly at Liz, but it wasn't going to do him any good.

"No," she said. "Haven't a clue."

"Oh, and there's a couple more coppers down the road, where, I gather, she lives. Presumably when she's not making *business trips* to South America. Is that who you mean when you say Betty?"

"Probably. But she's not a drug dealer. Her nephew was the drug dealer and he hid his haul in the caff."

"I'm still confused and I wonder if you would be kind enough to clarify things for me?"

"No, I'm sorry. I don't think that's possible. If you find out what's going on before I do, then please let me know. It was nice meeting you." But before she could get the door shut Angela, who'd obviously stopped to reapply her makeup and fluff up her hair, was there extending a gracious hand to Bob and smiling that I'm-going-to-be-a-local-celebrity smile of hers at him. Liz heard her say, "I'm sure I can help you."

Liz left them to it.

Ohmigod.

What a mess.

The PCs would have great fun with this.

Still, at least Moocher ended up smelling fresh and clean as a spring morning. But then, it had only taken an entire bottle of expensive shampoo, more than a few hours, a completely wrecked bathroom, several now-damaged adults and being threatened with a gun to achieve this end.

So, what would happen if the world at large discovered that Git-Next-Door was Julie's father?

Would life get back to normal? Was it her place to expose him as Julie's father? What if something awful happened to him if she did? Could she live with that? No, she didn't think she could. Damn! He'd just have to be made to do it himself and get all this stuff sorted out.

Liz was still wrestling with these problems as she dropped into the passenger seat of Hugh's car. The leather seat was the sort that moulded itself to your body when you got anywhere near it. She couldn't afford to be that relaxed, however, so she pressed the button that electronically shifted the back of the seat until she was sitting upright. Apart from anything else it would be easier to get out when they reached their destination. The car was so low-slung her behind felt very insecure, as though it would be scraping along the road when the floor of the car wore through, which had to be imminent.

She had finally got ready for her dinner with Hugh and they were on their way to a restaurant somewhere out in the country. There was lots of country around Bristol. Hugh was always trying out new restaurants recommended to him by some friend or other. This one was supposed to make fish a speciality, which would go down well with her.

"A euro for them?" he said.

Why can't he offer a penny like everyone else? "Oh," she said. "I was just wondering who else there is in Malvern Road that could be Julie's father and why Betty thinks we should know. After all, there must be loads of people in the road that we don't even know."

"No one that fits the profile, though," Hugh said absently as he took a fairly hairy bend.

She waited until they were safely around the bend, not that that wasn't where they normally were, before asking the obvious question, "What makes you say that? How do you know?"

It wasn't so dark that she couldn't see him flushing. It was only slight, but she could see it. "Come on, Hugh, how do you know no one else fits?"

"Because I've run through all the men of the right age in Malvern Road and none of them fit," he stated.

"All right then, how come you did that?"

"Because this whole question appears to be putting you in danger. Obviously I'm going to do what I can to prevent that."

The Before Charity Liz would have wanted to say, 'Why can't you mind your own business? Did I ask you to meddle?' and such-like things, but she wouldn't have wanted to hurt his feelings, especially *before* dinner. But if he was going to do things like this why couldn't he at least have done them in co-operation with her? Why leave her in the dark as though she were incapable of giving any useful input? Many feelings fought for expression, all of which, she knew, had something to do with why they no longer lived together, but she didn't want to ruin their evening and it would have been a waste of time anyway.

However, the After Charity Liz realised that maybe he never said anything these days because he had taken on board that she didn't appreciate the possessiveness this implied and anyway, if you're engaged to someone else it might seem a bit odd.

So she said, "If you've run through them, no doubt, with the aid of some private detective or other..." His flush deepened. "Then it's not possible that Julie's father lives in Malvern Road. So how come Betty is so certain that he does? And why have you dismissed Clive Oliver who I would have thought was a prime candidate. Talk about suspicious type characters!"

"Betty thinks so because of those papers she found in her husband's effects, but they're obviously not accurate so we must find some way of letting her know this before she causes any more chaos. As for Clive Oliver, I thought you liked him?"

Ah ha! Hugh must have been thinking about when he met her coming out of next door – he had never mentioned it, but she knew he wouldn't have forgotten it, even though it was none of his business at the time, what with him being engaged to that Charity woman. "I do like him, sort of, but he's still awfully shifty. He's always checking out of his nets and walks around as though his collar should be up and as though he's trying really hard not to look over his shoulder and he's awfully rich for someone who doesn't work."

Hugh smiled as though he'd realised he had nothing to fear from a quarter that he'd been worried about. "Anyway, he's not Julie's father," he said.

He said it with such certainty she had to ask, "What makes you so sure?"

"Do you really not know?"

His surprise was so unforced she began to feel uneasy. Apart from anything else, if Clive wasn't Julie's father, why had he let her think he was? "Um, no..."

"You know the name 'Belvedere McGuigan'?"

"Yes, of course I do. He's the thriller writer."

Hugh's silence was more than eloquent.

"You're kidding me! *That* is Belvedere McGuigan. Oh. My. God!" If she mentally cringed any further her brain would end up looking like a shrivelled pea. Perhaps it *was* a shrivelled pea someone put in there as a replacement. Who had run off with her brain then?

No wonder he was rich. No wonder he had all those books of that type. No wonder he was always looking out of his nets. It was well known that he was virtually a recluse. He never gave interviews. Of course he wasn't Julie's father. The very idea. She groaned silently, imagining all those biscuits she'd eaten and all those crumbs she'd dropped and how horrible she'd been to him when she discovered he hadn't been relieved of his finger. Aargh!

Belvedere McGuigan lived next door to her and she had done nothing but insult him and abuse him and eat all his biscuits. She went hot all over, a total body blush.

She felt so awful she could do nothing but sit there as stiffly as possible to stop herself leaping up and down because she didn't know where to put herself. She wanted to rip open her skull, tear the shrivelled pea out with her bare hands and feed it to a passing duck. Besides, if she stayed still enough the world might not notice her.

"Don't say anything though, will you? He obviously doesn't want people to know."

"Nah, I won't say anything. Don't worry." Catch her saying anything! Ha! If she could keep quiet about it then with any luck old Belvedere would never need know that she knew that he knew what a complete idiot she was. Groan. And he probably only agreed to keep quiet about his finger because he really didn't want to lose a finger – his fingers must be worth a bob or two when she thought of the books they'd written. And he probably only let her think he was Julie's father because he was a thriller writer. Thriller writers probably were incapable of setting you straight about anything. They probably want you to work it out. Yeah.

So that meant that Julie's father did not live in Malvern Road. Betty's old man must be mistaken or his papers out of date or confusing the trail. Oh, good. They could tell Julie to go away then and they could live happily ever after. Doing nothing but earning a living. And being nice to their neighbours. Of course.

They made it to the restaurant in one piece despite her feeling as though disappearing into the upholstery was what she wanted most in the world. She even managed to walk into the place, on Hugh's arm, as though she was used to walking around, physically connected to the man she loved, on an everyday basis. She was horrified - just touching him made her stomach tremble and her face hot, a reaction so foreign to her these days she had to work it out. And when she did she was almost shocked - and consequently, sympathetic to Sandra - of course – it was lust! Good grief. She'd almost forgotten what it felt like.

But nothing could spoil her pleasure in good food. After all, it was only another kind of lust. It was superb. The food. She had red snapper and seaweed in a racing-green sauce starter, followed by a monk fish puff pastry creation, topped off with steamed suet syrup pudding and custard and cream, oh, and just a teensy bit of ice-cream. She could barely move. It was just wonderful. She wanted to go to sleep, but she forced herself not to lean her forehead on the crisp white linen table-cloth and have a quick snooze. No, she engaged her companion in witty, fast-moving, entertaining chit chat: "Food," she said, gesturing at the table. "Good." her hands played a vital part in this conversation. They were positively Italian in their expressiveness. "Wonderful."

"You've eaten too much," he said.

How well he knows me she thought. She smiled lovingly at him and burped softly. "Um, yes, just a little. But, boy, was that yummy? Yes!"

Suddenly, the heavenly food having gone straight to her head, she leant forward and captured his hands in hers. He had nice hands. They were one of the things about him that she particularly liked. They looked like she imagined a surgeon's hands should look. A surgeon who plays the piano as well. A grand piano. A grand piano playing surgeon who was a masseuse in his spare time. Lovely hands. She stared at them unblinkingly as she endeavoured to cover and entrap them. Her hands were a bit smaller. Oh, boy, she had eaten far, far too much!

She really shouldn't be doing this now. One part of her knew that. Another part of her, the sucker for yummy food who ate too much and then got comatose until it had been absorbed into her system sufficiently to allow her to move a bit faster and her shrivelled pea brain to work again – that part of her was out of control.

Her voice belonged to that part as well. It came out of her mouth all thrilling and husky and said, "Hugh... Hugh, let's get back together again. We go well together, you and I. And you must have thought that once or you wouldn't have married me in the first place."

His hands were rigid in her grip and his face registered such pain she wanted to run away. It had never occurred to her that Charity had hurt him that much. Slowly he peeled her fingers away from his until they were no longer touching at all. He took a deep breath and started, "Now, Liz..."

Bad start, really, but she kept her peace.

"Now, Liz. It's very sweet of you, but I can't accept your generous offer. I know you don't really want to do that. I know you just feel sorry for me. And I'd rather you didn't. In fact, it's actually quite offensive, so don't do it again. I know I was a fool over Charity. Somehow, and I'm not sure how, I found we were engaged and then, suddenly, disengaged. And I'm still not sure how it all happened. But it doesn't alter the fact that I thought for a while we had a future together. I have to deal with this. And I refuse to drag anyone else into it."

"But, Hugh..."

He held up one of those hands she'd so recently admired. That was enough to stop a stampede of warthogs, let alone semi-conscious ones. She shut up.

"I'm more grateful than I can say that we can still be friends. I'd be devastated to lose you as a friend. You mean a great deal to me. But I won't have you sacrifice yourself for me because of my mistake. I know full well how you feel. I should have listened to you sooner and moved on with my life sooner. But I do thank you for trying to make me feel better."

Liz opened her mouth, but he hadn't finished. A strange little smile flitted across his face. "Next time I consider moving on I shall first of all look where I'm going. I might even ask you, as my friend, to check out the direction I'm about to move in, too."

She could have cried. Instead she said, "I love you, Hugh. I love you very much."

His smile nearly stopped her heart. "Thank you, Liz. And I love you very much, too."

Oh, how she wanted to be his little swamp dove again, his little sunny sand worm, not just his pal, Liz. But she seemed to be stuck in a position of complete helplessness on this score.

"Anyway," he said. "I'm glad we've got this sorted out. At least I can keep an eye on you now without you getting all defensive about it. Can't I?"

If that was the best she could get then so be it. "You certainly can," she replied gaily, her heart withering in a lonely corner of her breast.

"Thank heaven for that. I'm worried sick about you all the time. You've always got the police around or someone throwing things through your windows or dodgy lodgers or people with guns running amok in your house."

And she'd make sure to carry on like that, too, if that's what would keep him coming round. She smiled at him, but she had to swallow hard on the ache in her throat. It felt like she'd swallowed a Border terrier.

"Yep, you certainly can." She had intended being a bit more original than that but realised in time that that was her limit without bawling her eyes out. He patted her hand in a *friendly* way and her heart collapsed in a cloud of dust and ceased to exist.

Chapter Twenty-four

She got up late the next morning. It had been an exhausting few days. As soon as she made it into the breakfast room the phone rang and she was delighted to hear Lydia telling her the fridge door wasn't closed properly. She then asked Liz to call in and see her in half an hour or so, and to bring Moocher. She must have heard he'd been washed. Liz checked out the fridge for unwelcome inhabitants, fed Moocher and telephoned a few kitchen people to come round and give her a quote later in the week.

As she came out of her house, Clive came out of his. "Good Morning," she said, aiming for a pleasant, but nondescript tone. It took all her courage to stay where she was and not run, screaming, back into her house. But she knew she must have looked like someone who had dropped lots of clangers at the feet of an idol and now knew it. Not that the idol himself knew it, thankfully.

The idol looked at her suspiciously. "Good morning," he managed and then followed her down the pavement and up Lydia's path.

"Have you been summoned in, too?" she asked.

"Yes. No idea what for. Hope you haven't been telling her any of your daft ideas."

"What! I haven't been telling anyone any of my daft ideas about you. Not only that, but you should thank me because I've certainly had provocation enough to tell people."

The door opened and they both turned and gave Lydia polite smiles. Moocher sniffed her shoes. Lydia stood back and they entered her house.

She bustled about and got them settled with tea and biscuits and a bowl of water for Moocher. Idly Liz watched her, wondering why they'd been asked in at the same time. She hadn't even known that Lydia was on asking-in-for-tea terms with Clive. She wondered where Tony and Julie were and what they were up to now. Something vaguely unpleasant she supposed.

And, she didn't know what made it suddenly so clear to her, but some little thing, some little intuition, some little patchy makeup and she had it. The sudden revelation made her feel as though someone had hit her squarely between the eyes and dislodged that shrivelled pea. It ran around and around in her skull for a few nanoseconds and then fell out of her head and got stuck in her throat. She started to cough, spraying custard cream crumbs all around her as she catapulted out of her chair, grabbing at her throat with a feverish hand and feeling herself turning a lovely deep maroon to match the curtains. Clive was there, thumping her on the back. She had to use her other arm to keep him off her.

Why do people do that? As soon as you cough they start thumping you on the back. It's enough to *make* you choke. Why can't they wait for you to point, imploringly back-wards? Why do they have to just thump you on the back and look so awfully virtuous while they're doing it as though they're administering on-the-spot brain surgery and were sooo clever?

So there she was, dancing around trying to avoid Clive, coughing half her intestines up and absolutely staggered at her realisation. She had no idea what to do about it. It didn't make sense. In the meantime, thankfully, the dried pea dislodged itself from her throat and jumped back into her skull. Oh, good, brain in place again. She sat down. Clive sat down. Lydia was where she had been all along. She poured out another cup of tea and handed it to Liz.

"Thank you, Lydia," she said gratefully, and avoiding her look she took a long noisy slurp of the hot brown liquid. Anything to give her time. Time to think. "Sorry about that," she said, trying to laugh lightly and failing miserably. "Crumb went down the wrong way, I guess."

"Perhaps you should try chewing the biscuit before swallowing," Clive said.

She shot him a look of intense dislike until she remembered that Belvedere McGuigan was her literary hero. She changed her glare to an admiring glance and a titter. What a wit that man was! And, besides, given what she'd just realised, she might need him on her side.

"Oh, for heavens sake, Liz!" he said. "What's with this act you're putting on? I preferred it when you were simply insulting."

"I, uh, I... nothing."

"Oh, no! I know what it is. You've found out who I am, haven't you?"

"She knows who you are?" Lydia asked, apparently jolted from her calm.

282

"Yes, I do," Liz said, and then realised what Lydia had said. She turned to her and asked, "What do you mean? Who do *you* think he is?" Because, as far as she was aware, Lydia didn't know who he was. If she had known she'd have told Liz in one of their marathon chats. She wouldn't have been able to help herself.

Lydia engaged herself in brushing crumbs from the arm of the chair she was leaning on, as if there were any there. "Oh, I just heard it on the grapevine," she muttered as though she was going to burst into song. "You know, the whole thing with Julie..."

"Come on, Lydia, who do you think he is?" Liz pressed for an answer, moving closer to her in an attempt to watch her face which she was keeping it well averted.

"Julie's uncle," Lydia snapped. "Who else?"

"Julie's uncle?" Liz repeated in a silly I-know-nothing-really tone of voice. "Julie's uncle?" She sagged back into her chair again. That didn't make any sense at all.

"How the hell do you know that?" Clive demanded, leaping from his chair and slopping tea unnoticed onto the lacy tray cloth. He strode over the Persian medallion rug and towered above Lydia as she, keeping her head even further down, managed to look like she was going to disappear under a Mughal tapestry cushion. "Nobody knows that," he continued. "It's impossible for you to know that."

Liz just stayed where she was. Her mouth must have been so far open that if she'd got up to walk she would have tripped over her chin. "Julie's uncle?" she said again. If he really was, then it made everything else different too.

"Will you stop repeating yourself?" Clive thundered. "Who the hell did *you* think I was then?"

"I thought you were Belvedere McGuigan," Liz said. She couldn't think what else to say.

"The two things aren't mutually exclusive, you know," he retorted.

"You mean you're both Belvedere McGuigan *and* Julie's uncle?" Liz asked. She needed to be sure of her facts.

"You're *The* Belvedere wotsit? The thriller writer who's unbelievably rich and a recluse?" asked Lydia. Her voice seemed to have deepened alarmingly as though with jealousy or, perhaps, with fanatical obsession.

Clive turned from Liz and looking at Lydia he flushed ever so slightly. "Well, yes, I am as it happens," he said. Liz felt that he might have bowed if this had been happening a hundred years ago. Actually, she was afraid he would do it now. How naff. But, thankfully, he resisted.

"Bloody hell!" she roared in a most un-Lydia-like manner. Liz heard the pigeons from the shed roof outside take off in panicked, clattering flight.

Personally, she thought this was a bit over the top, however much of a fan she might have been. Although she couldn't be that much of a fan or she'd had known his surname correctly, in which case this was definitely over the top.

"Okay, Lydia. Calm down. He was your neighbour. That's more than most people can say. That's presumably why he wants it kept quiet. It must be very wearing if one just wants a quiet life and do nothing but write best sellers. Very wearing indeed to be constantly pestered by fans and the media and..."

"You've always got to go one better, haven't you," Lydia yelled. She banged her fist down onto her knee with such force Liz just knew her neighbour would have one wowzer of a bruise the following day. "I've never been able to keep up with you and you succeed beyond anyone's wildest dreams without even trying! It always was Clive this and Clive that, never Vincent this and Vincent that – not until Vincent pulled off one of the biggest robberies of the century that was, but by that time it was too late and being in jail forever didn't do much for my self confidence and for the last few years I've lived next but one to you and been happy to think that your life just consisted of fussing with your net curtains and getting your car parked in front of *your* house and such petty little concerns. I've gossiped and bitched with Liz about you."

Liz squirmed and looked around as though there would be another her that did that with Lydia, not the her that was present at this embarrassing scene.

Lydia continued with this astounding tirade. "I've felt quite superior to you. For. Once. In. My. Life! And now it turns out that you're some internationally famous best-selling bloody author!"

The silence that fell after this impassioned speech seemed to accentuate the smell of stewing tea. Liz could hear tiny whispers from outside of leaves rubbing against each other in a late spring waltz. The metallic taste of surprise startled her tongue. The clanking of cogs in the brain and the shrivelled pea, respectively, of her audience was almost audible. "You are Julie's uncle, then, Clive. Definitely Julie's uncle?" Liz said. "Ohmigod. That means that you're also Lydia's brother. And I'm beginning to believe that you didn't know that."

"What the hell are you two talking about," Clive shouted. "Everyone's gone stark staring mad. Why are you talking about my brother in that way, Lydia? Did you know him well? It sounds like you did. How? Where was he? I have looked for him long and often, but it's as though he never existed."

Lydia jumped out of her seat and strode up and down, back and forth, rubbing her hands, her large hands, over her face in a way highly reminiscent of someone in deep distress or uncertainty.

Liz looked up and clearly saw the scar, but then, she was looking for it by this time. It was big and looked as though the means of achieving it had been exquisitely painful. But Lydia persisted in her charade. "Did you really try to find Vincent? He always told me that you would be pleased if he rotted in jail. That you were always the clever one, the one everyone wanted to know, the one everyone was interested in, the one who'd go far. Well, you have, haven't you? Why would you be interested in Vincent?"

Liz decided she'd do best by keeping quiet for the time being.

Clive said, "Vincent was my big brother. I always looked up to Vincent. He seemed so far above me and he never wanted to know me because I was too young and then, of course, he left home so many years before I did. Do you know where he is?"

And Liz couldn't keep quiet any longer. "Clive, how many brothers do you have?"

"Just the one," he said. "Vincent, and even then I hardly knew him before he was gone." He looked so sad she felt a moment of deep pleasure for him until she remembered all the complications that were about to be unfurled over their unsuspecting heads. She sighed instead.

Lydia stopped her pacing and stared at Clive with what could only be described as luminous hope on her face. It was a heart-stoppingly wondrous expression. How lovely. Clive stared back at her, puzzlement making him look endearingly comical, which changed to a look of utter horror as Lydia slowly reached up her hand and taking a firm grasp on her blonde and immaculately curled hair, pulled it off.

Revealed to them now was a full head of greying hair cut close to the scalp. The evil-looking scar seemed to take this as permission to make itself more obvious. Lydia wore a delicate rose quartz necklace that nestled in the soft, high, neckline of a fine weave linen dress in a rich moss green. The dress fell in almost straight lines to just below her knees. Her shapely legs sported the opaque support stockings she habitually wore and now Liz couldn't help wondering if she truly did have varicose vein problems. On her feet was a pair of very classy, well-worn but highly polished, court shoes. She wore a bracelet which peeked through from under the cuff of her long sleeves, and dangly, clip earrings, both of which items of carefully selected jewellery, matched the necklace. Despite all this wonderfully co-ordinated and brilliantly modelled feminity, she now looked every inch a man.

A man, moreover who had successfully pulled off a highly complicated robbery, survived years in gaol and had hoodwinked not only all his ex-colleagues, but all his neighbours in Malvern Road and his own brother for the last however many years it was into believing he was a woman. A woman of means but lonely. Poor Lydia. Poor Thing.

Liz tried very hard not to think of the times she had taken that Poor Thing in her arms to comfort her when she was especially down. She tried not to think of the times that, in her scrappy underwear, she had happily waved to her from her breakfast room window or leaned out of her back door to wish her a good morning. She tried not to think, too, of the conversations in which they had spent so much time discussing such things as men and, well, and women, and other things like that... her teeth broke out into a sweat. Her skin tried to turn itself inside out so no one would recognise her and she realised there was only one thing she could possibly do to make herself feel better.

Yes, she walked across to Lydia who had no idea whatsoever that she was there, so engrossed was she/he with Clive and the dawning recognition and joy on his face as he realised that here was his adored and much missed older brother, and Liz kicked him as hard as she could on the shin. He immediately yelled and doubled over in a very satisfying manner. Clive caught him in his arms and the two stood there, arms around each other, glaring at her.

"What did ya do that for?"

"For the deception, that's what. For all that time when I thought you were a woman when in fact you were just another man. For all the things about which I shall think in the future that we spoke of in the past, that will make me burn with embarrassment."

"Oh, come on, Liz. We can still be friends. What's a few white lies between friends?"

Liz thought she might eventually come round, but it would take some time. "It might or it might not dawn on you, Lydia," she said. "But if you don't know I can't be bothered explaining. You're welcome to each other. Couple of right devious bastidgits if you ask me." She really wanted to walk out, but there were a few loose ends she wanted to tie up so she made herself some coffee and found some more biscuits while those two did a lot of noisy catching up. It was sweet. In a way. Her head still buzzed with shock. Her initial realisation had simply been that Lydia was a man. That was all. She hadn't even begun to guess the rest of it, hadn't even suspected there *was* any 'rest of it'.

Nevertheless, she was eager for Lydia to have a very sore shin for many days to come. She also worried that all this excitement in her usually humdrum existence was making her relish violence more than she should.

It was all a matter of perception. If you look for what you expect to see then you'll usually see it. If you look with no expectation, or a different expectation, then you're more likely to see what's actually there. Liz had been puzzled that Lydia's brother wasn't present when they called in and Lydia hadn't even mentioned him, which she thought odd. Also, Liz thought Lydia had been too hasty to find out what was going on, and had maybe been prepared to reveal herself in her true glory before they found her/him out anyway. Her makeup, which was always thick and applied with painstaking care, this time was hurried and patchy enough for Liz to mistake her for Clive when she had turned expecting to see Clive and, although it was Lydia she was looking at, it was still Clive she was seeing.

They were so similar it was breath-taking. She was amazed she'd never seen it before. But then, she didn't think she'd ever seen them together before.

Now, as she looked at her poor, lonely neighbour, she couldn't begin to imagine him as anything other than a man. She felt a nostalgic sadness for when he'd been a woman.

Moocher was completely unfazed by it all and merely continued his morning toilette. But that was him all over. He was such a laid back dog, that dog.

Chapter Twenty-five

Liz idly contemplated how to break the truth to Simon about Lydia, given that she was supposed to have the hots for him. Interesting how concerned Simon was about Stella for someone not at all interested in his ex-wife, though. As she was beginning to relax, Julie appeared in the doorway and shattered Liz's thoughts. She looked over Liz and Moocher as though they were not important, which Liz supposed in her scheme of things they weren't.

Taking in Lydia and Clive, Julie stood, transfixed, as she absorbed the full import of Lydia's wigless, and now almost makeup-less, head and face.

Liz watched her as she took one faltering step into the room, and then, as though she'd instantly seen, interpreted and worked out her new plan, she shifted to a longer stride and ran across the room to fling herself at Lydia.

As Lydia didn't hold out her arms, or do anything at all welcoming, Julie sort of bounced off her and had to step back to keep her balance. Her whole posture was one of lost-little-girl, rejected and unloved. Whatever failings she might have had, she was a magnificent actress.

"*You* are my father, aren't you?" she said, looking up at him shyly from beneath her eyelashes and twisting her hands together. She looked about fifteen.

"Biologically speaking," Vincent said. "But not in any other way, thankfully."

Julie flushed. Her face sharpened and she pursed her lips until her mouth resembled nothing so much as a cat's backside. She looked about a hundred and fifty.

Liz noted all this with some detachment. She was still trying to work things out.

"Hold on a minute. Hold on, Lydia..." Liz said. "Do you mean that you knew all along who Clive was?"

"Of course, I did. That's why I moved here. To be near him."

"And what about having Julie and Simon in as your lodgers. What was that all about?"

"I needed to keep a closer eye on both of them. My daughter because she's a nasty piece of work." Julie's face, incredibly, sharpened and aged even more. She looked the epitome of a nasty piece of work. "And Simon," Vincent continued, "Because he appears to have no sense of self-preservation and I didn't want anything to happen to him."

"Did you know who she was, then?" she asked.

"Of course I did! I've been paying for her existence since the day she was born. I have photographs taken of her at six monthly intervals. I must confess to finding it most amusing when you brought her round to show her how to get in without a key and she sat through all that tea and all those biscuits and all those questions, coming out with all those stories..."

Julie's face took on an interesting mottled effect.

"...without turning a hair," Lydia said. "She's quite a trouper, isn't she?"

Julie looked pleased.

Things were falling into place. Clunk, clank.

"You rang the police and told them Mark Scotter had broken into your house, didn't you? What was all that about him being your toy boy?"

"Just muddying the waters, Liz," he said. "That's all. And I did want him out of the way, especially after I found he was into drugs. He'd obviously come into the game expecting to get all the money when it was found. He'd have happily disposed of Julie and Tony in order to get it. He was not nice."

Briefly Liz saw the old Lydia peek through, but she went again, leaving Vincent very much in control.

"We also needed a bit of breathing space. I knew things were coming to a head. And I really wanted there to be time for us to have this little chat together." He beamed at her. "Just us old friends..." He beamed at Clive. "...and family together."

Liz ignored the blandishment. Clive gripped Vincent's arm even tighter and grinned so much he was in danger of losing his ears in the corners of his mouth.

"So, are you a dangerous criminal, or not?" Liz wanted to know.

"No, of course he isn't," Clive couldn't restrain himself any longer. "He only did that one job. Not only that, but he gave all the money back."

"He gave all the money back?" Julie looked as horrified as if a slug had savaged her ankle. "What do you mean? How come no one knows about that?"

Clive grinned and casting a brotherly and delighted look at Vincent he said, "It's a family thing. We knew."

"I thought it might make me more acceptable," Vincent said to his brother. "That was one of the times I nearly made herself known to you, when I was able to give that money back."

"Oh, silly…" Clive punched Vincent on the arm and Vincent punched him back. They were almost giggling.

"You knew it was me all along living next but one, then?" Clive asked, although they already knew that bit. He was revelling in it. He didn't look at all Gittish any more.

"Of course I did. That's why I bought a house here. To be close to you. To keep an eye on you."

"Oh…"

And there were more punches to the shoulder and more uncontrolled grins.

Julie was impatient with their boyish messing about. "What have you been living on then?" she asked. Practical to the last.

"I made some good investments with it before I gave it back," Vincent said. "So I could give it back with interest and have enough to keep me going after that. So you've been wasting your time, Julie, looking for the swag, because there isn't any." He stopped and frowned. "Oddly enough, I did that job in the first place because you were on the way and I panicked. Didn't know how I could provide for a wife and a baby. As it turned out your mother just up and left and next I knew, ages later, you'd been adopted and that was that. So, in a sense, that money was yours, but it's all gone back now."

Julie snorted, but Vincent ignored it. "What I have now is legitimately mine as far as I'm concerned. Anyway, I can't imagine why you thought you had a right to anything. You had a perfectly good home, two doting parents and every comfort anyone could want."

Liz felt obliged to stand up for her a little even though Julie was her idea of a cockroach in human form. "Yes, but she's lost both her parents recently and now you're disowning her anyway."

Vincent looked at Liz, his eyebrows raised. "I can't imagine why you should stand up for her after what she threatened to do to Moocher."

"Yes, but she didn't do it..."

"She was lying. They're both still alive and well and disappointed in their children, adopted or otherwise."

"Really?" Liz was surprised, but should have realised Julie would tell any tale if it garnered some sympathy for her cause.

"Yes, really. Not only that, but I think you'll find that she actually rejoices in the name of Lucinda Dell-Beckwithal rather than Julie Carrington-Smythe.

Criminy. Liz didn't stand a chance against such incredible fabrications.

"Come on, Lucy," Tony said. Liz leapt back in shock, not having heard him come in. "Let's go home. It's all fallen through. We're not going to get anything out of this crowd - we might as well accept that." He put his arm around Julie-Lucinda's shoulders.

"And I suppose *your* name will turn out to be Fauntleroy or Ethelred or something," Liz snapped, peeved that she'd been so taken in.

"Don't be silly," he said. "It's Anthony. What else would it be?"

"Oh, Tony," Julie sobbed into his chest. "After all I've gone through. After all these years of searching for my father, and he doesn't want me."

It was amazing. She'd just rolled, faultlessly, into another scenario, as though she needed to constantly live in a story of her own making, although this one was true. Tony looked down at her and gave a small smile, which she couldn't see, but Liz could. And she realised that he loved Julie. He really loved her. Perhaps he wasn't so bad after all. Liz smiled at him and saw him look quizzically back before gently leading Julie from the room. She heard him say, "I'm sorry about that, luv, but you still have a family that'll make it up to you."

Vincent laughed. "She'll always fall on her feet, that one. She's got such a nerve," he said and there was a strange note of pride in his voice. "She was trying to threaten me earlier with a cigarette lighter that looked like a hand gun. It was all I could do not to laugh at her. It would have completely destroyed her self-confidence." He shook his head and smiled in what Liz liked to think was a fatherly fashion.

"Anyway." Vincent thumped Clive's shoulder again. "We must go, before anyone comes along who will take more of an interest in our affairs than we want them to. Are you ready?"

Clive looked at his brother for a while before saying, "I'm ready when you are. Have memory stick, will travel." He patted his pocket. Liz assumed he meant he had his current book in there.

"Oh, there's just one thing," Vincent said, drawing a gun from his pocket and pointing it at her. "I don't like being kicked by people who are supposed to be my friends."

Liz stared at the gun wondering if, after all the experience she'd had recently, she could tell the difference between a real gun and a cigarette lighter. Um, not with enough certainty. She stood still.

"You can't blame her," a new voice to the scene said, and her blood instantly congealed. Hugh had turned up and it would be just typical for him to get hurt instead of her. It seemed to be the way things worked out. "When you consider the deceit you practiced on her, I'm surprised she only kicked you." Out of the corner of her eye she could see movement that must be Hugh. He moved slowly as he approached Vincent as though creeping up on wildlife.

He might as well have held a huge placard above his head saying, "I'm going to talk and talk and talk and lull this person with a gun into a false sense of security and then I'm going to jump on him and wrest it from his grip and we'll all live happily ever after."

Did Vincent only threaten her with the gun because he'd seen Hugh coming in, Liz wondered? He must have seen Hugh before she was aware of his presence. How strange. Liz had difficulty believing he would actually shoot her just because she'd kicked him. But then, he had produced a few surprises recently. What was one more?

Seemingly oblivious to the fact that everyone in the room knew what he was up to, Hugh advanced painstakingly on Vincent. "Mind you, she has to thank you for calling me every time you thought she might need me. That was very kind of you and keeping the conspiracy with Melanie quiet too, so she wouldn't know about it. Of course, as we all know it didn't work, unfortunately, but I was still glad to be able to keep an eye on her."

"There's no reason why it can't work now," Vincent said. "Now you've got shot of that woman with the inappropriate name."

"No, she got shot of me, as you so charmingly put it. Because I made a fool of her by being around here, lusting after my ex the whole time. The picture in the paper was merely the straw that finished it off."

"But now you and she can get back together, can't you?" Vincent was trying very hard to be patient. Liz could hear it in his voice. She decided to keep quiet. Maybe Vincent could succeed where she'd failed in convincing Hugh she loved him.

"No. I know she has mentioned it, but I also know it's only because she feels sorry for me after the Charity debacle. I know very well how she feels. I have been hearing it for the last two years even if I didn't really take it in until too late."

"Okay, stop right there, Hugh. You're getting too close and I refuse to be wrestled to the ground by someone as pig-headed and blind as you are. You will force me to do something very unpleasant. Liz loves you. Why don't you buy my brother's house from him? He and I are about to go away and probably won't be back. Then you'd both have your own houses, right next door to each other. She won't feel hemmed in. She'd have her attic bolt-hole to go to when she needed to. You'd both have your own space. It's ideal."

Liz peered at Hugh's face from under her lashes. It had his stubborn, not-listening look plastered across it. Vincent wasn't going to succeed. It was hopeless. Moocher got up and ambled across to her. He always knew when her spirits had taken a downward plunge.

Before he reached her Vincent thundered, "Stop! Right there!"

Moocher was so surprised he did stop just as he'd reached where Hugh stood. Moocher turned his head sideways and looked enquiringly at Vincent, tail slowly waving side to side. Both her dog and her man were out of her reach, which made Liz feel uneasy. "Sit," Vincent commanded.

Looking even more surprised Moocher did sit. Liz didn't know who was most taken aback at that point. Keeping his eyes on Moocher as if willing him to stay, Vincent said, "Liz. My shin really hurts where you kicked me. I am going to take my revenge. So. It's up to you. Which one shall I shoot? Hugh or Moocher?"

It was Clive who reacted aloud. He stared at his brother and gasped, "You can't!"

"Watch me. You should never let people get away with stuff. They'll think they can take advantage whenever they want. In fact get your gun out and keep it trained on Liz. I don't want her doing anything stupid."

Clive was aghast but still did as he was asked by his newly found brother.

Liz's brain seized up. What did he mean by giving her such a choice? This couldn't be real.

"Come on, Liz. Haven't got all day. Which one shall I shoot?"

He didn't look like he was messing around. Anything but. And she believed him. Her self-indulgent descent into violence was going to cost someone she loved their life. She turned and met brown eyes steadily gazing at her, the love for her plain, and an understanding she would never have expected to see reached out to her to let her know it was all right. Her vision blurred and her throat hurt so much that getting sound out through it was like vomiting up razor blades.

"No!" she said. "No, I'm not going to choose. You can't do this. I don't believe you will do this."

"That's okay," he said. "I know who you'd choose." And he pointed his gun at Hugh, squinted theatrically and Liz could have sworn, tightened his finger on the trigger.

"Moocher…" she shrieked. "Moocher!" Oh, God. She'd given the death sentence on her dog. She kept her eyes on Moocher's. She wasn't going to chicken out of it. She would keep contact with him until his life force flickered and went out.

A heavy, waiting silence fell into the room. Clive shifted his feet, Vincent sighed heavily and aimed his gun at her lovely loving dog.

Hugh and Liz both jumped at the same time, colliding in the middle with a colossal crack, Moocher hidden behind them. Liz felt as though she must have been shot, but it was Hugh who, white faced and thin-lipped with pain, clutched his shoulder.

Another silence, this one patently full of disbelief, fell over the assembled company.

"You chose me," was all Hugh managed to say, his eyes staring in shock.

"Yes, and then because you couldn't face the thought of us getting back together, you chose to commit suicide by jumping in front of Moocher. Thank you very much!"

He seemed struck dumb, whilst she battled with white-hot fury and toe-cringing hurt. She looked for blood on him but could see none. She could see none on her. And Moocher was fine, puzzled but absolutely fine.

Vincent and Clive clutched each other, looking terrified.

"Did you shoot," one of them said.

"No, I thought it was you," the other replied.

"I never would have shot any of them."

"No, nor me."

Weird.

Liz looked back at Hugh, who was clearly in pain. He smiled weakly at her. "You *do* love me," he whispered. "You chose me."

"Yeah, and then you tried to kill yourself by jumping in the way of the shot," she snapped.

"There was no shot!" Clive or Vincent asserted.

"I heard it, and anyway, look at him." She nodded at Hugh's colourless face.

"I think the shot-type noise might have been my collarbone breaking," he said.

Liz got to her feet, her hand on Moocher's head. "Serves you right," she squeezed out between her gritted teeth, but she couldn't hold his gaze.

"Oh, for heavens sake," Vincent said. "Get it sorted, you two. It's time we were off. I've done the best I can for you. If you can't see it, then, tough! You can get two people together as often as you like. As I did. Repeatedly. All those times when I rang Hugh to tell him Liz could do with him around, without telling her that's what I was doing. But it's impossible to make other people see sense. At some point they have to do it for themselves. It's time we weren't here." And he and Clive moved towards the door.

"You're just going to go. Just like that?" Liz suddenly felt the loss and, approaching Vincent, she hugged him quickly. He was so surprised he didn't have time to hug her back. "I'm sorry I kicked you so hard," she said. "Will you keep in touch?"

"Yes, why not? We can trust you, I know. Also, would you like to take charge of my house? Rent it out, take care of it. Just deal with it. Take a hefty commission."

"And mine," Clive said and handed her his keys. "I don't think we'll be back for a long time. You could rent mine out to my fan club – that might make more money than ordinary tenants. But it's up to you. Do what you like. You could move in while you're doing up your own house. The commission from looking after both our houses could be enough to enable you to do what you want. I'm not sure accountancy suits you. Or you could just sell it to that lunkhead over there and get back together, but in separate houses."

"That reminds me, Clive," Vincent said. He put his arm around his brother's shoulder as they moved to leave the room. "Your third Bertie Elfen Lee novel where he goes undercover as an auditor

302

– your informant about the safe cracking wasn't quite right about using dynamite in that way. I don't suppose most people will have noticed though. In future, I could, maybe, if you wanted, check out your books for such details..." His voice trailed off.

"Oh, would you, Vincent? That would be great!"

And they were gone.

Chapter Twenty-six

Hugh didn't get in touch with Liz for seven weeks. Maybe he was waiting for his collar bone to heal. Maybe he was waiting for her to regain her equilibrium. Maybe he was afraid. Maybe, though, he was simply waiting for everything to be in place. That is, when he did finally get in touch, he'd bought and moved into the house next door to hers into what had been Clive's house.

And Liz didn't get in touch with him, either, and she had forbidden his only remaining mole – Melanie - from ringing him up and reporting on her movements. That had to stop. They had to sort this out themselves.

After that seven weeks she was in full possession of everything required to rent out rooms in Lydia's house. The commission from this, plus the rents from her own lodgers enabled her to be independent of any other demands. And she had a full house again, only awaiting one more lodger. She still managed all this and her accounting from her eyrie in the roof. Any accounting clients she had she chose to have – she didn't have to have them. She could now settle back and take her time choosing just exactly what she did want to do with her life. She'd been unable to decide so far, there were so many interesting directions she could take.

So when Hugh emailed her she was already completely independent of him, and he knew she would be. Of course, that was why he emailed her when he did. He knew her so well. He was actually, despite the Charity business, quite a bright chap.

Obviously, she knew he hadn't chosen death over life with her. Of course she knew that, unthinkingly, he'd tried to save her grief over Moocher by sacrificing himself. But, honestly, there were limits. And she had just made the most complex statement she would ever make in her life – choosing a man over her dog. And to have him chuck himself in front of a bullet at that stage – well... Well – it was downright careless!

He was just too trusting. If she was a Charity type person or a Tortoise-woman person or a Julie or a Tony, Hugh would be easy money. He would play into their hands so gullibly he wouldn't stand a chance. He really needed her around to keep him unhurt and unfleeced. Whether he realised it or not - it was her duty to look after him.

If he wanted to believe it was *his* duty to look after her – well, there was such a thing as give and take in these relationships and what harm could it do for her to let him believe it was that way round?

It was clear that they were made for each other. She'd sacrificed her dog for him and he'd sacrificed his life for her. Yes, they were equal partners in each other's future.

So when his email showed up in her inbox it was to arrange a meeting at *his* house next door. To which she agreed.

He kept her waiting five days from the email. He knew she was hopeless at waiting. He knew she was boiling up something the whole time she had to wait.

When the day finally arrived after what seemed like a few years, she rang what used to be Git-Next-Door's doorbell. Hugh answered it. The two of them stood there, motionless, for what seemed like a fortnight and then he held out his arms. She simply walked into them. She belonged in them. No one else should be in them but her.

How they made it up the stairs without breaking any other bones she didn't know. But they did. Only to discover that Hugh had imported an *enormous* bed into the front bedroom, luxuriously draped in shiny, slippery sheets and throws. On the floor were fur rugs so deep that as clothes were thrown around in frenzied haste they sank out of sight to be lost in their depths. Along the side, lit by shimmering lamps, were plates of every conceivable biscuit to be found in a supermarket's repertoire. Freesias crowded the room delicately scenting the air. He'd even obtained some Bonzo Dog vintage postcards from somewhere to replace the ones she'd had nicked by an errant lodger. What a man! What a hero!

Not that she really noticed this lot beforehand. Things were way too rampant and thrilling for an inventory at that stage.

Hugh took her breath away. This time when he murmured, "Now, Liz..." into her ear her every fibre trembled with anticipation. He held her, body and soul, in his capable, piano-player-crossed-with-a-surgeon's hands and, there was no mistake, she held him, body and soul, in hers.

Moocher stayed downstairs. He was such a sensitive dog, that one.

And it was like regaining life, like realising that although the world carried on full of deceit and nastiness none of it would matter for as long as they had each other. In fact, if they carried on this way, and other people carried on in a similar way, then the world couldn't possibly be full of nastiness. There'd be no room for it.

That wouldn't last long. Just the moment he demanded to know where she'd been or who with, or she reacted angrily, pushing him away and feeling smothered, then they'd be back to hating each other. But this time they'd know it was all part of the game. They'd know it didn't really matter because they both had their own boltholes, that either of them could invite the other into when they wanted. They were two individuals who could choose to stand together when they wished.

She'd forgotten how wonderful it was to be loved so completely. She could swear they both looked about ten years younger after their second round. She sat up in bed and gazed at the over-the-top décor that no one meeting Hugh would ever imagine he'd put in place. She loved it.

As he'd gone to the trouble and produced such a blinding array, she had to force herself to eat some biscuits with bubbly enjoyment. But she had already discovered that the biscuit thing had only been because of the lack-of-Hugh thing. In the previous seven weeks she'd gone right off biscuits – even custard creams – even those meringue ones dipped in chocolate – and as a consequence had lost half a stone without even trying. That was handy because her smart jeans no longer threatened to cut her in half when she sat down in them.

"My luscious dahlia," he said. "I have something I want to say."

"Oh?" she felt her muscles tense in readiness. "Let me guess. The whole thing with Charity was a joke to make me see the error of my ways?"

The way his face darkened and his eyebrows grew together, beetlingly, she surmised that wasn't it. She would never, ever, mention Charity again. She stuffed a chocolate crispy thing in her mouth to shut herself up.

"No. That's not it. This is something I've given a lot of thought to. I think we belong together, don't you?"

She nodded her head vigorously, spraying crumbs over the bed. "Yeah, I do. Yeah."

"But I realise that I'm a bit heavy handed sometimes and it makes you want to leave before you get crushed to death. I wonder if I'm afraid that because you are so special you will, in the end, find me boring." He dropped his gaze to the throw and started to pull threads from it, which he then tried to push back. Impossible job, of course.

So he didn't see her jaw drop so far it nearly bounced off the bed, flying back to cut the end of her tongue off. "What?" she finally managed to squeak out. "Sometimes you're a bit pompous, but you're never boring. It's not just you, you know. It's a lot to do with my childish urge to resist, on principle, suggestions from other people and go dead against them even if in doing so I'm making life difficult for myself."

"You're not childish. Enthusiastic, caring, full of joy, not childish."

"Stop arguing. I am childish. Sometimes. But anyway, this time we know all this stuff so it won't happen, will it?"

"No. We'll be on the watch out so it can't happen. And we could give each other more space, mentally and physically."

"And we can make more use of each other's strengths. Talking of which, would you kindly sit in on the interview for the final lodger to keep my gas bills paid, please?" And so she took the first step to complete coupledom, by asking him to do something she didn't need him to do.

He looked pleased to be asked but immediately blanked his face to look only businesslike. She had her poker face on anyway and signified that she was delighted he'd acquiesced.

And then maybe she could get pregnant soon and move in to his house to be pampered properly. She didn't say that aloud, but clutched it to herself as a delicious secret. Hugh would be *so* chuffed to become a father. It would be lovely to produce a child and put it in a Christmas stocking as a surprise for him. He'd make a fabulous Dad and would be so delighted she knew it would keep her in happy tears for a week. Unfortunately, she wasn't convinced it could be done totally in secret. Damn!

Chapter Twenty-seven

He was much too broad across the shoulders to fit through the dog flap so she didn't even mention it. He looked the type to never, ever forget his keys anyway. He looked the strong, silent and thoroughly dependable type. He looked the type who would clean the bath before he got in it *as well as* after he got out of it. She was sure he would always pay his rent on time, unprompted. Yes, he would go to bed, sober, alone, at ten and get up at six. He was a tax specialist. He had a clean driving licence.

He looked as boring as square-cut meat-paste sandwiches.

He seemed to be mind-numbingly fussy about washing and cleaning facilities. (That was a shame, but she promised him some building work, a new bathroom and a complete spring-clean before he moved in.)

His litany of references was as tedious as it was long.

His sex appeal was as magnetic as a cistern's.

He wouldn't know how to tell a lie, white or otherwise.

He was exactly the type of lodger that she was looking for these days.

Liz glanced at Hugh. She was glad she'd asked him sit in on the vetting of any new lodgers – seeing as how she'd been so bad at it, and he was delighted to be asked again. He smiled at her to show his approval of Wayne. It merely had the effect of making her forget why she was there. God, he was a sexy beast! She couldn't wrench her gaze from his lips.

Suddenly, Wayne said, "Is that a *finger* your dog has in his mouth? Surely not..."

Eek – not Stella's pickled finger! She whipped around and sure enough Moocher had a finger in his mouth. Two sensations assailed her. Relief that he hadn't actually eaten it before. It would make him a cannibal, almost. But also dread – how to get out of this one?

"Moocher. Come here. There's a good dog." She waved her hand at him enticingly. He looked suspiciously at her and suddenly sprinted towards the back door and clatter-thunked out into the garden.

There was the definite sound of people holding their breath until she spoke. "We, er, we have someone who lodges with us who works in... um, works in the local joke manufacturing plant. That's just a finger from one of those arms you see sticking out of people's car boots." She looked over her shoulder. Good grief, where had these incredible powers of fabrication come from?

She wondered who the hell that was who worked in the local joke manufacturing plant that didn't exist. Ohmigod. What was happening to her? She was turning into someone else.

Liz saw Hugh's lips twitch and waited to hear what he'd say, when Simon erupted from the hall into the breakfast room. "Stop that dog. He's got Stella's finger. She wants to take it back to the lab where she got it from." He chased out through the back door and she could hear him and Moocher playing a happy game of catch out there, cheered on by a few lodgers who watched from next door.

Wayne's mouth fell open.

"Did you know that, Hugh?" Liz said, feebly, knowing he already knew, considering this was Simon's room they were interviewing Wayne for... "Simon and Stella are getting back together. Isn't that good news?"

"This is the house of happy-ever-afters," Melanie announced as she trailed through to join Simon in the garden, carefully not looking at Wayne but flushing delicately up the back of her neck.

Wayne's eyes tried to leap out of their sockets to follow her. She was wearing her Sunday afternoon resting gear, which consisted of a lot of frilly not much. "Do I get the room?" he finally croaked, his mouth obviously having dried out so much he could barely speak.

"Yes. You'll fit in just fine," Liz said. "Here's your key and now if you'll excuse me, I'll be back later."

Shyly she dropped her gaze from Hugh's, made off down the hall and out the front door, Moocher at her heels. They jumped over the wall, she opened the door and dashed upstairs, tearing off her clothes as she went. Throwing herself onto the big bed she hugged a Christmas stocking to herself, although it was only August, and waited for the one man in the world who could make her life complete.

Susan Alison's next book is another frothy romp, this time involving Stephanie Lawry, quite a few other humans, a couple of dogs – oh, yes, and a polar bear – in:

Out from under the Polar Bear

Read the first few pages now…

Chapter One

Who would have thought she was allergic to him? Who'd ever heard of that? Dazed, Stephanie Lawry stumbled over the edge of the pavement. 'Oh!' She put her hand out to save herself. Finding nothing there, she fell over. Shrieking brakes and blaring car horns fractured the crisp morning air.

'Tired of life, love?'

'Get out the road.'

'Silly cow!'

Pushing herself up, Steph stared around as though seeing Bristol anew. The news she'd just received was startling enough, but she was also surprised by her reaction to it.

She was allergic to her fiancé.

She should be devastated. In fact, she felt nothing at all. Although she *was* pleased it wasn't the clap – her initial suspicion. Or crabs, or some other pox.

The consultant had been very kind, obviously expecting her to wail and declaim that life was no longer worth living. She'd thought at first he meant because of the allergy to Keith, but apparently she was expected to wail over the possible difficulties it might cause in conceiving a child. He'd provided her with a glass of water and some faintly aromatic tissues to weep into. Even an arm around her shoulders, which she'd found a tad over the top. But she was expert these days at that oh-so-casual shift away so the unwanted limb slid off.

When he started rattling on about artificial insemination with washed sperm, she'd bolted for the great outdoors and death by traffic.

She staggered back onto the pavement and leant against a handy wall as she considered the situation. Dr Stainsworth, with a habit of getting too close to people, had explained about the infertility that could arise with this condition. Apparently, if Steph was allergic to some men's semen she was also likely to be allergic to some foods. Something to do with the proteins. She didn't want to think about that too deeply.

She could imagine the conversation with her fiancé. 'The fact of the matter is, darling, I'm allergic to you.'

Keith would stare at her over his half-moons - why, oh why wouldn't he get vari-focals? Anyway, he'd stare at her over the top rim, his eyes would get smaller, his lips would thin before parting to deliver some conclusive statement. Something like, 'Don't be silly, Stephanie,' and then he'd carry on reading the pink pages, the matter settled to his satisfaction, but not to hers, as happened so often. She snorted and hastily pulled herself up straighter, looking around in case anyone had heard her unladylike eruption. Maybe if she went for hypnotherapy she could stop this snorting thing that her mother hated. Keith wasn't too happy about it either...

Why was she still with him? She shook her head. Maybe it was simply too difficult not to be. How feeble! How unfair to Keith. All she knew was that she didn't see him in quite the same light as when they'd got together. Maybe he felt the same.

Anyone else in the world would be happy with her situation. She had a good fiancé, a good career, her own house. She was just ungrateful.

She slunk off down the road to find her car and go home. She'd worry about telling Keith when she absolutely had to tell him, and not before.